AN
EPITAPH
FOR
JEZEBEL

AN EPITAPH FOR JEZEBEL

L. DIVINE

www.kensingtonbooks.com

DAFINA BOOKS are published by

Kensington Publishing Corp.
900 Third Ave.
New York, NY 10022

Copyright © 2024 by L. Divine

All Kensington Titles, Imprints, and Distributed Lines are available at special quantity discounts for bulk purchases for sales promotions, premiums, fund-raising, and educational or institutional use. Special book excerpts or customized printings can also be created to fit specific needs. For details, write or phone the office of the Kensington special sales manager: Kensington Publishing Corp., 900 Third Ave., New York, NY 10022, Attn: Special Sales Department, Phone: 1-800-221-2647.

The DAFINA logo is a trademark of Kensington Publishing Corp.

ISBN: 978-1-4967-4996-3
First Kensington Hardcover Edition: July 2024

Library of Congress Control Number: 2024932357

ISBN: 978-1-4967-4998-7 (ebook)

10 9 8 7 6 5 4 3 2 1

Printed in the United States of America

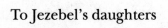

To Jezebel's daughters

Part One

Monaka: Nightfall

"**Y**OU KNOW I DON'T USUALLY DANCE ALONE," I SAY, SPINNING around the brass pole. We've just begun the private dance and I'm already missing my partners. I close my eyes and pretend they're with me, remove my top, and allow my breasts to fall with the beat of the music. My panties will stay on, at least for the time being.

"You should do it more often," he says, unfolding several hundred-dollar bills and placing them in the small basket at the center of the table. Unlike other clubs, clients at The Honey Spot aren't allowed to make it rain all over the dancers. Instead, the offerings are collected from the baskets and divided among all of the dancers at the end of each shift.

"Open your eyes," he commands, snapping me out of my fantasy. "Remove your veil."

I toss the sheer gold fabric offstage and reclaim my large hand fans—a signature part of my routine and our exclusive game.

"Slower," he commands, crossing, uncrossing, and then recrossing his painfully thin legs. "Slower, Monaka. Slower . . . That's better," he says, performing the action he wants to see emulated onstage from his seat in the audience. If it weren't for the crisply pressed three-piece all-white linen suit—and the strict rules in place against such things—I'd swear he'd be the one dancing instead of me.

I follow his instructions, slowing down the pace until my movements feel more like yoga poses than a pole routine.

"Very good. Lovely, Monaka. Simply perfect," he says excitedly. "Now face the mirror."

I spin slowly toward the back of the wall and catch my reflection in the antique bronze-framed glass wall, seeing his likeness as well. He's a strange-looking man. I should talk. But there's something off-putting about his pasty skin, tall and extremely thin frame with nicotine-yellowed teeth that give him an air of death, or at the very least a sickness that sticks.

My benefactor always keeps his eyes covered by the type of designer shades only a person with money to spare—if there's such a thing—can afford. I'm surprised that he can get away with something so flashy in this small hick town. They don't like anything too different around here.

The music directs my hips as they sway back and forth, causing my audience to shift in his seat.

"May I join you?" he asks, rising from his seat. His question, more of a command, lingers in the air for a moment—he knows better. The main stage is holy ground, and there's nothing sanctified about this man.

"Dancers only," I say, pointing to the rules clearly written on the wall just like they've always been for the twenty-plus years The Honey Spot's been in operation, then around the stage, which takes up a third of the great room. "You know this here's a women's only domain."

My benefactor winces. He momentarily pauses before forcing his pencil-thin lips into an awkward, painful smile. I can see that my words hit a nerve, even if he doesn't want to admit it.

"But I have a gift for you, my sweet." He reaches inside his shirt pocket and retrieves a small pink velvet box.

"I can't. You've already given me so much," I say, eyeing the lovely and expensive shopping bags filled with designer lingerie, three pairs of shoes that Carrie Bradshaw would envy, and various gold and diamond jewels to tote. He spared no expense for his birthday show, even though I'm the one being spoiled.

"This is the last gift for the night, I promise."

Against my better judgment, I silently give him the permission he so craves—also part of our game. HoneyMama would kill me if she knew I had a man, or anyone not ordained by her and her alone, on the main stage. If I weren't afraid of losing out on a lump sum that could pay a quarter of my medical debt overnight, and the fact that there's always been something about this man's demeanor that makes me believe he could easily snap at any time, I'd tell him to fuck off. But instead, I stand against the pole and await my next surprise, anxious for this night to end.

He mounts the steps as if he's danced here for years and joins me in the center of the reflective stage. "Close your eyes."

I do as I'm told.

He covers my face, eyes to chin, with a multicolored silk veil, tying it behind my head a little too tightly for my taste.

"Is this the gift?"

"Hush, my sweet," he says, running the back of his heavily scented hand down the left side of my neck, giving off salamander vibes.

I try to ignore my repulsion for the familiar cologne and focus on my true love, my one-and-only partner, the real sweet one. I wonder what she's doing right now, and how nicely her bright eyes will set off the diamond and sapphire earrings—another gift from earlier this evening.

"Now, where were we?"

The music changes in tempo with Radiohead's eerie melody filling the room. His hands move down the bare sides of my body and follow my every movement.

"I told you—the stage is for dancers only," I say, attempting to free myself from his grip, but every sway of my hips is accompanied by an uncomfortable hard grind.

He ignores my plea and continues to dance. His manhood pokes me in the back, causing me to damn-near jump off the two-foot edge into the audience. I'm losing patience.

"Please let me finish," I say, catching my footing. I turn to face him, but can barely make out the faint image through the thick material.

I can feel his eyes on mine, searing through the delicate yet resilient material.

"I could've been a dancer, too, you know," he says, his voice becoming many octaves higher as if he's trying to find the right note to sing. "I can dance just as well as any other bitch in this establishment."

"HoneyMama only hires women," I say, growing more unsettled by the minute. What's this dude's problem? He knows the rules all too well, and who the hell is he calling a bitch?

It's a well-known fact that HoneyMama caught hell when she first opened a strip club where strictly femme—not necessarily female—dancers ruled. They also weren't too keen about the fact that the club was nudity optional, per the discretion of the dancer's routine. In other words, the original patrons were a little more than pissed at the fact that The Honey Spot became a successful Black-woman-owned-and-run strip club where men—white men in particular—weren't in control, and there wasn't a damned thing they could do about it.

"Again, only dancers allowed onstage." I've never felt completely comfortable with doing private dances, and this client is starting to freak me out.

As much as I hate to admit it, my baby might be right: I need to wrap up my off time marauding with Couverture—the sooner, the better.

Couverture, or C as she's not so affectionately known as, is the number one and most feared dancer at the Spot. She also happens to be responsible for all side hustles as unholy as they are. No matter how good the extra loot is, it's not worth the trouble she always manages to find, along with the wealthiest clients.

"Trust me. I know all about HoneyMama's rules," he slurs, more than a little hate in his scratchy voice. "Do you know how exhausting it is to get rejected, over and over, and over again, by a fat, mediocre at best, mulatto bitch of a whore like Josephine 'HoneyMama' Thibodeaux? Cocky cunt."

I push my veil down to find my client completely naked, save his panties, nude high-heeled shoes, and matching satin gloves—each identical to my own gifts that he also provided. He removes his customary shades to reveal a stunning pair of damn-near-white grayish-blue eyes—lash extensions, makeup and all.

My client, now completely unhinged, is crying while smiling—never a good combination in my book.

"I don't understand what's going on, but you're making me feel very uncomfortable," I say, backing away from the pole. "You need to leave."

"Shh, Monaka," he says, holding me by the waist to stop my imminent escape. "The dance isn't over yet."

"Dulce!" I try to scream, but his strong grip stifles the sound to a mere murmur. My client turned opponent covers my mouth with his left hand while his right masterfully constricts the fallen veil around my neck.

"Hush, my pretty," he whispers into my ear. "It'll all be over soon."

I drop my fans and try to fight, but the slick gloves simply slide across his smooth, pale skin. My attempts to scratch, slap, and punch are all in vain as he traps me between the pole and his embrace. Pictures of The Honey Spot, Dulce, HoneyMama, and Couverture fade to the back of my mind as I desperately try to remain conscious. I don't want to die, not like this.

"I've always admired your perfect poise, Monaka," he says, controlling our renewed routine. "You dance so elegantly, like a gazelle onstage, not like the whores so many dancers have become under Couverture's tutelage, but I'll deal with her later."

I attempt to grab hold of the pole but there's little friction between satin and brass. All the things that were once so attractive about this stage have now become enemies to my survival.

He spins me around to face the empty chairs and tables in the ghostly audience. "You were a bright and shining star in this overindulgent, gaudy place. It looks like a bad replica of the inside of a genie's bottle, don't you think?" He tightens his grip on the knotted veil, slowly taking my breath away.

I try to wedge my fingers between the silk fabric and my throat, but again he blocks my attempt.

His satin-covered fingers grip the knot tighter, but the veil slightly loosens from the moisture caused by my falling tears.

I seize the opportunity and bite down hard on his gloved hand.

"You stupid cunt!" he screams without giving an inch, and neither do I.

I don't know if I broke any skin, but I'm not letting go of him until he lets go of me, no matter the repercussions. I'm not going down without a fight—never have.

He lets go of the veil only long enough to recover. With the same hand, he punches me hard in the back of the head. Warm blood trickles down my neck.

"Hail Mary, full of grace," I mentally pray as my consciousness begins to fade. I haven't recited the prayer in quite a while, but now seems as good a time as any to ask for a little help.

He hits me again.

I fall to the ground and continue the prayer. "Blessed art thou among women." All I can think about is escaping. I again catch our reflection in the mirrored background, still unable to make out a clear image or path of retreat.

He kneels beside me; his left fist rises above the back of my head. This time, the blow causes a cracking sound loud enough that it echoes against the hard floor.

He stares down into my bloodied eyes and smiles wickedly at his handiwork.

"Monaka, a gentle gazelle among dancers," he whispers, slowly winding his narrow hips and flat ass up and then back down toward the floor behind me, like one of the moves we perform during partner routines.

Me and Dulce were the best duo at the Spot. My Dulce. My love.

Our twin shoes rub together, now blemished by identical scuffmarks.

"Now look what you've done! We could have been so good together," he shrieks, bastardizing George Michael's near-perfect lyric. With that final rebuff, he reclaims the viselike grip on the knotted veil, taking away the few breaths I've managed to catch between chokes.

"Holy Mary, Mother of God," I think as the image of Dulce and the scuffed nude stilettos fade into the background. "Pray for us sinners, now and at the hour of our death. Amen."

Chapter 1

"*T*HAT'S IT, LADIES. MOVE YOUR MIDSECTIONS BACK AND FORTH; *semicircle to the left, semicircle to the right.*"

I subconsciously obey the memory, winding my wide hips in the seat along to Bob Marley's raspy voice the same way I learned to do at The Honey Spot way back when.

"*Bend your knees, keep bending and let your backsides lead the way down. Now drop it low to the floor. Then slowly wind your way back up. We're in no rush. Pull your belly button in toward your spine and stretch your shoulders back. Breathe in. Breathe out. Focus your movements. Feel your hips open up, the wider you spread your knees apart. Repeat at least a hundred times per day to keep your power—and your patrons—in check.*"

I recall the powerful feeling that mastering a brass pole brings, remembering the first dance class I took with Honey-Mama. She was the oldest, and the baddest, stripper in Atlanta at the time—still is the baddest, as far as most people are concerned. And she's one of the only female owners of a lucrative strip club outside of Las Vegas, Nevada. Most Atlanta dancers who are serious about the craft drive the fifty-plus miles to Indian Springs, Georgia, for HoneyMama's classes when they want to increase their cash flow and get a break from the norm. Tips are everything when you dance for a living. And the more control you have over the tippers, the better.

Professional dancers used to scare me until I became one of

them. I was introduced to the dance game when I was only sixteen years old, and became addicted to the power that money and attention brings very quickly. It wasn't until I worked at The Honey Spot that I truly understood what it meant to embody feminine power and how to use it to my advantage while making a damn good living. The first time that I walked into a strip club, I thought it must've been how visitors felt when they landed on Wonder Woman's Amazonian Island: captivated, entranced, and afraid that with the wrong move those powerful, sexy women could crush a person under their five-inch stilettos. Not necessarily the prettiest women on the block, but the way they wore their scantily clad bodies with such confidence and strength made me want to be just like them.

I wrote all of these feelings down and more in my first feature article, "An Epitaph for Jezebel," although it wasn't well received by HoneyMama or the dancers at the Spot, and I don't blame them. I admit, dealing with the bitter breakup from my boyfriend at the time, Drew, plus the untimely death of one of my co-dancers, gave a bitter tone to the article that landed me on the Atlanta map as one of the freshest new voices in journalism. That was over a decade ago, and a lot's changed since then.

Most journalists are forced to write obituaries early in their careers before moving on to other stories. We write pre-death announcements for celebrities, and short and sweet ones for rich society folks filled with the most clichéd epitaphs Google can find. We rarely write obits for regular folks, unless a family member sends in a request or there's a probate sale at stake. Death only makes the news if it's graphic or tragic enough to catch the attention of the masses. If it bleeds, it leads. In most people's eyes, there's nothing tragic about the death of a stripper. I saw enough working the dance scene to know that too many of our stories go untold.

I want to do hard reporting, but my editor, Charlie, doesn't think a cute stripper-turned-writer has the balls to write the real shit—as he put it—which is why he called me first thing this morning when he heard about the murder of one of the Spot's own. He gave me the story, not because he thinks it's worth telling, but because he's sure there's a salacious side to it that gets muddied by the small fact that a woman was killed, which is why I didn't bother telling Charlie that HoneyMama already called me last night. He doesn't need to know all my business. Besides, a good reporter keeps her informants to herself. I just took it as a sign that it's time for me to go home.

My cell rings with a call from the paper. Damn, now what?

"Keke," Charlie grunts, interrupting my vibe. "Did you make it out there yet?"

"Almost," I say, reluctantly lowering the volume to listen to my boss bark more orders.

"Text me when you hit the ground. And make sure Pete stays on task. That kid's easily distracted by anything. I can only imagine how focused he'll be with a harem of freshly waxed pussy walking around all willy-nilly for the taking."

"I keep trying to tell you, the Spot isn't like that." I constantly find myself on defense with Charlie, especially when it comes to any topic dealing with women and nonwhite folks.

"Keke, please," he says in between cigarette draws. Like most places I've worked, most people don't give a fuck about codes regarding indoor smoking. "All strip clubs are exactly like that."

"Not HoneyMama's club."

"Well, if it was so goddamned wonderful, why did you leave?"

After a moment of silence, he continues. I have no rebuttal for that smart-ass remark, at least not one I care to share.

"Exactly. Now go get my story."

The long drive down I-75 is almost unbearable. The air conditioning in my Toyota Corolla broke over a year ago, and I still haven't found the money to get it fixed. Once I moved north, I never looked back, no matter how much I missed Indian Springs.

Hopefully, this will be my first hard-hitting story, no matter what kind of filth Charlie's expecting. Pete wasn't my first choice of photographers, but no one else would take the assignment. I just need him to document the story with a few photos to accompany my piece. One weekend should be enough time for him to get the job done.

When I got the call last night from HoneyMama, or Honey as she's affectionately known, I was shaken to my core by how her smooth, sweet voice hadn't changed. Knowing her, she probably looked the same, too. I only heard from her once after my article was published, and that was the last time we spoke. Although I was happy to hear from Honey, I wish she had called under better circumstances. I never would've imagined that one of her girls would be murdered, especially not at the Spot.

Most dancers hear Indian Springs and envision country boondocks, which it pretty much is. But for some of us, it sounds like heaven incarnate, and that's exactly what it was, until last night. HoneyMama's like a mother to all her girls, and most of them need her influence in their lives. She routinely scouted Atlanta clubs for the cream of the stripping crop, offering them a way out of the male-owned clubs through their craft, if they were willing to leave the city behind. If it wasn't for her, I'd probably be strung out on drugs or dead, just like Mocha, and now Monaka.

The drive from Fulton to Butts County is just as long, miserable, and boring as I remember. Once I cross the narrow bridge leading into the small town of Indian Springs, the official state park sign welcomes me back. A few of the girls swear the springs are magical for more than just the sulfur-filled water cascading over the black rocks. They say the springs themselves can heal any ailment. They also say the Native Americans who once populated this entire area thought so, too, but so much for that theory. As long as I lived here and bathed in the luminescent water, I shouldn't have any issues, but Lord knows I've got plenty.

Like weight, credit scores, and everything else in life, careers go up and down, and mine has been no exception. Who would've thought that ten years ago I was as fine as the best of them—young, fit, and juicy, with money in the bank? Now that I'm a full-time writer, I'm just juicy, with thickness to spare. Since taking my job at the *Metro Journal*, I've been stressed out and broker than I've been since I was a teenager, with the gray hairs and rubber checks to prove it. Who says that taking the supposed high road is the best path? Sometimes I wish I'd never left the Spot, but there's no magic time machine to turn that desire into a reality.

When I pull up to the brick-and-iron gates at the entrance of the refurbished antebellum-mansion-turned-nightclub, red dust from the long dirt road leading toward the parking lot rises to greet me—as if my car wasn't already dirty enough. I creep forward, mindful of the rocks and other natural speed bumps along the path that force me to take in the scenery.

The ancient pine and oak trees lining the plantation provide plenty of shade for the various squirrels, rabbits, birds, and other country wildlife that inhabit the massive estate. The natural shade also grants me a slight reprieve from the sweltering sun. As usual, the ominous storm clouds from earlier came and went, taking my fresh silk press with them.

At the end of the narrow driveway is a clearing that reveals The Honey Spot, in its entire splendor. I've always loved the tall columns and high beams of Southern architecture, minus the Confederate flags prominently displayed on most of the other structures in this area. The house hasn't changed much since its original days when the owner also owned several of Honey-Mama's ancestors, including her great-grandfather, Joseph Thibodeaux. She has the pictures and certificate from the national registry of historical homes to prove it. Most of the other plantations around here have either been turned into hotels or museums, but HoneyMama held on to her house and made it a home for all of us.

The brilliant white mansion looks like it's been steam cleaned recently, eliminating any remnants of the yellow pollen that coats any and everything, starting during the spring and now in the summer, too. Four massive columns stretch from the second story down to the first, highlighting the eight picturesque windows in the front of the home where admirers can catch a glimpse of the preshow when the thick drapes are drawn. There are two large ceiling fans on either side of the wraparound porch that perfectly match the restored hardwood floors. Aside from dancing, HoneyMama's favorite pastimes are decorating and cooking: she's always had a way with making her club feel more inviting than most.

I park my tired vehicle and notice the numerous police cars and ambulances present instead of the customary Mercedes, Jaguars, and other high-end cars. I exit my car and immediately tug at my unforgiving slacks. There are few sidewalks in these parts of Georgia, causing me to second-guess my open-toed shoe choice. With my legal pad and digital recorder in hand, I'm ready to get to work, anxious for the chance to vindicate myself in HoneyMama's eyes, no matter how uncomfortable coming home is.

Three of the Spot's dancers are seated around one of the four patio tables, chatting it up, while watching various people enter and exit though the front door. I hope they're enjoying the warm weather before the heat becomes intolerable in the next hour or so. During the summer months, the sun doesn't have to reach high noon to make you wish for winter to arrive early—ten in the morning will do that just fine.

"A real shame, ain't it?" one of the nosey locals says to another onlooker standing in front of the house, smoking a cigarette. Both women look as if their faces have been molded into permanent frowns of pure disdain. Years of hating will do that to anyone.

"We've been waiting for something like this to happen," another lady says, joining the conversation. They each look like they could use the Spot's services. One six-week dance course could change even the frumpiest housewife into a bona fide diva.

There are about a dozen or so people standing around for no other reason than to catch the latest gossip. I'm surprised Honey-Mama hasn't enforced the "NO TRESPASSING" signs prominently displayed at the entrance to both the property and the house. On more than one occasion, she's greeted unwelcomed guests with one of her several shotguns, but I guess that wouldn't go over too well, with this now being the site of a criminal investigation.

"It was just a matter of time before this house of whores fell, just like the Good Lord did to Babylon," a newcomer says to the other ladies, who fervently nod in agreement. "God don't like ugly."

Don't they know that there's nothing ugly about the Spot? You can tell that by observing the care HoneyMama puts into each aspect of her property. She's never taken for granted the blood, sweat, and tears that went into its creation, not to mention the quality of her dancers.

I walk past the outsiders without making direct eye contact with any of them, intent on my destination. The last thing I want is to be pulled into a pointless conversation demonizing the Spot.

Still strong, prominent, and sexy as hell, the women of The Honey Spot are the best and only advertisement HoneyMama's ever needed to promote her business. She always encourages her dancers to mingle with the locals, earn their trust, and make them feel good just by being in their presence. After all, time is money.

"Well, look what the cat dragged in," Dulce—one of the veteran dancers—says, taking a long drag from her cigarette. Dulce looks nearly the same, with the exception of tiny spider lines creeping along the sides of her eyes, which only seem to highlight her high cheekbones and reddish-brown complexion. They all look timeless, as if age passed them right on by and landed square on my ass.

"It's nice to see you, too," I say, stepping up the five steps leading onto the front porch, where the casually dressed women lounge.

If they were sipping on sweet tea, instead of Evian water, I'd swear these ladies were preparing for an octoroon ball. Each of the women glare at me, none inviting me to join their midmorning chat. I recognize all but one who looks like she's heard about me, the prodigal dancer I've unwillingly become in my dance sisters' eyes.

"I hope you weren't expecting us to be all happy to see you, with open arms and shit." Dulce blows her cigarette smoke directly in my face, making me want to slap the taste out of her fuchsia-covered mouth. "We knew you'd eventually come back to beg our forgiveness for that piece-of-shit article you wrote."

I haven't talked to any of my former coworkers since I left Indian Springs, and this is why. Dulce and I used to be close, but I see the tides have definitely turned for the worse. I've always admired her no-nonsense, straightforward Nuyorican attitude. But now that Dulce's focused that hate on me, I'm not feeling her vibe at all.

"I'm surprised the bitch had the nerve to step foot anywhere near the Spot," Couverture says. This woman and her thick Jamaican accent still shake me to my core. "We may be all the way out in butt-fucking Egypt, but we still remember how to kick a traitor's ass like we're in the A."

There's something about C—as she's commonly known—that makes me feel like the sixteen-year-old foolish girl I was when we first met at The Pimp Palace, the club we were both dancing at when HoneyMama rescued me. C took me under her wing and quickly taught me the rules and regulations at the Palace, one of the most popular and raunchy clubs in the South. She schooled me on who the highest tipping clients were, which deejays had our backs, how to get moved from the C team to the A team, and, most importantly, that the only friends strippers have—if any—are other strippers.

"I actually came to investigate Monaka's murder at Honey-Mama's request."

I can't believe these broads still intimidate me like we're in high school. I have a job to do, but they're not letting me get by so easily.

"We know that, Poindexter," C says, poking fun at my glasses. She takes a sip of her cold water and crosses her long, glittery legs, displaying a fierce set of leopard print boots. I could use a bottle myself, but I'll be damned if I ask them for a thing. If memory serves me correctly, there's a cooler on the back porch that's usually packed with complimentary nonalcoholic drinks for the customers.

"Just because we didn't go to college doesn't make us stupid, you know," Dulce says, lighting another cigarette with the butt of her last.

"Whatever," I say, done with our mini reunion.

I glance ahead through the front door into the busy foyer, where various investigators and others are discussing their theories of how Monaka may have fallen to her demise. I need to be inside gathering information for my story, not out here. But before I can make my exit, C continues the unwanted conversation. I guess they've missed me as much as I've missed them.

"I see when you left us, your pretty figure and skin took a hike and never came back. What goes up must come down, huh, Brandy?" C asks, calling me by the dance name HoneyMama gave me. "Or in your case, it's actually the reverse. Ain't that some irony for your ass?" She laughs loudly at her wit. C always did have a way with words.

"Good one," the newest dancer says, another one of C's protégés, I assume.

I look hard at the newbie, and she shuts her glittered mouth. Professional or not, I can only take so much before setting a broad straight.

"Thank you, Tiramisu. I'm just telling it like I see it," C says, caressing Tiramisu's bare left thigh with the back of her middle finger.

Someone needs to tell Tiramisu how ridiculous she looks with that platinum-blond weave set in a high ponytail. It looks more like a used mop than a professional hairstyle. Even with her fit physique, Tiramisu looks older than me and I'm guessing she's only about twenty-eight. She has dark circles around her bloodshot eyes with tiny wrinkles that age her otherwise even skin tone. The living ain't easy when you're a mark for predators like Couverture. She'll suck the life right out of fresh meat, just like the succubus that she is.

"You might want to rethink your new style, *chica*. Fat isn't a good look on you." Dulce can be a mean bitch when she wants to. I used to think her sass was funny, but now it just hurts.

"I don't have time to fight with a bunch of bitter bitches." I strategically walk around the cat fest toward the front door. I think we're all too old to scrap like we're pledging a sorority, but I can't put anything past angry women. "Where's Honey?"

"She's at the springs, cleansing," Dulce says, reminding me of the mandatory cleansings HoneyMama subjected all of her girls to whenever she deemed necessary. If a new girl was hired—which wasn't very often—we'd all have to participate in the ritual officially making her an ordained dancer at the Spot.

Tiramisu and C suck their teeth in unison at the thought of being dipped in the cool water at the back of the five-acre property. Dulce glares at them both before refocusing her energy on the noise inside.

"She said for you to wait for her at the main stage," Dulce says, pointing to the screen door, where policemen are talking inside. Words like "brothel" and "trick" linger in the still air, reiterating my main purpose this morning. In this moment, Monaka's voice is the only one that counts.

I guess I can start my investigation without my former benefactor's physical presence. I'm sort of glad HoneyMama's not here. If her heat is anything like theirs, I'll need more time to armor myself against the impending flames.

Chapter 2

*T*HE SUCCULENT COUCHES AND PLUSH PILLOWS STREWN ACROSS the soft-carpeted floor are still tempting, even for the most pious person, which I'm far from being. The entire motif is designed to be enticing, enchanting, a place you can't wait to get inside of and never want to leave. Most of the women who work here are some shade of brown, so the red, orange, and gold hues are perfect complements to the near-nakedness prevalent throughout the Spot. The soft scent of honeysuckle creeps up my nose slowly at first. Then powerfully—much like a good fuck—the overwhelming sweetness takes over my senses, almost making me forget why I'm here.

"Please walk around the yellow tape, ma'am," a tall, thickset officer says in his native Georgian accent. His cheeks have permanent sunburns, and I can't help but stare. "Haven't you seen a crime scene before?"

About half a dozen of his comrades laugh, one after the other, some not sure what's funny, but too stupid or scared to object. For as long as I've been writing for the *Metro Journal,* I've endured all kinds of *isms:* racism, sexism, and classicism are among the top three. The white, country cops that I'm forced to deal with shell out the worst of the trifecta. The combination of me being both Black and a woman with the nerve to consider herself a serious journalist is at the top of their ever-growing list of Black pet peeves.

"Yes, I have," I say, noticing how he's now eyeing the dancer's stage. "Have you?"

I can see the rise in his pants as he continues to follow Monaka's lifeless form from the pole and down the wooden steps leading from the stage into the audience, where we're standing.

He looks at me hard, the smile from his chapped, thin lips morphing into a scowl as his friends' chuckles turn on him. I've always hated cops, and not just because they want to screw strippers one minute, then harass them the next. Mostly, I can't stand them because they have the power to act on their hypocrisy, and that's more than I could take back in the day. No matter which profession I seem to choose, law enforcement is apparently an inevitable part of it. At least in my current position, I can talk back with a little less fear of being arrested for pissing off the wrong officer.

Seeing Monaka lying on the floor conjures up old images of Mocha's death, as well as grateful guilt that it's not my murder under investigation. I walk past the men and around the yellow caution tape toward the familiar stage. The room looks the same, except for the reflection staring back from the mirrored background isn't nearly as golden as it used to be.

"Excuse me," I say, pushing past the gawking male investigators as I continue my trek across the floor.

I pass empty tables and chairs, usually filled by men and women alike partaking in homemade sweets while enjoying a daily show. Brightly colored tablecloths highlight the overall décor, as do the matching candles in the center of each. Colorful images of nude women or their silhouettes line the walls, all procured from local artists.

This stage—the golden stage, as we call it—is where dancers graduate to after performing on the smaller, multi-poled stage in the back of the house. My hands want so badly to feel the cool material against my skin, but I freeze in my tracks. Once a mistress of the pole, I'm now way too heavy and out of shape to even give it one go-around, though I wouldn't mind trying for old times' sake.

I almost feel like the young woman I was when I worked here, almost twelve years ago, remembering how anxious I was for my turn to dance with the brass rod. The sensation of simply being near it still humbles me.

I hate to agree with C, but the stripper pole is definitely a metaphor for life: what goes up must eventually come down. I hope the old saying applies to my weight, too. It has gone up and down all my life, but this time it seems to be stuck at the top and, as all dancers know, that shit's dangerous. Friction is the key to controlling the slide up and down the slick rod. The more inexperienced the dancer, the more difficult it is to reach the top. And once at the top, successfully working your way back down is pivotal to both your money and your safety.

"Please don't contaminate the crime scene, little miss," the same beefy officer scolds while loosely chewing on a toothpick. The forensic investigator looks up from his meticulous dusting, shakes his head in disgust, and exits the stage.

"I won't." Damn, this jerk is working my nerves. If he weren't such an asshole, he might be slightly attractive in an *In the Heat of the Night* sort of way—Bubba could get it.

I navigate through my overstuffed purse to find my recorder and get to work. But no matter how hard I try to remain focused on the task at hand, all I can think about is dancing on that stage.

The scene's all too familiar, eerily similar to Mocha's lifeless body lying in the dry brush that hot summer day. Fortunately, Monaka's fresh body is absent the stench that rotting flesh brings with it, but the sick, heavy feeling in the pit of my stomach is the same.

I hold back the tears stuck in my throat as all eyes are on me, the only other woman in the dimly lit room besides the victim. I don't want to appear any more unprofessional than these men already assume me to be. Lord knows it's taking everything in me not to break down, right here and now. I also don't want word to get back to my editor that he was right about me being too soft to cover the hard news that makes headlines.

I'm acutely aware that I need to suck it up if I want to be taken seriously.

Seeing Monaka's body on the otherwise-immaculate floor isn't the way I'd hoped to meet her again. I make my way over to where the only slightly covered body lies. Someone should've at least closed her eyes.

The same officer eyes me from across the room and walks over to where I'm standing. Damn. Now what?

"Where'd you say you were from?" he asks, further irritating me. I wished they'd all leave. Whatever work they have to do can be done elsewhere over coffee and donuts, I'm sure.

"The *Metro Journal*," Pete says as he walks into the room full of men equally fascinated by the erotic yet disturbing scene. My current companion lets out a deep grunt and eyes the badge displayed prominently against my cleavage. I guess he's not a fan of the paper. Tell the truth, neither am I, but it's a steady paycheck for the time being.

Pete flashes his badge for the officers, then hurriedly walks over to the bottom of the stage, ready to shoot. As a young, entitled, and wealthy white Southern gentleman himself, Pete fits right in with the rest of the men staring at our fallen beauty.

I press through various old recordings in the digital memory and attempt to ignore the officer's obvious disdain at my presence. He finally walks back toward the entrance of the grand room and leaves me to my work.

"Hands and feet bound; dried blood causes her black hair to stick to her forehead; vacant eyes wide open." I pause the recorder. When my mother hears about this, she won't be able to contain saying, "I told you so."

"Hey, Keke," Pete says, wiping the sweat from his tanned brow line. He places his briefcase down on one of the tables closest to the stage and removes the cap from the expensive camera lens. "You forgot to mention how far this place is from the city."

"I know you have GPS," I retort, in no mood for Pete's complaining, privileged ass this morning. He's a Buckhead brat, through and through who just happens to be Mark's youngest son—the paper's publisher. If it weren't for his wealthy father's ties to the paper, I doubt he'd have a job, even if he was on the newspaper staff at Harvard, as he likes to tell anyone who'll listen.

"Calm down," Pete says, taking shots of the Spot in its entirety, before turning his attention to the stage in front of us. "It's just an observation."

"You're late. That's my observation," I say, turning my recorder back on.

"The victim appears to be in her mid to late twenties, of African-American and Asian descent, wearing black stockings and red high heels; long, straightened black hair appears to have been bound in traditional geisha style, but now loosely cascades down the stage steps; red chopsticks still intact at the crown of her head."

I pause the recorder and take a deep breath. After being in my line of work for so long, I've become slightly desensitized to gruesome sights, but this one's too close for comfort.

"Did you get this?" I ask Pete, pointing at the intricate way Monaka's legs are wrapped around the bottom of the pole. No way she naturally landed like that.

"You know I did." The bright flash temporarily blinds me and anyone else in the room within range of the camera.

I have the feeling that most of the pictures he takes of this crime scene are going to end up on the Internet, which is his new side hustle. It's already a stressful situation when a dancer is taken advantage of, but to have to worry about exploitation even in the afterlife is enough to make me sick.

"She still looks good, though, considering," Pete says without missing a beat.

Yeah, considering Monaka's as dead as a doorknob on the stage she once worked with so much life. Unfortunately, now the audience doesn't have to pay to see her work her pole magic.

"Monaka. Her name's Monaka," I say, loud enough for all within earshot to hear before continuing with my recording.

Pete looks like he wants to shush me, but he knows he'll lose a finger if he tries. Everyone looks at me—the emotional lady journalist—like I've lost my mind, and that's just fine with me. Long as they all recognize that this body isn't just another dead stripper, but a person who deserves some fucking respect, I don't give a shit what they think.

"Two large peacock-feathered fans lay mangled in both hands," I continue. "The iridescent colors in the feathers match her airbrushed nails."

I again pause the recorder and marvel at how well she was put together. Monaka could work the hell out of each of her tools, as well as all of the other God-given talents she possessed.

"Red, peep-toed stilettos intertwined, and tied with some sort of thin rope at the base of the stripper's pole."

The positioning of the shoes reveals scuffmarks from repeated abrasive rubbing—also a hazard of her chosen profession. I don't know who did this, but from the looks of it, Monaka was giving a private dance. Back in the day, I avoided being alone with clients at all cost. Sometimes being too close can be an extremely dangerous thing.

"She's a beauty, ain't she," another admiring officer says, staring down at her bare breasts and stomach.

I need to get a list of names and badge numbers. The dozen or so men present are treating this like a field trip, instead of the tragedy that it is. They all need to be investigated as prime suspects.

"Yes, she is," Pete says, momentarily pausing his voyeuristic lens. "It's a shame she had to end up like this." As if he really gives a damn.

"Looks like the body bag is finally here," another cop adds, heading outside to meet the coroner.

The forensic investigator follows suit with his little black bag of tools for evidence collection in tote. I hope they find the nut job who committed this heinous crime, sooner rather than later.

"Blood is still present on the steps at the bottom of the stage, seemingly uninhibited so far by the dozens of investigators on the scene," I say into the small device, finishing up my last observations. "Doesn't appear as if she had a chance to put up much of a fight."

I turn off the recorder and bend down to stare into Monaka's open eyes. I wish I could close them. She doesn't need to witness the debauchery surrounding her untimely death. At least she looks peaceful now. There's going to be nothing but chaos surrounding her name until the locals run out of shit to talk about, which'll be never. Monaka's murder has been the hottest case to hit this side of Georgia in a long, long time, and the vultures are out to feast.

"Keke, the coroner's coming in to remove the body," Pete says. "I'm going to get a few more shots here, and then work on the rest of the scene."

I guess that's supposed to be my cue to finish my recording, but I don't know what else to say. Everyone's looking at this as just another murder, but for me it feels like déjà vu—Monaka's only here because I left ten years ago.

"This isn't personal, Keke. This is your job now, not that," Pete says, pointing at the recorder in my hand, then up at the stage. "Get the information you need and let's get on with it. We've got a story to print, and this could be our first major headliner. Front-page shit. Don't blow it." I know Pete is right, but I can't help feeling sad, especially for HoneyMama, who still hasn't returned from the springs. All the water in the South couldn't remove this scene from my memory or hers.

"All right; almost done," I say, reluctantly moving from the bottom of the stage and placing the recorder back inside my overstuffed bag. One day, I'll clean this thing out, but until then, it serves as a purse, travel bag, and suitcase, depending on the occasion. "I'll meet you around back."

I glance around the ancient room one more time, still able to hear soft sounds of the seductive music that played in the background for our opening dance. HoneyMama can put on a show like no other. Other strip joints couldn't care less about talent—the main element that separates the Spot from the rest.

When I first started working here, HoneyMama received no love from the residents of Indian Springs, including the owner of Red's Café, across the way. When she returned here from Louisiana, most of the houses were dilapidated, and there was barely any semblance of a town—only deserted buildings, the woods, and the springs at the edge of the property.

Honey said it was when she first dipped her head in the flowing water that she was saved from her abusive marriage and decided to make a home out of the inherited house. Now she helps save other women in situations like the one she was in. I will always be grateful for that. I just wish we could've helped Monaka when she needed it most.

"Ma'am, we're going to have to ask you to move away from the crime scene. Think you've got more than enough fat to chew on for one day," another officer says, snapping me back into the present reality.

I know he didn't mean anything by that last comment, but I can't help feeling that was a cheap shot at my weight. Two men from the coroner's office approach the stage with a stretcher and black body bag. The forensic investigator returns to the scene ready to continue his task, while Pete and a couple of others take shots of their entrance from the foyer. I'm not sure what's wrong with me, but if I try to move now, I'm bound to trip and fall, unlike the professional that I am.

"Come on, Keke. Let's go," Pete says, coming back inside to rescue me. He offers his right hand and I accept, glad for the assistance.

"Bag her up," one of the coroner's men says. I don't want to leave the stage or Monaka alone with these jerks, but I have no choice.

"Thank you for that." I hate the fact I have to thank Pete for anything. He works my nerves on a good day and makes my ass itch on a bad one.

"No problem," Pete says, ushering me away from the main stage, out of the house, and onto the front porch, where C, Dulce, and Tiramisu have been replaced by investigators, cops, and neighbors alike. "Do me a favor and have your breakdown some other time," Pete whispers into my right ear. "We've got too much work to do."

Pete abruptly releases my hand and heads to the back of the house. Just as well. I'd rather take in the lush scenery alone while I gather my thoughts.

Chapter 3

*I*GNORING THE BUSY CHATTER, I WALK ALONG THE PORCH AND ADmire the picturesque rose gardens lining the side of the house. I'm tempted to sit in one of the two oversized rocking chairs on the back porch, but leisure time will have to wait. I need to get the rest of the description down before HoneyMama returns and my real work begins.

I enter the main parlor leading to the backstage, where most of the dance and yoga classes are held, and notice the announcements posted on the corkboard. *"Sensuality is about more than sex,"* the hot pink words on electric blue paper read, immediately catching my attention. HoneyMama holds many sessions on the art of seduction, and this is one of my favorites.

Maybe I should sign up for a couple of classes while I'm here. I feel all dried up inside, instead of juicy and ripe like I did when I was dancing. Now I'm in my midthirties, with no kids, no steady man, and I make less money with more work. At least when I was stripping, I enjoyed my work and stayed fit while doing it.

They do more than simple dances at The Honey Spot: It's more like seductive theater. Each of the girls chooses music that best suits her personality, with the outfits to match. Those who can sing might do that, too. No matter the routine, there's always a captivating dance number enjoyed by all.

"Excuse me. Is the other stage this way?" a plainclothes officer asks as I continue to silently read the board. Is it that obvious I know my way around?

"Yes, sir. It's through the hallway, past the fainting couches," I say, pointing directly ahead. He marvels at the intricate molding lining the ceilings and continues his trek toward where the others are gathered.

I hate that all these strangers have the right to poke around HoneyMama's home. She doesn't even allow shoes in here, yet these men have been given carte blanche to invade her sacred space in every way possible—dirty feet, dirty minds, and all. I choose to delay the inevitable for a moment longer and return my focus to the bulletin board.

"How to find your honey spot. Sunday mornings, eleven till noon," the simple line reads. Now that's a new one. HoneyMama's always coming up with new ways to make money flow.

If someone gave me a map with explicit directions, I still wouldn't be able to find my spot. It's been too long since I could even get close to hitting it without damaging myself. I could honestly get more satisfaction from stripping. I envy all of the women who still dance with HoneyMama in these backwoods of Georgia, even though I do hate driving down here, and I sure as hell don't want to live here again. However, being back does feel like the sweetest thing ever.

I make my way through the room of chattering bodies and other idiots toward the backstage, where Pete's fully engaged in conversation. I don't blame HoneyMama for retreating to the springs. Her peaceful home is gone for the moment. Even if the crime didn't take place in here, I suppose the entire house is subject to molestation.

I've always appreciated the intimacy of the back room as opposed to the grand room that houses the main stage, which is about twice the size of this one. There are multiple entrances into both rooms, giving them an open feel, even when the place is packed.

"Long time, no see," Drew, my former coworker and ex-boyfriend, says, walking into the crowded room through the side entrance. Idris Elba ain't got nothing on this man. After all this time, Drew still looks good enough to devour.

"Boy, this here's a crime scene," the same officer who earlier checked Pete's credentials says, assuming Drew's just another nosey neighbor. The officer uses his stubby index finger to draw an imaginary line between himself and Drew. "You can't cross this border unless you have the proper credentials."

Drew looks over the stunted cop's head and down at me. He could easily move the uninformed man out of his way, but chooses the path of least resistance. I've always respected Drew's ability to stay cool, even in the most heated situations.

"Here's my badge. And it's Detective, not boy." Drew flashes a grin as he displays his shiny bronze star. He glances at the man's uniform and notices the badge loosely pinned above the protruding left chest pocket. "Officer Cannon," Drew says, acknowledging the shaken cop's badge as he returns his own to his back pocket. "Can I cross the line now?"

"No need to get smart, Detective." Officer Cannon looks like he wants to spit chewing tobacco all over Drew's yellow Polo shirt. Finally he walks away, allowing us to properly reunite.

"Impressive, Detective Drew," I say, meeting Drew halfway. Last time we spoke, I was explaining to him why his shit was strewn across the front lawn in front of our love shack up the road.

"Keke, how've you been, girl?" Our embrace momentarily provides an escape from the sadness. His body has always had a way of doing that to me.

Pete and his new friend look at us and whisper about the two Black people in the room displaying public affection. Let them talk: Drew and I are the only ones who actually belong here.

"I've been good," I say, pulling away from our embrace. "From the looks of it, I'd say you've been doing pretty well yourself." He was the security guard and deejay at the Spot for three years, until we both went our separate ways. HoneyMama also helped Drew finish his college degree.

"You look beautiful, Keke."

"Thank you," I manage.

Even if it's not true, I enjoy surrendering to his fantasy world. Our love was as addictive as heroin. And I'm still jonesing for that high, no matter how deadly it inevitably is.

The creak of the antique screen door is the only sound in the room as the men all pause in awe. Without looking behind me, I instinctively know that HoneyMama has entered the building.

"She's here," Drew says, smiling widely and clearing his throat in anticipation of HoneyMama's approach.

I turn away from Drew, anxious to see with my own eyes.

"Gentlemen," she says to no one in particular.

With the sway of her right hip, and then her left, HoneyMama moves through the large space, her small yet full body completely taking it over. The sweet sound of tiny bells sewn around the hem of her bright, multicolored dress flows freely in the warm breeze, mesmerizing us all. It is her house, after all, lest the men forget.

"Excuse me, Ms. Thibodeaux," the same jackass of a cop who sweated me so hard in the main room says apprehensively to HoneyMama. "We'll have to take another statement as soon as your time permits, ma'am. There are a few more details that need to be addressed."

"In a moment," HoneyMama says, floating by her admirers while cooling the muggy air with the wave of her hand fan. "I need to greet my prodigal children first." She walks toward the men gathered at the entrance of the dance room and places her wicker basket full of flowers next to one of the two fainting couches on either side of the doorway.

"Umm, yes, ma'am, Ms. Thibodeaux. No rush," the same almost-attractive officer who spoke with such authority toward me says nervously. HoneyMama has a way of making a grown man feel like a five-year-old boy.

She touches the officer's hand to reassure him that she'll indeed give him the information he's requested, but on her terms, not his. HoneyMama's audience follows her eyes to where Drew and I are posted in the hallway. She tosses her long tresses over her left shoulder, smiles, and heads our way.

Pete—like everyone else—stares in complete wonder at her power to command attention. He's one of the only few present who's never been graced by HoneyMama's aura—everyone from here to the city knows who she is.

Visibly, HoneyMama is a white woman. She was raised in New Orleans by her mother, Betty, and her aunts. Ms. Betty didn't intentionally pass as a white lady; everyone just assumed that she was one on sight, and she didn't object. And her father, Joseph Thibodeaux III—a very proud Cajun man who loved his liquor almost as much as he loved his women—left Louisiana for Georgia when HoneyMama was much too young to remember.

Mr. Thibodeaux became a very wealthy real estate investor across the South after inheriting a portion of his father's land. When he died of too much partying and old age, Sugar Daddy, as he was affectionately coined in Indian Springs, left a house to each of his seventeen children spread all over the South by various mothers from Alabama to Florida. If you let the old folks tell it, every woman Mr. Thibodeaux met melted at the mere sight of the man. According to these same old folks, HoneyMama looks, acts, and operates just like her father did, whether she knew him well or not.

Standing a good five inches shorter than my five-foot-six frame, HoneyMama reaches up to wrap her arms around my shoulders and squeezes tightly. Apprehensively, I bend down and allow my head to find its nook in her right shoulder and return the love tenfold.

"HoneyMama," I say, unable to verbalize everything I'm feeling. I want to repent for my disrespectful behavior, for leaving the way that I did. I want to tell her I love and miss her. I want to beg for her forgiveness, but I can't seem to do anything more than let her hold me.

"Brandy," she says, coating me with her signature homemade fragrance of honeysuckle, lavender, and gardenias. She slowly rocks me, acknowledging my inability to move, before letting go. "You look good, girl."

"Thank you," I say. "You look beautiful as always." HoneyMama blushes at my compliment. No one would guess she's old enough to be my mother, or that she's given birth to three children.

"Drew, I'm so glad you were able to make it," HoneyMama says, hugging him just as tightly. "When I saw all of those police cars swarm the property early this morning, I didn't know what else to do." HoneyMama's deep drawl lowers in pitch. She's only speaking to us, not everyone else present, no matter how hard they attempt to hang on to her every word.

"Anything for you, HoneyMama," Drew says, returning the affection. "I am so sorry about Monaka. She didn't deserve to die like this; no one does. If I were still working here, this never would've happened." Drew lets go of HoneyMama and takes us both by the hand. I imagine he's feeling as guilty about Monaka's murder as I am.

"It's not your fault, Drew," HoneyMama says. "You hear me?"

With tears welling up in our eyes, we grip tighter, sharing a moment only we can relate to. "You know we're a family here, and we will get through this together."

HoneyMama's words hit a chord I haven't felt in over a decade. A large part of me died when I left both the Spot and Drew. We were a family, and I have missed my people.

"With you and Drew working together, I know I'll get the answers I need," HoneyMama says.

After a long minute, Drew releases our hands and enters the back room, ready to throw his hat in the investigative ring.

HoneyMama looks at me and I can see the sorrow in her eyes. The stress of Monaka's death is beginning to take its toll. Dealing with spiteful neighbors is enough to make anyone tired. The small taste I got of the talk around town must be nothing compared to what HoneyMama's been hearing all morning, not to mention the misinformation already being channeled through the local media.

The *Spring Review* has never had to be concerned with actual facts, because the local paper doesn't go any farther than Indian Springs—no wonder HoneyMama called Drew and me to help. The longer the murder goes unsolved, the more time people's imaginations have to run wild. We've got to get to the bottom of Monaka's murder and vindicate The Honey Spot and its owner. I owe HoneyMama at least that much.

Chapter 4

*T*HE MORNING AIR IS FILLED WITH THE PUNGENT AROMA OF THE sulfur water that populates this area and the natural springs it's named for. Even if the majestic water is supposed to be good for every ailment known to humanity, I've never been able to get past the smell of boiled eggs.

Last night ended late, and I knew that I'd need to get an early start this morning if I wanted to beat the majority of Atlanta traffic. I ended up getting a room at the only hotel in town, which was more like a bed and breakfast, minus the breakfast. I'm starving and in no mood for the morning newsroom briefing I'm running late for, but if I don't show up, Charlie will have a field day with my ass.

No doubt Pete's already filled our boss in on the visual details of Monaka's murder. Now I need to do my job and make Monaka a real person in Charlie's eyes rather than just another murder victim for his headline.

I have to convince my boss that me staying in Indian Springs is a smart investment, especially if he expects me to get up close and personal with the dancers again. They have all but formally exiled me.

"Shelley, I'm running late," I say into my cell, slamming my car door with everything I need for the day in hand.

"Okay, okay," she says, recognizing my exasperated tone. I'm always in a rush this time of morning. "But real quick, have you spoken to Ian since your date last week?" Shelley asks, referring to the first date I've had in a long time.

I met Ian at a news writer's conference downtown during the annual Black history month festivities, for the second time in two years. This year, he followed me around until I agreed to leave the hotel and have a drink with him. The date ended at my apartment, and he didn't call the next day as promised: typical. Once he did call, two weeks later, he made it a point to make plans with me, even if I think he was only interested in getting inside my panties, because I didn't let him get it all that first night.

Since then, Ian's been fairly consistent, but something tells me he's in no hurry to commit. Besides, I can't fully trust a man who doesn't keep his word, no matter what the self-help books say about why men don't call immediately after the first date.

"Shelley, this is neither the time nor the place to talk about Ian," I say, balancing my smartphone between my right ear and shoulder while trying to hang on to my coffee and bag without dropping either one. I press the parking garage elevator button, praying it's not on the top floor. I have two minutes to make it upstairs without getting the late look from Charlie.

"Actually, I think it is," Shelley says as I step inside the empty elevator. I can hear her newest baby suckling at her breast as we speak. "Don't go fucking shit up with your new man because you're hot and heavy for your ex."

I called Shelley last night and told her all about how delicious Drew looked, even if he is off-limits.

"Shouldn't you watch that dirty language in front of the baby?" I ask, placing my items on my disheveled desk. The lower reporters don't have any privacy; that's why I take all my most important documents with me. Shit has a way of walking away around here.

"Hey, missy. I've got four kids, and you, none. So let me worry about the parenting skills, okay? You worry about getting a husband and not just a man, which is where Ian comes in and Drew falls out. Don't go screwing up your new relationship before it even begins."

"Relationship? What *relationship*, Shelley?" I ask in between bites of my blueberry scone. "We've been dating for five months and only slept together a handful of times, and they weren't all that great."

"Yes, but the condom came off the last two times, so it's serious whether you like it or not. Take your *Nikes* off, girl, and stay your ass put somewhere long enough to get to know a man before moving on to the next one," Shelley says, telling it like it is, as usual.

The newsroom is bustling with reporters and writers moving rapidly from one section to the other. I better join the stampede before I get run over.

"I know you've got a big ass, but your last name isn't Kardashian. You're moving too fast, Keke. Mark my words, Ian's a keeper."

"Yeah, but what if he doesn't want to be kept?" I glance around the busy workspace and read my coworkers' body language to gauge the energy. If everyone's in a relatively good mood, I know Charlie's in one, too. If they look tense, like they do now, then I know he's out for blood.

"No man wants to be kept at first. It's your job to show him what he's missing by not being kept by you," she says, her baby cooing in agreement. "You've got a lot to offer, missy. Stop selling yourself short. And please stop settling for less than you deserve."

"McCoy, let's hear it," my boss says, stepping into the open space from his adjacent office and scaring me half to death. "I haven't got all day." He loves to yell early in the morning and scream late in the afternoon.

"Shelley, I gotta go."

"Whatever, Keke. You know I'm right. And tell that uptight dimwit of a boss to get off your ass and get some. Maybe he'll loosen the hell up," Shelley says, making me laugh at Charlie's displeasure.

I hang up my cell, take a sip of my coffee, and face Charlie, ready for the briefing.

"Thank you for joining us this morning, Ms. McCoy," my boss says, clearly irritated. "Let's hear what you've got for us, that is, if you're finished with your little girl talk."

The other twenty or so reporters gather around the large worktable in the center of the room. When I first started working here, this was my favorite time of the day. I used to love to listen to all of the fascinating stories people were working on, each with a different focus. To know that this is where the pages of the newspaper were first born really got my blood flowing. Now it's just the daily cuss-out that I wish I could skip.

"Well, actually, that's what I wanted to talk to you about," I say, flipping through my notes. I listened to my recordings last night several times and jotted down the key points. I know Charlie's only interested in the meat—screw the details. "There's so much more to this story than a simple murder."

"So what?" Charlie says, chewing on the butt of his unlit cigarette. "I sent you down there to get the story on a murdered stripper, nothing more." Charlie's face turns a deeper shade of red. He doesn't like the paper's time or money being wasted.

"Yes, Charlie. I get that," I say, scanning my barely legible handwriting for a few juicy facts to convince him that there's more here than meets the eye. "But this murder is the first tragedy to hit Indian Springs in decades, and I know there's more going on there."

Charlie looks to Pete for confirmation, and he nods his head in agreement.

"What do you think is going on here, Pete?" Charlie asks. Why is he asking the photographer about my story?

"I don't know, but there's definitely something suspicious about the way the girl was killed, right down to the way the body was positioned," Pete says, displaying his photos for all to see.

"Damn," Jacob, a senior City Hall correspondent, says. Every man in the room—which is the vast majority of reporters present—takes a second too long to check out the photos of Mon-aka's lifeless body.

"I can see that." Charlie bites down hard on his cigarette as his bloodshot eyes carefully scan the pictures. "Get as much as you can out of this story, you hear, McCoy? I want to know what they don't want to share."

"Got it," I say, elated that he's going to keep the story going. "In order to do my best, I need to be where the action is," I begin, ready to plead my case further. He's got to allow some sort of budget for travel and lodging.

"It's only an hour away, right?" Charlie asks, again looking to Pete for confirmation. "That's close enough to drive back and forth, McCoy. Now, Nick, tell me all about the fire that killed the three kids in Little Five Points. That's a good one," Charlie says to another coworker, who covers the city beat, but I'm not giving up so fast.

"Charlie, my car's already on the fritz, not to mention the cost in gas," I say, interrupting Nick before he can answer. He and Charlie look at me like I've lost my mind. "It would be more cost effective for the paper if I just stayed in Indian Springs for the time being. I need to earn the women's trust if I'm going to do my best work."

Charlie glares at me, still shocked that I interrupted him. "Ms. McCoy, this paper's not going to foot the bill for a stripper re-union," he says, insulting me in front of everyone. The nerve of this pig. "I know you may have a sense of nostalgia for your for-mer life and all, but you're a reporter now and you don't need to be in residence to get the scoop, right, Pete?"

Again, why is he asking Pete, who's technically junior to me in status, about my story? And what the hell is his problem, calling me out like that? This jerk is too much for me sometimes, but until I find a position at a better paper, I have to bite my tongue and take the shit he constantly shovels my way. The MeToo movement never made it to the *Metro Journal*.

"Well, actually, the girls are quite tight-lipped around strangers.

And Keke isn't considered one of them anymore." Great. Another thing I have to thank Pete for, damn it.

"Fine; whatever," Charlie says, writing on a piece of paper and handing it to me. "Tell Sally I said to write you up a payment voucher. You'll have to save all the receipts, and you only get two meals a day, so make 'em count."

"Thanks, Charlie. It'll be worth it, trust me," I say, taking the slip from him before he changes his mind.

"You've got two weeks, McCoy. Make it work," Charlie grunts before returning his attention to Nick.

"Will do." I collect my things and head down the hall to his secretary's cubicle. The older white lady has been here since the start of the paper decades ago and isn't budging from her post.

Pete follows me for his "thank-you," I suppose, but I have half a mind to kick him in the balls, since I can't serve Charlie properly.

"Hey, Keke. You're going to need more pictures, aren't you?" Pete asks, falling into stride with my quick pace. The sooner I get out of this building, the better.

"I don't think so, Pete, but thanks for having my back in there."

"No problem," he says, stepping in front of me before I reach Sally's desk. "Listen, Keke. I think we'd do better working on this project together, don't you?"

"What do you really want, Pete, and make it fast. I've got to get on the highway before it gets too hot to bear." I glance at the wall clock, anxious to get on my way.

"The same thing we all do—recognition, and eventually out of this hellhole." I agree with him so far, but my coffee is getting cold and he's already worked my nerves enough for one day, and it's barely nine in the morning. I can't imagine two weeks with him by my side. "Look, for a headliner, you're going to need good pics," Pete says, reminding me of the days I used to love to look at the colorful pictures in my daddy's newspapers. He has a good point: the right picture is worth a thousand words, and a promotion.

"Fine, but you can't stay. The dancers won't appreciate it at all if I have a hungry young buck following me around all the time. Now move out of my way."

"Great. And don't worry, you can have my travel vouchers. I can pay my own way," Pete says, dangling his BMW key chain in my face. "See you at the Spot."

Some men are always looking for easy prey, and in their minds, strippers are the most vulnerable of them all. I saw the way Pete eyed the dancers yesterday. I hope he knows what he's doing. HoneyMama's girls are well trained in their art form. Pete had better be careful before he winds up a victim himself.

Chapter 5

*I*T TOOK A WHILE FOR ME TO PACK UP MY BELONGINGS, MOSTLY BE-cause I haven't done laundry at all this month. I went by Shelley's house to catch up on my wash and fill her in on the details of my love and work life, which took all afternoon. It was nice to see her and what I'm not missing by being a stay-at-home mom. Her beautiful Craftsman home near Emory University—where she's also a permanent PhD student due to her continuous maternity leave—is gorgeous and always a mess. I love my friend, but I was glad to get on the road and away from her screaming brood.

After finally checking into the small hotel up the road, I walk back to the Spot to see if I can catch HoneyMama before she starts prepping for tonight's work. I could also use the exercise. It's a beautiful evening, and, unfortunately, the buzzards are also out to feast. The town folks are overly excited about the tragedy, each with their own "whodunit" theory to share with anyone who'll listen.

"What are you doing here?" Dulce asks, taking a drag from her cigarette. She's the only person sitting on the front porch, watching the sunset, I assume.

I look at the unfamiliar faces populating the once-private estate freely roam through the grounds. They're in the parking lot, the garden, and even toward the edge of the property where the springs are.

"My job," I say, passing her by. I'm in no mood for her attitude. It's too hot out here to play around. These sandals weren't made for both walking and sweating. "Where's HoneyMama?"

"She's in the front room preparing for Monaka's last dance," Dulce says dryly.

"A last dance already?" I'm not completely shocked that Honey-Mama would want to honor Monaka so quickly, but it is too soon.

Much like cowboys, HoneyMama honors fallen dancers by performing in their honor. We've only had to participate in the celebration once before.

"Yeah," Dulce says in between drags. "She says it's bad luck to leave the dead unsung for more than twenty-four hours. I say it's because she's already lost a day's worth of income, damn the chalk outline on the main floor."

"You know HoneyMama is not like that," I say. "If nothing else, she wants to make sure Monaka's memory is honored before the shit really hits the fan. This might be her last opportunity to do that."

"You always were an ass kisser, Brandy," Dulce says, taking one last puff before tossing the lit butt onto a wet spot on the wooden deck.

"I know you're grieving, Dulce, but don't push me," I say, stepping over her trash. "I can and will push back, remember?"

Dulce glares and wisely bites her tongue.

I walk through the foyer into the open living space, where several dozen guests await the service. I'd love to see another club owner honor one of its fallen dancers like she does.

When I first started at The Pimp Palace, I was a broke-ass teenager who needed a job. And to the men running game, I was fresh tail. I was introduced to the pole first, as the owners always want to make sure the new girls have some sort of coordination on their feet. I can remember the stench when I first walked into the thick air-conditioned room. I'd never smelled anything like it. Well, maybe in the girls' locker room after volleyball practice—I wasn't on the team for very long.

"Keke, there you are," Drew says, diverting my attention. "I was wondering where you went last night."

"Had to check in with the boss," I say, shaking Drew's hand and avoiding the hug he was going for. I can hear Shelley in my head telling me to stay as far away from him as possible.

"This is my partner, John Miller," Drew says, introducing us. "John, this is Keke McCoy. She's a reporter for the *Metro Journal*."

"Nice to make your acquaintance, Ms. McCoy," John says, tipping his cowboy hat toward me. The toothpick in his smile barely hangs between his perfectly straight teeth.

"Likewise," I say, allowing his full, soft lips to kiss my hand. "Well, aren't you the Southern gentleman." It's been too long since a man charmed me like this.

"Always," John says, pulling back slowly. His light green eyes complement his bronze skin and thick mustache, momentarily causing the heat in my body to rise to my cheeks.

"All right, you two," Drew says impatiently. Glad to see he's still feeling me enough to know flirting when he sees it. "Let's find HoneyMama before the service starts and say our proper hellos."

"HoneyMama," John says, smiling. "I love it. Nothing like coming to a whorehouse where the madame's name starts with 'honey' and ends with 'mama.'"

"This is not a whorehouse," Drew says sternly. He'd better check his friend before HoneyMama hears him slandering her business. "It's a dance club—that's all."

"Well, if that were so, we wouldn't be here, now would we?" John glances around the vast space, taking it all in. Like Charlie and many others, I can see John's already made up his mind about what happened. In his eyes, Monaka was just another Jezebel who got what she deserved.

"Innocent people get killed, too, John," I say, attempting to shed some light on his closed mind. Drew looks like he wants to beat his partner's ass and we can't have that. "Not just harlots and hookers."

"Yes, Ms. McCoy. But you have to admit, the harlots and hookers get killed more than most innocent folks, like you and me," he says, shifting the worn pick from the left side of his sly smile to the right. If he only knew about my past, he'd bite more than that toothpick.

"It looks like they're about to start," Drew says, noticing the lights dim throughout the home.

"It's time for Monaka's last dance," Tiramisu says, opening the double doors that lead to the back of the house.

I guess I'll have to catch HoneyMama after the show. If I had known what I was walking into, I would've at least brought flowers, like the other patrons.

Dulce steps inside and glares my way. The rest of the dancers usher the guests into the room while she walks as if she's in a daze. It appears that Dulce's taking Monaka's death harder than the others. I need to have a one-on-one with HoneyMama to catch up on the group dynamics at the Spot. Like Pete said, I'm no longer one of them and need help figuring it all out.

"How can a dead woman dance?" John thinks he's funny, but Drew and I shoot daggers at him to let him know that he's not.

"The last dance is for Monaka, in honor of her life and talent," Drew says, visibly disappointed in his partner. He always was quick to jump to our defense regardless of who the offender was. "Whatever money is earned goes toward the funeral arrangements, and to the dancer's family."

"You should feel honored to be in the presence of Honey-Mama and her dancers, especially tonight," I say, watching the guests file into the room. They each receive a white rose as they're escorted to their seats. "It's rare that she has a fallen dancer, but when she does, she puts on the best performance you'll ever have the pleasure of witnessing."

I step in front of them both and lead the way. Like most homecomings, this one, too, is bittersweet. If only John could walk a mile in a dancer's shoes, maybe he'd have a little more appreciation for the art form.

As I move from the light violet-and-blue foyer into the back dance room, the lush décor, overflowing in hues of orange, red, and gold, immediately calms my nerves. There are dozens of mirrors hanging from the gold-speckled walls throughout the large room, with curtains that can be released with ropes to serve as dividers for private sessions with the dancers. Plush gold couches and armchairs with orange pillows engulf the fifty-plus guests and twelve dancers alike. Kashmiri silk carpets and velvet curtains help to create an intoxicating ambiance—not just for entertainment, but one of complete healing and joy.

"Damn," John says, horrified. "I think I've died and gone to whore heaven."

"Shut up and sit down," Drew says, directing his partner to take a seat at one of the four tables closest to the stage.

Pete notices our table and joins us. Lucky me.

"This is my colleague, Pete Harper," I say, being cordial. "Pete, this is Detective John Miller and Detective Elijah Drew. They're working on Monaka's case."

"Nice to meet you both," Pete says as he focuses his camera on the stage. "I should be able to get some great shots tonight."

I have to admit, the right pictures of this dance will accompany my story nicely.

"Everyone, please take your seats and enjoy the complimentary biscuits, honey butter, and tea at your tables," a young dancer I don't recognize says from the double doors as several other barely clothed dancers enter the space. "The show's about to begin." She closes the doors behind her and turns off the lights to allow the candles to finish setting the mood.

"Don't mind if I do." Drew takes a warm biscuit from the basket in the center of the table and slices the butter. I can smell the honey from here.

"Would you like some maple syrup with that, sweetie?" another dancer I don't recognize asks.

Drew nods his head affirmatively and watches as she pours the hot liquid onto his saucer.

"Me too," John says, putting his saucer in the air like a child asking for seconds.

The dancer gladly obliges.

Pete looks on in amazement at the way the Spot operates. I smile at the men, knowing they're already out of pocket for all their cash and then some, which is all a part of the master plan.

Several dancers always function as hostesses to the audience, while the main girls are onstage. There are no lap dances at the Spot, just pleasure keepers that keep the clients full and happy. Butts County refused to grant HoneyMama a liquor license, which is where the idea for sweets and drinks came from.

The unusual twist only added to the Spot's unique ambiance and lore. The desserts have become a staple in Indian Springs, with a café around back, where the kitchen's located. The kitchen door used to be used for the colored help's entrance when her father owned the house, but now HoneyMama uses it to serve all the clients who come for fresh baked goods during the day.

"Well, all right now," Pete says hungrily.

Drew looks at my coworker and gives him an unspoken warning to calm the hell down. Even if it is a show, we should all remember why we're here.

Although he often frequents the high-end gentlemen's clubs on the white side of town, I know Pete's never seen anything like this before. The Spot is more like an erotic, interactive concert with extremely talented dancers rather than a simple strip joint. These women can make a man nut in his pants just by the way they serve the sweet treats—no dancing or contact necessary.

Tiramisu walks through the crowded room, up the three steps to center stage, and completely commands our attention. There are five crystal vases lining the front of the stage, each holding a few yellow and red roses dripping with honey. She takes a flower out of one of the antique vessels, slowly rubs it against her full lips, down her neck, and eventually reaches her breasts, delicately circling her bare nipples and allowing the honey to fully penetrate her dark skin.

"I've never wanted to be a flower so badly in all my life," Pete says, shooting away. I would snap at him, but I think most of the patrons feel the same way, including John, who hasn't chewed on his toothpick once since sitting down.

The deejay changes the music, cues the rest of the dancers to leave their captivated clients and approach the circular stage. Each woman wears a jeweled veil in complementing colors that will be removed when it's their turn to dance. The women, also wearing matching gold mesh skirts, with bare breasts, sashay barefoot up the few steps leading to the stage.

The room begins to glow as they provocatively dance to Beyoncé's "Naughty Girl," apparently one of Monaka's signature songs—each dancer has a few she's known for. Tonight, Monaka's dance sisters will perform to all of her favorites.

HoneyMama enters the room from the side entrance with a microphone attached to her ear and approaches the stage.

"Welcome, dear hearts, to Monaka's last dance," HoneyMama says, eliciting applause from the crowd. She's the only one with a top on, for what it's worth. It's the same material as the skirts, and blends in perfectly with her even-toned vanilla skin. Honey-Mama's the oldest and, by far, the sexiest woman onstage. Not the best dancer, but she is the one who possesses that pull that makes her—and her club—irresistible.

I glance around the room and notice several other women enjoying the show. All of the patrons are having a good time, or so it appears. One in particular catches my eye from across the room. He's a strange-looking man, not because of his ambiguous features, but more so because he's wearing shades inside of the already-dim room.

"What's with the diva over there?" Drew asks, noticing the same peculiarity. "Doesn't he know that Cazals went out of fashion years ago?"

I smile at Drew's fashion update. He's never been shy about his sense of style.

"I don't think he got the memo," I say, eyeing the last biscuit. I'm tempted to eat the square treat, but I don't want to be greedy. Besides, I'm sure I'll get my fill by the time my two weeks of investigating are up.

"Shh, you two," Pete whispers. "You're interrupting the show."

"You're not supposed to watch, Pete," I say, irritated. "You're on assignment." I tap the top of his expensive camera, reminding him to get more shots.

"Maybe you can't understand it because you're a woman and all, but watching the show is unavoidable." Pete opens the shutter and shoots a couple of quick shots before again losing his focus. And he had the nerve to question my professionalism yesterday when I almost broke down near the main stage.

"Walk and chew bubble gum, Pete," I say, snapping my fingers in front of his eyes. "And, in case you haven't noticed, there are women also taking it all in."

Pete looks around the room and smiles. "My kind of women."

"Not mine," John says, sitting back in his seat and tucking his thumbs in between his jeans and thick leather belt. With his complementary cowboy hat and boots, John looks like he just walked out of an episode of *Yellowstone*. "I prefer a good ole Southern belle, a Christian woman who knows her place."

"And how does your wife feel about that?" Drew asks.

"Funny, Detective Drew," John says snidely. "Very funny."

The song changes to Sade's "Jezebel," the perfect conclusion to this evening's performances. So far, the new girls have done an excellent job paying tribute to Monaka's memory. I'm sure Dulce and C, both veteran dancers, will stop the show in the finale.

"I missed the joke," I whisper to Drew.

"John's wife left him last week, for the third time," Drew says aloud, damn the low voice. I'll ask him about the tension between him and his partner later.

"She'll be back," John says, resuming his oral fixation. "She always comes back."

Drew and I exchange looks as John stares intently at the women onstage. It's as if he's fighting his body's natural urge to experience joy. HoneyMama needs to give John some special attention. One private dance from her and he'd be a new man.

As the women conclude their dance, HoneyMama begins her strut offstage and into the audience to officially greet her guests.

"Hey, Keke," Pete says, without looking away from the stage.

"The headline for your story should be 'The Honey Spot: Where the women are as sweet as honey, and thick like it, too,'" Pete says, throwing back the last biscuit. He signals one of the hostesses to bring more to the table.

"I'll think about it," I say, noticing Dulce approach the stage from the side entrance. She doesn't look like she wants to be here.

"And for our finale, may I present to you Couverture, Dulce, and Tiramisu. Enjoy the show, ladies, gents, and everyone in between." HoneyMama steps back and allows the women to take center stage.

Dulce approaches the pole first, solemnly taking the brass rod in her hands and swinging her left leg up parallel to the pole. I never took Alanis Morissette as a club artist, but the song suits Dulce's mood perfectly, and she's working the hell out of it.

"Damn, these must be the biggest women in here," Pete says, eyeing Tiramisu and C dancing in the background. "Haven't they ever heard of Weight Watchers?"

"No, Pete," I say, tired of his juvenile conversation. Usually, Drew would be the first in line to check Pete, but I beat him to the punch. "Ain't no skinny girls up in here. These are professional mamas, sisters, lovers, and girlfriends. In other words, these are real women with real strength and sensuality who are forces to be reckoned with, not toys to play with."

"Okay, Ms. McCoy, calm down," Pete says, gesturing with both hands for me to chill. "It's just an observation. I'm surprised they can make it up the pole carrying all that luggage," he says, pointing at C. I hate to admit it, but she's the best pole artist in the place, and she knows it.

"Well, get your camera ready because you're in for a treat."

Tiramisu and Couverture come to center stage and work the hell out of one of the three gold poles. Their dance is synchronized perfectly to the upbeat rhythm of the classic Janet Jackson song playing in the background. The women's hips move synchronously to the hook as they begin their pole sex together in perfect harmony.

Each woman is different and unique in her talent. C's main talent, outside of the pole, is pussy popping. Her ass is full and round, and she works it beautifully up and down the pole. C holds on tightly and climbs up to the top, nearly touching the ceiling, while Tiramisu seductively dances around the stage. Then Couverture fully extends both her legs parallel to the pole without missing a beat and works her way back down in expert fashion.

"Why are these girls making me hungry in more ways than one?" Pete asks, damn-near drooling. "Their names alone sound good enough to eat."

HoneyMama used to serve the dessert each girl was named for, but the tasty treats proved to be too exotic for the patrons' taste buds.

"That's because HoneyMama named all of her girls according to their best attributes," Drew says, equally captivated by the dance. He can't stand C any more than I can, but the girl's got skills too flawless to ignore. And Tiramisu's not bad, either.

"So, what was your dance name, Keke?" Pete asks. "Not that you need a stage name—Keke McCoy already has such presence."

That's what my dad used to say, but I don't think he intended this stage to be where it shined.

"I won't reveal my Spot name, but it was just as befitting as the rest."

Drew smiles, already in on my little secret.

"Well, can you at least give me a rundown of how these girls got their names?" Pete asks, enjoying his second round of biscuits. He'd better be careful. Pete's in his early thirties, and his party lifestyle is starting to catch up to his waistline.

"Women, Pete. These women were named by their employer, benefactor, and friend." I roll my eyes, but I think the correction went over his head. It's okay for those of us who know the women to refer to them as girls because it's out of familiarity, but Pete's just being a sexist jackass.

John also looks curious to know their origins, but doesn't want to admit he's interested.

I take out my recorder and use the opportunity to get more information on tape for my article. I almost forgot about the significance of the dancer names.

"Well, I can only speak for the women that I know," I say, starting with the dancers onstage. "Tiramisu, because she dances light on her feet like an angel. Dulce because she's as sweet as jelly, and shakes like it, too. Couverture, or C as we call her, is one of the best dancers in Georgia, and her ebony complexion and thick build have women and men alike wishing that she could be sold and packaged like a Godiva bar."

"Damn," Pete says, fully appreciating the appropriate monikers. "That's what I'm talking about."

I look around at the other dancers circulating around the large space and wonder what their names are.

"You forgot one," Drew says, pointing to one of the hostesses in the crowd.

How could I forget Crazy P?

"And Praline because she's a straight nut. She also specializes in making dudes come in their pants."

Drew laughs at my description because he knows it's the truth. She's the shortest and loudest girl I've ever met. She's also one of HoneyMama's favorite hostesses.

"Language, please," John says, making a cross sign with his fingers from his forehead to his shoulders. "I've never known a lady with such a vulgar mouth."

"That's not vulgar," Drew says, laughing at his partner. "But C could make you repent all day, every day." Drew would know. Unfortunately, he and I both have suffered under her spell on more than one occasion.

"What about the dead chick?" Pete asks unsympathetically.

"Could you be any crasser?" I say, ready to be rid of Pete's ass for the night.

"My bad!" Pete says. "Dead woman," he says, slurring the last word a bit. At least he's learning. Still disrespectful, but learning.

"See, now that's the reason I didn't want you to come," I say. "You have no filter at all. Where's your sensitivity for the victim?" I click the recorder off, done with the explanations.

"And your problem is that you're too damned sensitive to be a serious journalist, Keke," Pete says, repeating Charlie's words almost verbatim. "You need to learn how to separate the victim from the story if you want to do this right. Otherwise, you're setting yourself up for failure, and I don't like failing."

Pete's right about my sensitivity, but I'll be damned if I admit that shit in front of present company.

"What's the significance of Monaka's name," John asks, refocusing our attention. "It may have something to do with why she was murdered."

"Monaka is a type of Japanese dessert, very delicate and shaped like a flower," Drew says, taking a sip of his sweet tea. "Monaka was the sweetest, kindest, and gentlest woman I've ever met. Her name suited her perfectly."

John and Pete are speechless, and so am I. Out of all the dancers I've worked with, Monaka was the last one I would've imagined this happening to. She was soft-spoken, kind, and never caused any trouble.

"Let's have a moment of silence for Monaka," HoneyMama says, reclaiming the stage.

All the patrons and dancers bow their heads in unison. I glance around the room and notice that the strange man with the sunglasses hasn't moved a muscle. What the hell's up with him?

"Thank you so much for joining us this evening," HoneyMama says, directing her dancers to mingle with the crowd and pass around the collection baskets. HoneyMama doesn't allow patrons to throw money at the women—she says it's degrading to both the money and the dancers. "Please know that all donations from tonight's event will go toward Monaka's funeral services. And don't forget to take some biscuits home to share with your loved ones."

While everyone else applauds, I watch the strange man leave through the double doors. If I didn't need to talk to Honey-Mama, I'd follow him. Something about his energy just ain't right.

"HoneyMama put a lot of thought into the names, didn't

she?" Pete asks, wrapping several biscuits up in a napkin and stuffing them into his bag.

"HoneyMama puts a lot of thought into everything she does," Drew says, claiming a biscuit from the basket before Pete takes them all. If Pete would wait a minute, he'd see that the women are about to disperse prepackaged biscuits for the guests to take, greedy ass.

"I guess that's why she's the mama, huh?" John says sarcastically.

I don't know whose ass I want to kick more, John's or Pete's. Drew, on the other hand, looks insulted enough to kick the shit out of them both.

"Actually, HoneyMama's daddy gave her that nickname when she was a child and it stuck," I say, noticing C count her donations. She claims two bills for herself before placing the rest of the wad into the collection basket. At least she's a consistent bitch, damn the occasion.

"Just like honey, I suppose," John says to me dryly.

I look away from C's trifling behavior to focus on John's uncalled-for hate.

"Yes, John. I suppose so."

Chapter 6

*T*HE REMAINING GIRLS DESCEND BACK INTO THE EXCITED AUDIENCE to collect their hefty cash offerings and personal requests. Christmas has nothing on a good night's haul. HoneyMama notices the activity and heads our way. I'm a little nervous about talking to her. Our relationship has been almost nonexistent since publishing my article.

I thought I was doing a service to the sisterhood by talking about the pimps and hustlers in the game. But HoneyMama didn't see it that way. She said there's enough negative attention cast on our profession as it is. She wondered why I didn't choose to talk about the positive side of dancing, and so did I for a long time. Eventually I stopped questioning the need to tell my story my way, but it still stings.

"Keke," she says, coating me with her signature fragrance. "Glad you made it."

"Me too, HoneyMama," I say, returning the love, although the only scent I have to offer after my long day is a mixture of coffee and sweat.

"And Drew. Thank you so much for coming," HoneyMama says, moving from me to my ex, coating him with the same sweetness.

"Of course," Drew says, standing to return her affection. "Monaka would've been honored."

"I hope so, baby. I hope so." HoneyMama turns her attention to our guests.

"You remember my partner, John," Drew says, tilting his head toward the stoic man by his side.

"And this is Pete, a photographer from my paper," I say, formally introducing Pete. But just like John, I hope he won't be around long enough to become memorable. "He's going to be taking a few photos to accompany my story."

"Well, welcome, gentlemen," HoneyMama says, smiling at them both. "I do hope you enjoyed the show, even under the circumstances."

"I did, ma'am," Pete says, almost dropping his camera. He's been itching to speak to her since yesterday afternoon. "It was lovely."

"Lovely, considering," John says, clearing his throat.

"Considering what?" HoneyMama asks, instantly noticing the slight. Her pale nipples poke through the sheer material causing all the men to work extra hard to divert their attention away from the obvious. Looking away doesn't help.

"Considering what type of establishment you're running here," John retorts. He attempts to remain stoic, but the bulge in his pants betrays him.

"John," Drew says, placing his right hand on John's shoulder.

"Oh, no, Drew. Please let the man speak." HoneyMama winks, ready for the judgment. Whatever John's got to say can't be new. She's heard it all before.

"No disrespect intended, Ms. Thibodeaux," he says, dabbing the corners of his mouth with a cloth napkin. "This just ain't my cup of tea."

Drew squeezes John's shoulder tightly, a warning to temper his comments toward HoneyMama. Drew's mother wasn't in his life much as he was growing up, so he'd be damned if the closest thing he's got to one is disrespected anywhere, anytime, or anyplace—especially, *not* in her own home.

On cue, Praline comes over to our table with her serving tray in hand.

"Did I hear someone ask for tea?"

"Yes, Praline," HoneyMama says, gesturing around the table.

"Please serve everyone a little something sweet, would you, my lovely. It's getting a bit bitter in here."

John glares at his partner; Drew stares right back. He finally removes his hand and John rubs his affected shoulder. John looks like he wants to throw a punch, but knows better. Not only will he more than likely lose his job, but he'll also lose an eye, a tooth, and anything else Drew can manage to beat out of him in the allotted time.

"My homemade pralines can make even the wickedest man smile," Praline says, placing the caramel-colored confections on the table, along with a kettle full of jasmine tea for the four of us. Even if it's hot as hell outside, the subtle scent of the fragrant elixir cools the heat building at our intimate table.

"Don't mind if I do," Pete says, digging in.

I think Pete's died and "gone to honey heaven." That's how the dancers refer to clients who get caught up in the rapture of the Spot. I know he's used to the traditional tobacco and liquor favors at the gentlemen's clubs in the city, but I haven't heard him complain once about missing out on his other vices.

"Thank you, Praline," Drew says, taking a nut-filled dessert and devouring it in one bite. I could sit and eat an entire tray, damn the consequences.

At first, John tries to resist Praline's offerings, but it all smells too good to pass up, not to mention the regular night show is about to begin.

"Y'all relax. Let's catch up and leave the men to their vices," HoneyMama says, pointing me toward the basement door, where her living quarters are located.

"See y'all later. And, Pete, control yourself." I follow Honey-Mama through the crowded room toward the side entrance.

She opens the door, checks over her right shoulder to make sure I'm right behind her, and proceeds down the flight of stairs.

When you look at her from behind, HoneyMama looks even better, her ass and thighs are as firm as ever. She looks as young as I do—probably younger, if I'm being totally honest. And her body's definitely in better shape than mine. I've been off the stage for too damn long.

"You look lovely this evening, Brandy. Red's always been your color," HoneyMama says, once we're out of earshot, thankfully. The last thing I need is Pete calling me by my dance name in front of Charlie. Whatever little respect our boss may have for me would be out the door.

"Me? I look like shit compared to you. How do you do it?"

We make our way into the basement, where the walls are lined with the type of family photos you'd expect to see at a nice little old grandma's house. There are photos of her parents and her as a child, her mother, and aunts, and of her father and his father. The living album almost makes me nostalgic for my childhood home—almost.

HoneyMama looks up at me from the bottom of the stairs and smiles. She flicks the light switch on the wall and takes a deep breath.

"You know the Spot keeps me busy, girl." She opens the beaded drape that serves as the entrance into her private domain. The space is larger than my entire apartment.

Freshly peeled oranges, laced with honey and cinnamon, permeate the incensed-filled air, causing me to take a step back upon entering to completely absorb the aroma. Even though the aroma is the same upstairs, it's more potent in the enclosed space. The intoxicatingly sweet smell's impossible to duplicate. I've tried at home many times and have come up with something between a honeysuckle and jasmine fragrance, but nothing quite as pungent as the fragrance these women create. It stays in your hair and clothes for days.

"Step into my office," HoneyMama says, walking across the intimate living room to open one of the three doors on the opposite wall. Her office has the same décor as the main dance room—only, orange and red are the dominant colors in here.

She takes the copper carafe full of water off of her desk, pours two glasses full, and offers me one.

"Thank you." I take a seat on the red velvet couch across from her desk and claim the cup she's placed on the side table. What I really want are those pralines the men are enjoying upstairs. "I'd like to get started on our interview, if you don't mind. I know you have to get back to your clients."

"How come you haven't been by in so long?" she says, ignoring my request. HoneyMama takes a seat in her oversized chair and props her freshly pedicured feet up on the antique wooden desk. "New man?"

HoneyMama's always known how to cut right through the fat to get straight to the sore parts.

She takes a sip from her glass.

"Just busy working," I say, sounding as guilty as I feel.

"Brandy, are you still concerning yourself about that article you wrote a decade ago? Girl, get over it. I have."

She lights the vertical incense stick in its marble holder on the small table behind her. It's cluttered with pictures of her dancers, like most doting mothers would display their children.

"To tell you the truth, Brandy, I didn't know what to think when I read that article. I was glad you were doing your thing, of course. But your take on stripping really surprised me. I remember after you read *Memoirs of a Geisha,* you wanted to call me Mama-san for weeks," she says, rekindling fond memories of our book club meetings.

"It surprised me, too," I say, much more honestly than I care to be at the moment. "Again, I'm so sorry for hurting you."

In all fairness, before working at the Spot, my experiences with stripping were all bad. And the article actually came from the journals I kept during that time period. When I started dancing at the Spot, I didn't write as much because I was too busy enjoying life. Unfortunately, my inspiration for writing came during my most painful times—still does.

"Yeah, I'm sure," she says, sounding unconvinced. Honey-Mama takes a cigar out of the top drawer and lights it with her engraved golden Zippo. I swear she channels Mr. Thibodeaux whenever she smokes. "Let's discuss this once, Brandy, and move on." She takes a puff. "Shall we?"

"Okay." I make a quick adjustment in my seat and prepare for the impact of her words.

HoneyMama turns her attention to the wall behind her, where she has several framed newspaper articles dating back to when her father owned the property. She also has the stripper's creed, which she made us all recite every day before work, displayed in the center, and my article right beneath it. I feel honored and ashamed at the same time.

"What I don't understand is how the personal statement that I encouraged you to write for your intern applications turned into this?" HoneyMama says, pointing at the article. "Your power has always been in telling your truth. But this . . . this is not the entire story, Brandy. You know it."

"You're right," I say, feeling like a student in the principal's office. I know it wasn't the most favorable piece I've ever written, but it's still valid. "I meant no disrespect to you or the profession. However, I did tell a part of my truth that needed to be told at the time."

HoneyMama puts her feet down on the plush rug and places her elbows on the desk, blowing cigar smoke in my direction. "I can respect that, Brandy. And I'm proud of your strength. I know it's not easy being back in the lioness's den," she says, a sly grin on her face.

"Not at all," I say, glancing at the photos around the room. "Even if your dancers aren't nearly as forgiving as you are, Honey."

"Well, all of that's water under the bridge, as far as I'm concerned. That was one experience. This is another," she says, glancing at a photo of Monaka on the wall.

Once hired, all dancers have their professional headshots taken, also courtesy of the Spot.

"In your current article, I want you to shed some light on the reality of our lives inside *this* house, and only *this* house." HoneyMama takes another puff. "No mention of other clubs, even if you're trying to make us look good—we don't need that kind of help, understood?"

"Yes, of course," I say, thinking about the angle Charlie wants me to take. The two approaches are completely dichotomous, but, somehow, I have to make them work. "I'm sure anyone who's ever been here knows better than to believe any of the bullshit people are saying about the Spot."

"You would think so, but these folks around here are wagging their tongues faster than a dog wags its tail, with no truth behind a single word. To think that my own neighbors would spread rumors that I may be responsible for one of my girls being hurt is unacceptable." She pulls hard on the cigar, causing its amber glow to quickly spread up the Maduro wrapper toward her red-stained lips.

"I hope this article will help with your reputation, and the reputation of the club." I take my tape recorder and notepad out of my purse. "I'm ready whenever you are."

HoneyMama nods her head.

I push RECORD and begin with my prepared questions.

"Ms. Thibodeaux, let me first say thank you for allowing me the rare opportunity to interview you and the dancers at your club, The Honey Spot. I will ask a series of questions, and we'll just go from there."

"Questions?" HoneyMama says, relaxing back in her chair. "Can I hear them first?"

"Yes, ma'am," I say, not surprised. HoneyMama hates surprises.

"The five questions are as follows:

1. How did The Honey Spot come to be?
2. Who/Where were you before?
3. How has the Spot changed your life?
4. How well did you know the victim?
5. Where were you the night of Monaka's murder?"

"Do I have to answer the questions like that?" she asks, crinkling her nose.

"No, of course not," I say, embarrassed by the formality. "Let it flow. I'll get the answers I need from our conversation. Just answer the questions being as vague or as precise as you like."

"Does that go for all of the girls or just me?"

"They're for all of you," I say, surprised she'd think I'd show favoritism. I've always been pretty straightforward.

"Well, don't let the girls be too vague, especially Couverture and Dulce," she says, taking the final puff from the first cigar as she uses it to light her second. "I want you and Drew to get to the bottom of this and soon, you hear?"

"That's the plan," I say, noting the two names.

I can see the sorrow written all over HoneyMama's face, conveying the stress of recent events. I've got to help vindicate HoneyMama and the Spot—I owe her at least that much.

The alarm on her cell phone rings, indicating that it's time for her to get back onstage. No show can commence without HoneyMama's blessing.

"Before you go, can I ask if you have any idea who could want Monaka dead?" I can name a couple of jealous dancers off the top of my head, C being number one. But this feels like more than simple envy.

"I don't, but I can say that it's the ones closest to you who can hurt you the most. My mama always told me to keep my friends close and my enemies closer."

Ain't that the truth.

"Then I'll go straight to the source," I say, rising with Honey-Mama and heading back upstairs.

"Our interview will have to continue after the show," she says, straightening her translucent outfit before leading the way back upstairs. "What time do you need to be back in the city?"

"I don't," I say, gathering my things. "My paper approved me staying in Indian Springs until the story is done."

HoneyMama grips the brass doorknob and allows me to step in front of her.

"Well, then, Brandy," HoneyMama says, smacking me on my ass as she opens the door leading out into the lively dance room and approaching the table where the men are seated. "Welcome home."

"Welcome home, indeed, Ms. McCoy," Drew says, smiling at

both HoneyMama and me. All of the men are quite content, even John's uptight ass.

"Thank you," I say, attempting not to blush, but I can feel the heat flush from the top of my curly bun to the bottom of my feet.

"Drew, I know Brandy knows her way around our little town, but I'd feel more comfortable if she had an escort back to her room." HoneyMama's not slick. She was almost as crushed as I was when we broke up.

"So you're staying in town?" Drew asks, rising to the occasion. "Isn't that convenient."

"Convenient for whom?" Pete asks, chiming in without taking his eyes away from the stage for a second. "And who the hell's Brandy?"

Damn, I hoped he missed that part.

"Keke McCoy's Brandy, and Brandy's Keke McCoy," Drew says, standing beside me. "I'll be back, John. Try to enjoy yourself."

"Yeah. You too." John looks at the two of us with a smirk on his face.

Pete also looks at us with a crooked smile. I don't know what kind of girl they think I am, but they're only half right. My days of sleeping with another woman's man are over, even if he was mine first.

"I can find my way back alone," I say, walking toward the double doors. "I'll see everyone tomorrow."

"Oh, no you don't, missy," HoneyMama says, adamantly claiming my hand before I can make my grand escape. "In case you forgot the main reason you're here, there's a murderer on the loose. I would feel more comfortable if my girls were protected at all times until he or she is found. That includes you, Brandy." HoneyMama takes my hand and loops it through Drew's bent arm. "See to it that she gets in safely."

"Yes, ma'am," Drew says. "Will do."

Chapter 7

A COUPLE OF HOURS AGO, DREW WALKED ME BACK TO MY ROOM and tried his best to get inside, in more ways than one. I told him that we're just friends and will remain that way, as long as he doesn't try that shit again. No matter how badly I wanted to rekindle our fire, I knew it would've been wrong on so many levels. He's engaged to a maniac, and I'm sort of dating someone. But it felt good being with him again, until he was gone.

When he left my room, my tears began to fall. I feel powerless to stop them and the flooding memories of our good times together. I can't remember the last time I cried so fucking hard. I don't know if it's because seeing Drew again brought up all of the feelings I had buried deep inside, or if I just want to believe that after all of the shit we've been through, there's a light at the end of the long, dark tunnel that was our relationship.

I still love Drew, but I love myself more, and that's always been the problem with us. In the relationship, he loved his freedom more than he loved me. And I loved myself just enough to have some dignity and get the fuck out when it was getting too deep. Most women will put up with all of the baby-mama drama, the other women, the phone calls, the emails, and all of the other indiscretions that were so vividly brought to my attention every single day of our existence together. I'd rather spend my time in a relationship making love and doing other productive activities, not looking through his cell phone to see who else he's fucking. Unfortunately, I still have that same insecurity in my current relationship—if I can even call it that.

My current lover-friend, Ian, is a strange bird. He's damnnear emotionless and the true definition of "aloof"—completely opposite of Drew. What Drew and I shared was real, passionate, unrestricted good love. But after all of the good fucking, and all of the bills are paid, or not paid—money really doesn't matter when you're that deep in love—what do you have? I know I lost more than I gained, except when it comes to my weight, which packed on after I left Butts County. By all calculations, our relationship was not a good investment. However, it's a lot more than I have right now as I try to come myself to sleep.

"Damn, another text from Drew," I say aloud, even if I'm the only one around to hear my frustration. He ain't saying shit, just trying to get back in my panties and my head, but I'm not letting him. Drew's text is loaded with all kinds of innuendos. I'm trying to get off now and don't need his help. Just the smell of him on my skin is enough to keep me wet.

My cell vibrates again, interrupting the good feeling. I lean over and snatch the illuminated phone to check the message. **"You know you miss me."** Drew's always been straight to the point. **"See you tomorrow at the Spot. Maybe we can have a drink or something afterward, friend."**

I turn my phone off, knowing it will automatically turn itself back on promptly at six in the morning. I should reply with a resounding **"Fuck off,"** but I know he'd like the attention. The silent treatment is all Drew's getting out of me tonight.

My usual nighttime routine consists of indulging in several chocolate generic Oreo-type cookies, smoking a joint—if I can afford some good herb—and drinking half a bottle of threedollar Chardonnay from Trader Joe's. Sad, I know. But it's what I need to wind down after a long day of working with the assholes at my newspaper. Whoever said racism was dead in America never lived in the South, because it's not only alive down here, it's more rampant than herpes on a college campus.

Tonight's the first night I've spent away from my tiny apartment in years. The beds are comfortable in my rented cottage by the main road, but Indian Springs is much noisier than I recall. It doesn't matter much, since I haven't slept solid in months. I was just hoping that being by the springs again might help me relax naturally, but no chance.

I can't even hear the water that runs behind the Spot anymore. It used to be loud enough to drown out all of my thoughts, but all I can hear are cars, loud motorcycles, and trucks speeding up and down the two-lane highway disturbing what little peace I have. Seeing Monaka's lifeless body lying at the bottom of the stage is a picture that'll never leave my psyche, no matter how many glasses of wine I down before bedtime.

I remember the first time I spent a night completely alone in my first apartment in Indian Springs. It was behind one of the neighbors' houses barely big enough for one person. No furniture, no television, and no man around to comfort me then, either—some things never change. But I did have an old birthday gift from Dulce I'd forgotten about and learned how to use it that night.

It was my first vibrator. I had it tucked away in a box for almost a year and found it just when I needed it most. There was also an instructional DVD inside. When she found out that I hadn't opened the box, she immediately made me go there, with her in the room—I became an expert later that night after she left.

"Mami, *have you had my gift in the box all of this time? Ever heard that if you don't use it, you'll lose it?*" Cynthia said—I never called her Dulce back then.

When I opened the unassuming box, a pretty pink surprise awaited me. I took the pearl necklace out of the box and put it round my neck, much to the amusement of my very informed instructor.

"*You shouldn't have, but thank you,*" I said.

I remember opening the birthday card, but stuffed the box inside my already-packed closet, completely forgetting about it until I moved off of HoneyMama's property and into my own place. HoneyMama makes the new girls stay in the house for their first year, just to make sure they stay focused on the job. After that, you're free to live wherever you like.

"Fuck your thank-you, puta*! This is how you treat my gift?" Cynthia said, shaking the box at me. "Mira, it's jewelry with a twist."*

After taking several photos of me with the necklace ignorantly draped around my neck, Dulce told me to press my finger on a small button in the center of the short, thick charm and it began to vibrate. Nowadays, I proudly pack a vibrator in my suitcase—damn the security checks at the airport or anywhere else. I never leave home without one.

Dulce said using the little toy would feel just like someone going down on me. It didn't work that well, but I guess it depends on the head you've been accustomed to receiving. And, if I do say so myself, I taught Drew how to eat my pussy just right, much to my detriment, now that he's tasting someone else's.

After twenty minutes of using the excited battery-operated companion, I get chafed worse than when I dare to walk around in a skirt with no baby powder in between my thick thighs. I can remember a time when my thighs didn't rub together. I can also remember a time when I didn't need my own finger to fuck.

I love the feel of a real dick. I mean, don't get me wrong. I buy the best toys I can afford. But nothing can substitute for a nice dick, for real. The smooth tip, the ribbed, pulsating shaft. Nothing online or in the kinky store can substitute for one of God's best creations, indeed. It takes me a clit-numbing hour to get a decent couple of nuts alone. Drew could make me cream all over the place with a good four-minute finger fuck. And, if he got a chance to lick my pussy, it was really all over, just like my night is. Maybe I'll sleep better after I wear myself out.

After a long night of pondering and pseudo-coming, I'm abruptly interrupted from my slumber by a buzzing phone. This time, it isn't Drew.

"Good morning, masa," I mumble. It's way too early to be talking to this human buzz kill. I know it's going to be a rough day if it's starting out with Charlie's voice.

"I love it when you talk dirty," Charlie says. He can be such a pig. "How's the murder at the titty club going?"

"Is that what we're calling it now?" I ask, kicking the sheets off of my naked body and allowing the cool air to fully wake me.

Pretty soon, this air will feel like hell with a side of sunshine. I better enjoy it while I can.

"Call it whatever you want, Ms. McCoy, as long as you get me the full story, you hear?"

It's only six in the morning and Charlie's already harassing my ass out of bed. I guess he misses the only Black girl being in the office to unload his shit on. Charlie knows I need the job and takes advantage of it every chance he gets.

"And don't bring your ass back to the city until I get it, you hear me, girl?"

"Charlie, you know I'm a grown woman, right?" I let him push the envelope because he signs my checks, even if they're smaller than my mother's feet. But no one calls me a girl unless it's before he makes me scream out "Daddy!"

"Full story: hookers, pimps, hoes, and all," Charlie continues, ignoring the correction, much like Pete did last night. Sexist ass-holes. "And nothing less, Keke. I smell a Pulitzer out of this one. You're our street girl. Get the grit, Keke. I want dirt." Charlie hangs up the phone and just in time, too. When he gets on his "You're our street girl" campaign, I start fantasizing about the many ways I can tell him to go fuck himself in the face—that would be real street for his ass.

I replace my cell on the nightstand, slide out of my queen-sized bed, slip into my house shoes, and make my way into the bathroom for a quick shower. The earlier I get out and dig for the truth about Monaka's murder, the sooner I can get back here to write. I'm still on the fence about having drinks with Drew tonight. I have a feeling it'll do more harm than good.

"Me and my pudge," I say, eyeing my bare frame in the floor-length mirror. Clothing is highly overrated. No matter how big I get, I love being in my own skin.

I look at the yellow sundress draped over the closet door,

ready to wear. I didn't bring many choices in attire, because I don't think I'll be here for more than a week or two. While I'm here, I plan to make the most out of it, starting with getting as much out of the dancers as I can, with today's round of interviews.

After last night's late show, the girls were too tired—or busy—to talk. So was I. HoneyMama gave me permission to attend the morning roundup with the A team—me and Monaka's former dance partners. In HoneyMama's opinion, it's the best place to start digging for information, and I agree. Whether or not they'll volunteer the truth is a whole other story, but I've always been good at getting people to give me what I want, eventually.

Chapter 8

"GOOD MORNING THERE, MISS," PASTOR BRIDGES, THE LOCAL clergyman, says as I walk down the dirt path leading from the cottages into the rest of town.

There's only one main road that runs through this side of town. Whether going to church or the liquor store, we all have to walk down it, one way or another.

"Looks like it's gonna be another scorcher, don't it?" He removes his straw hat and wipes the sweat off of his forehead with the back of his bare forearm, making his already-glistening skin even brighter. If he weren't a churchman, I might try to hit on him. But by the look in his eyes, I can see a hint of recognition. As one of HoneyMama's girls, his judgmental ass wouldn't come near me with a ten-foot pole—his loss.

"Yes, it's going to be a hot one. Thank Goddess for Honey-Mama's freshly squeezed limeade to cool our hot asses down. Nice to see you again, Pastor Bridges," I say, leaving his jaw on the ground, where it belongs. I know I look different, but he'll always see me as one of *those* Honey Spot girls, and that's just fine with me. I didn't take kindly to his judgment back in the day and refuse to deal with it now.

"Brandy, over here," Pete says from his table on Pinky's patio, the only café within a fifteen-mile radius. The locals here definitely keep their businesses in the family. "How about some breakfast?" He offers me a seat in front of his delicious spread. It looks like heaven on a plate, with sausage, eggs, biscuits, grits, flapjacks, French toast, and fresh fruit on the side. Damn, this dude can eat.

"No thanks. I'm good with coffee," I say, pointing to my travel mug. The truth is, if Pete weren't here, I'd devour much of the seven-course meal all by myself. "And I want to get started early with my interviews. I'm supposed to be there by nine." I glance at my watch, noticing it's only eight now. I should have plenty of time to check my email and gather my notes before the meeting.

"Sounds like fun," Pete says with a mouthful of food. "Why do I get stuck with the boring shit, like talking to cops and the neighbors and shit?"

"The same reason you get to eat like a pig and still look like a stick." I snatch up a biscuit from his plate and continue my trek toward the Spot. I catch Pastor Bridges looking at me from across the road and give him a slight smile. I'm not as bad as he thinks I am. Well, not anymore. If the good pastor only knew the kind of debauchery I used to be involved in, he'd kiss my feet for turning so holy.

Before I met Drew, I wasn't much into relationships, which at the time I equated to slavery. When I felt like fucking, there was no shortage of willing participants, and I'd dispose of them at will if any one of them became too attached. It wasn't until Drew came to work at the Spot that I even considered a real relationship. Perfect timing. I had just moved out of the main house and into my own apartment, up the road, and Drew was my first overnight guest.

Most men can't handle dating a stripper, especially not one at the Spot. HoneyMama doesn't get involved in our personal lives, unless she has to, and most men can't stand her presence. But because Drew was my coworker, he understood the life and didn't mind seeing me onstage at all—he knew it was all his for the taking when we got home.

After Drew and I broke up, I tried to get back out on the dating scene with the same vigor as before, but my spot seemed to have dried up a bit. I don't know if it's because my job has me constantly tired, or if it's because I'm just not that interested in sleeping around with randoms. Whatever it is, I can't wait until I get all of my mojo flowing again. Maybe then, Ian will start acting more interested in a steady relationship rather than the bullshit he's serving up at the moment.

Whenever Ian and I do have sex, it's pretty good, but he's the most selfish lover I've encountered in a long time. And the sex is too damned sporadic for me. I like my dick on a consistent basis, not every now and then. He hasn't texted me at all this week, which is not unusual for him. Lack of communication plus a lack of good cunnilingus equals a dry pussy always, every time.

I walk up the long dirt path leading to the front of the house, the same path I drove up the day before yesterday. All of the nosey folks are still out and about, as well as a few police officers—to what end, I don't know. But they're here, and from the looks of it, not going anywhere, anytime soon.

"Morning, sunshine," Mr. Graves, the groundskeeper, says to me from his post at the bottom of the porch. He's been keeping the property since Mr. Thibodeaux owned it.

"Good morning, Mr. Graves," I say, walking up the broad steps. HoneyMama said to meet her around back in the kitchen. I can already smell the sweet potato biscuits baking, which causes my stomach to growl. I hope he didn't hear that.

"Brandy, girl," he says, leaning down and kissing me on my right cheek. "It's so good to see you."

I can't help but smile wide at the sight of my old friend. Mr. Graves has always been one of my favorite people. Fiercely loyal to HoneyMama, he lives in one of the two remaining structures on the back end of the property, near the springs. The other is used as a guesthouse for the company HoneyMama rarely receives, or to temporarily house folks in need, including a few of the locals at one time or another.

"It's good to see you, too." He's wearing the same blue-and-white-striped overalls, long-sleeved, white shirt, baseball cap, and work boots he always dons. "How's your family?"

"Oh, you know my Gloria. Sweet as peaches, tough as nails. All three of my chirrin' done gone off and moved to the big city, just like all you young people do," he says, winking.

"Mr. Graves, don't be like that." I take a freshly clipped rose from his wicker basket and bring it to my nose. The potent fragrance instantly calms my nerves.

"Shit, I ain't mad at 'em, though," he says, continuing with his morning duties, clipping flowers and doing a perimeter check of the property.

Very little happens around here that Mr. Graves doesn't catch, at least not during the day. He's not responsible for anything that happens after dark.

"They come home every first Sunday for church and supper, so ain't that much changed, as far as I'm concerned. But you can't tell Gloria that. No, Lawd! My wife just about lost her mind when the last one went off to college. She think them chirrin' walk on water, and will tell anyone who gives her the time of day the same thang."

"I know she will," I say, remembering my conversations with Gloria. She was never disrespectful to HoneyMama, but would always try to save our sinning souls whenever she got the chance. Their children were Gloria's models for how the rest of the world should behave. Little did she know, her sons frequented the Spot as soon as she went to sleep. Her daughter's just like her, much to her approval, and stayed as far away from HoneyMama and her girls as possible. I know Gloria's got plenty to preach about with Monaka's murder.

"Ms. Thibodeaux's waiting for you 'round back," he says, nodding toward the far end of the house. "The other ladies should be here shortly."

"Yes, sir." I take that as my cue to head to the kitchen, and do just that. If HoneyMama wanted us to know something in confidence, she'd tell Mr. Graves, and he'd relay the message. She never worries about him betraying her trust, which is why she'll never replace him.

I walk around to the far end of the wraparound porch and

peek through the back window above the door, whose creaky entrance announces my arrival.

"It's about time you got here," HoneyMama says, removing a large silver tray full of sweet potato biscuits from the oversized oven. The fluffy orange treats are Drew's favorites.

"HoneyMama, I'm a half hour early," I say, propping myself up on one of the six barstools surrounding the kitchen island, which fills the center of the open space. There's also a breakfast nook near the entrance, where her cat, Jambalaya, is posted on the semicircle bench, gazing out of the window.

"Time's relative, Brandy. You know that." HoneyMama takes off her oven mitts and wipes her hands on her red-and-white-gingham apron. Underneath, she's wearing a black strapless bodysuit with matching heels to envy. She makes domesticity appear sexy as hell.

"Okay, so next time, I'll know to come way earlier than the suggested time." I've missed our banter. She, Dulce, and I could talk shit for hours about any- and everything. As much as Shelley would judge, my bestie would fit right in.

"Now you get it." HoneyMama smiles.

It's a privilege to be back inside of HoneyMama's kitchen. The new girls are never allowed in until invited. The bright yellow Martha Stewartesque kitchen is the envy of many housewives in town. It contains state-of-the-art equipment, with all of the original fixtures, including a wood-burning stove in the corner, next to the back door.

"Have you seen Corrine yet?" HoneyMama sets a platter of biscuits in the center of the table next to a tray with various tea selections.

"Corrine who?" I ask, taking one for myself before the others arrive. No matter how much HoneyMama bakes, there's never enough to go around.

"Coco goes by her full name now. Corrine, Drew's alleged fiancée."

The copper teakettle whistles loudly as HoneyMama turns off the stove. She takes the kettle and pours hot water into two coffee mugs on the kitchen counter.

The heat in my body grows as hot as the kettle water at the mention of Drew's ex-side chick turned main woman. I don't care what she calls herself. To me, Coco will always be a manipulative home-wrecking psychopath. I've seen her flip from loving girlfriend to a cold-hearted bitch in the blink of an eye.

"No, I haven't had the pleasure," I say, choosing a tea bag. There's also sugar, honey, cream, and butter, with a stack of china saucers, teacups, and butter knives for serving. "Why did you call her his 'alleged fiancée'?"

"Because to be engaged means that there's a real intention to marry," HoneyMama says, joining me. She sets the mugs down before choosing her own bag to steep. "Drew ain't marrying that girl, and anybody with good sense knows it."

"Oh," I say, gazing out of the window. I already know Honey-Mama's trying to play matchmaker. She was responsible for our first go-around, and I'm not about to fall prey to her seductive reasoning again.

Mr. Graves, making his way around to the back of the house, continues to leisurely sweep the porch, humming to himself, as always. It almost feels like nothing's changed—with Mr. Graves contently performing his duties, while HoneyMama's in the kitchen doing her thing—but so much has.

"So, Brandy. We never did get into whether or not you're dating anyone." Knowing HoneyMama, I realize this is just the beginning of the inquisition. This, I assume, is why she wanted me to arrive early—so she can get all up in my business.

"I am, but it's a bit shaky," I say, taking a sugar cube from the china dish and adding it to my tea.

Every time someone asks me about my relationship status, I get a knot in my throat. What do I say? Am I single? Technically, I suppose. But I'm fucking a man I think I'm in love with, even though there's no formal commitment. No matter how many times Ian says he's not seeing anyone else, I just don't trust him. The days between me texting or calling him and his reply, coupled with the fact that he's rarely available on weekends, is enough to drive any woman insane.

"Shaky, huh?" HoneyMama says, sipping her tea.

"Yeah, to say the least," I say, trying to control my thoughts. If I weren't here right now, I'd be checking his Facebook status, not that there's much to check. Ian's the most reclusive man I've ever met. "Sometimes I think the ups and downs of love just aren't worth the trouble."

"Sounds like a girl in love." HoneyMama reaches across the table and gently pats my hand. "Take a deep breath, Keke. This, too, shall pass."

"Will it ever?" I say, almost screaming. "I'm tired of worrying over this man. If it's not one thing, it's another. I do everything that's asked of me in my relationships and more, but it's never enough." The tears are flowing freely, and it feels good to let them fall. It hurts loving when the love isn't returned.

"Keke, let me ask you an honest question," HoneyMama says, passing me a napkin.

"Uh-oh." I attempt to blow my nose like a lady, but no such luck. Jambalaya looks at me like he's going to pounce if I interrupt his slumber one more time.

"Do you date up or down?" HoneyMama asks, stirring cream into her black tea.

"'Up or down'?" I am unsure of what she means.

"Yes—up or down, financially, spiritually, sexually. Are the men you date on your level, Keke?"

"HoneyMama," I begin, but my thoughts drift off as I contemplate the question for a moment.

"It's important to ask this question and be honest in your response. After all, if you've hit rock bottom, it's essential that you find out how you got there, who's down there with you, and if he helped you get there. Only then will you truly heal, honey bun."

I think about all of the men I've linked up with in the past, including Drew and Ian. "From what I can recall, every one of them had been on my level financially, or above it. Spiritually, well, I guess so. Mentally, I honestly can't say." I can't say because I feel like I'm a bit on the crazy side, more often than not, but that wasn't the question.

"Okay," HoneyMama says, looking at me quizzically. "What about the men you dated before your current lover?"

"Oh, well, that's easy," I say, recalling my repeated disasters. "I attracted depressed, miserable men, or previously depressed, miserable workaholics who were sexually repressed. And married men—let's not forget those."

"It's the married ones who remind me why I'll never walk down the aisle again," HoneyMama says, and I almost agree.

I actually dated a married man for three years. He works at a competing paper and still calls every now and then to see if I'll slip up. By the time I found out a year later during a casual conversation, I was already sprung. It was some of the best sex I've ever had, but I finally got strong enough and ended that shit.

"Well, damn. Seems like you should've stayed with Drew." HoneyMama winks again. "You mean to tell me you haven't met one good guy in Atlanta since you moved back?"

I shake my head in frustration and at my own track record. I've probably slept with more men in the past ten years than I care to admit. But the Jezebel in me has needs, too.

"I met one nice guy, but he was a perverted bastard with the smallest dick I've ever seen."

"And your current lover? How is he in bed?"

"Oh, I love Ian's dick," I say, shivering at the thought. "It suits me perfectly, unfortunately." That's why I can't completely shake him, even though I might need to, if he keeps coming up missing in action.

"Yes, the dick must fit nicely," HoneyMama says, recalling a memory without sharing.

"A penny for that thought," I say, helping myself to another biscuit.

HoneyMama smiles coyly and continues to sip her tea. "That memory is worth a whole lot more than a penny, young lady."

"Must've been some loving," I say, laughing. HoneyMama's a hot mess.

"Still is," she says, chuckling at her own wickedness.

Mr. Graves looks through the opened window to see what all the ruckus is about, but knows better than to ask. The last thing he wants is to be involved in our girl talk. He smirks, tilts his hat forward, and continues sweeping.

"But seriously, Keke. I want all of my girls to be happy, and you deserve to meet your match." Jambalaya, tired of being alone, makes his way from the window post to the bottom of his master's stool. She reaches down and he leaps up, settling onto her lap. "No one should ever settle for less than they deserve," HoneyMama says, stroking her pet back to sleep.

"I hear you, but it's not that easy to find a good mate these days, or so the statistics say." That's one downside of working for a newspaper: I'm constantly inundated with the negative side of life. My married dick would always tell me that's why Black men should be allowed to cheat openly and as often as they feel. His logic was there are so few good men out there that Black women should be willing to share. Complete bullshit, I know, and he served it up liberally.

"Girl, please," HoneyMama says, tossing her head back, causing her long, dark hair to fall over her bare right shoulder. "Fuck the statistics. You can have, be, and do anything you want."

"I think you've been watching way too much *Oprah*," I say, helping myself to another biscuit. This time, I take the ladle out of the honey jar and sweeten my already carb-loaded breakfast a bit. Jambalaya looks up at me as if he wants a taste. I wish he would try to take a bite; it'll be the last thing his fat ass eats.

"Keke, do you remember when you wanted to apply to college, but talked yourself out of it in every which way possible?" HoneyMama asks, conjuring up old memories. "You thought you didn't have it in you to attend a university, even though you'd already earned straight A's in community college. You've always been your worst critic, chile. When are you going to stop beating yourself up and bask in the glory that is you?"

"'The glory that is me'?" I choke back the tears. "'The glory that is me' is tired, overworked, underpaid, overweight, and underloved."

HoneyMama looks at me like she wants to slap the taste right out of my mouth. I bow my head and take another bite.

"I told you the same thing then, that I'm telling you now. We're never done learning, sweetie. Not until we're six feet under or ashes in the wind," she says, her thoughts drifting off to Monaka, I assume. "You're still here, Keke. Make the best of every day you have on this earth. If you don't, you might as well just slap Goddess in the face, because that's what you're doing by wasting what precious time we've been given."

"You're right," I say, remembering the days that I thought I'd never be able to afford a degree. Then HoneyMama offered me a partial scholarship if I got into a university, and so I did.

"Not only are you an excellent dancer and baker, Keke, you're a writer, and that's your gift—your soul's blessings. You choose how to share it with the world."

Obviously, HoneyMama hasn't seen me dance lately, but I'll take two out of three for argument's sake.

"I don't feel very blessed these days," I say, damn-near licking the honey off the china saucer. Mr. Graves keeps his own bees and makes the best honey and honey wine in Indian Springs— yet another source of income derived from The Honey Spot.

"Well, that's all on you, my dear." Damn, HoneyMama can be merciless when she wants to be. "I know sometimes it's difficult to see what others see in you, but nobody can force you to look in the mirror and see your good."

"HoneyMama, I hate to say it, but the truth of the matter is, I have less than I left here with." Pretty soon, my tea is going to turn to salt from all of the tears shed if we keep up this conversation. "I'm still single, broker, and fatter than I was a decade ago. I should've never left."

HoneyMama shifts on her stool without disturbing Jambalaya's slumber. Her hazel eyes narrow as she homes in on my pity party for one.

"You know what your main issue is, chile? You think you don't deserve to be happy, healthy, and whole, just as you are. When you first started working for me and I promoted you faster than any of my other girls at the time, you felt bad because you thought C and Dulce should've been put on the A shift before you."

"But they started stripping long before I did. Hell, C pretty

much brought me into the game back in the day," I interject, recalling the first time I met C at my great-aunt's house. If it
weren't for her and my cousin, who knows how my life would've
turned out? "They were senior to me in every way."

HoneyMama ignores my reasoning and continues.

"Then, when you graduated from Georgia Perimeter with
your associate's degree, you didn't think you deserved to go any
further, because, as a mere stripper, you thought you wouldn't
need the education you so craved," HoneyMama says, almost
quoting me verbatim. Damn, her memory's good. "Now, after
the degrees have been had and the job earned, you still sit before me with the same bullshit-ass pitiful thinking, and not as
the evolved young woman you've become."

Jambalaya opens his eyes as if to concur with her wise words.

"Do yourself a favor and call yourself only good and delicious
things from now on, like I do all of my girls. Be sweet to God's
chile and stop beating her ass up every chance you get."

I catch my breath, afraid to make a sound, for fear that even a
sigh might be misconstrued as an excuse. HoneyMama's right
and she knows it. Hell, even the damn cat knows the gospel
when he hears it.

Chapter 9

*I*T'S BEEN SO NICE HAVING HONEYMAMA ALL TO MYSELF THIS MORN-
ing. I don't remember the last time my day started with pleas-
antries and tea. During the week, it's mostly coffee and Charlie's
yelling.

"I should put some more biscuits out," HoneyMama says, taking the last one from the now-empty tray and drizzling it with
honey. "I love to see my girls eat."

"And we love you feeding us," I say, taking the last bite on my
saucer.

I'm glad to see not much has changed around here, especially
not HoneyMama's baking. I've had three biscuits in the hour
I've been here, and would eat another one if she put it down in
front of me.

HoneyMama and I stop our conversation at the sound of several footsteps rounding the long porch. I guess the cavalry has
finally arrived. We break up our morning chat, ready to get back
to work.

"Morning, ladies," HoneyMama says, welcoming most of the
A shift inside.

Praline, Tiramisu, and Dulce strut in, looking and smelling
hypnotic. Each of them is dressed in an all-black ensemble,
ready to rehearse tonight's dance routine after our meeting.
Dulce and Praline are both sporting formfitting leotards and
leggings, while Tiramisu's wearing a tennis skirt and tank top.

And they're all wearing matching thigh-high stiletto boots. From the outside looking in, it seems they have no confidence issues whatsoever.

"Morning, ma'am," they reply in unison. The dancers take a seat around the island and dig into the prepared breakfast. Unlike me, they'll burn off the rich treats with calories to spare within thirty minutes of practicing their routines for tonight's show.

"What's she doing here?" Dulce hisses while claiming a teacup. "I thought this meeting was for dancers only."

"For real," Tiramisu says, following suit.

Praline's silent for the moment because of the biscuit in her mouth, but I know she has an opinion about me, too. I wonder where C is. Not that I miss her, but as a member of the premium dance clique, she should be here.

"Brandy's still and will always be a part of this family. She will always be one of our best dancers and bakers," HoneyMama says in my defense. "I hope you'll help me get the treats ready for tonight's show, Brandy. We're serving tea cakes, your specialty."

"I'd love to," I say, unsure of how my schedule will unfold, but I'll definitely take time to bake with HoneyMama if she's asking.

"Looks like you've been baking plenty these days, *mami*," Dulce says, sneering at my hips. "Make sure to leave some cakes for the clients, no?"

If I could smack the trick and still maintain my professional decorum, Dulce would be on the floor by now.

"Ladies, be sweet," HoneyMama says, gently nudging Jambalaya, who obediently makes his way down to the floor. "We're here to discuss solutions, and, of course, Brandy's part of that discussion."

"Morning, ladies," Drew says with John in tow.

Why didn't HoneyMama tell me they were coming? Damn, I'm not prepared to deal with Drew this morning. My pussy's still slightly numb after attempting to mimic his touch last night.

"Good morning, baby," HoneyMama says, accepting Drew's kiss to her right cheek.

"You look as radiant as always, ma'am," Drew says as he reaches down to pet Jambalaya, who purrs at the affection. Spoiled brat. I've never been a cat lover, but Drew loves pussies of all kinds—and they love him right back.

"And you look as handsome as always, sir," HoneyMama says to Drew, and then smiles at his uptight partner. "And how are you this morning, Detective?"

"I'm just fine, Ms. Thibodeaux," John says, obviously uncomfortable with all of the love going around the open space, not to mention the scantily clad women capturing his attention. "Thank you for allowing us to speak with y'all this morning."

John remains standing in the doorway as Drew makes himself comfortable at the kitchen island with the rest of us. It almost feels like old times—almost.

"Morning, ladies," Drew says, displaying his perfect set of ivory teeth. He's got more play from that perfect smile than most men acquire with a Bentley.

"Hey," the women say unenthusiastically. Ever since Drew became a cop, my guess is the dancers don't trust him as much. I won't know how they truly feel about him until I ask them myself.

"Well, don't be shy, John. There's plenty to share," Honey-Mama says, gesturing around the bountiful spread. "Don't see anything you like?"

John turns beet red as he stares into HoneyMama's welcoming eyes. "I'm fine, ma'am," he says, clearing his throat. "Thank you."

"Suit yourself." Drew pours a generous helping of honey onto his plate. "Thank you for the hospitality," Drew says in between bites. "Again, sorry that our visit's not under better circumstances."

"Me too." HoneyMama's eyes drift to outside, where Mr. Graves has wandered far out back toward his house. "Monaka had so much life left to live."

"Yes, she did," Dulce says. She's the only one not eating, other than John's statuesque self.

"She was spunky, I'll give her that," I say, sipping my tea.

I first met Monaka at the auditions for my replacement. She looked like a slightly shorter, plain version of Kimora Lee Simmons. A little less than six feet tall, that girl wasn't afraid of a thing, not even C, who hated Monaka from the start. Anyone could tell that Monaka was a brave chick back then, and I'm sure she didn't go down without a fight.

"If you don't mind, we have business to handle," John says, shifting his weight from one cowboy boot to another. "Do any of you ladies know who'd want to hurt Monaka—better yet, kill her?"

"Bitches be hating," Praline says, true to character. "I bet it was some trick who got mad 'cause she wouldn't give him none. Wouldn't be the first time." Her hood ass is straight out of Decatur and she displays it proudly. "Or maybe even one of his hoes. Like I said, bitches be hating for no damn reason."

I hate to agree, but Praline might be onto something. The one thing HoneyMama couldn't keep out of the club was jealousy. The girls—like any other people in any competitive environment—all want to win. Win what? HoneyMama never could figure out.

"Envy's a dangerous thing," HoneyMama says, blowing on her tea. She looks at Praline hard, as if she's trying to read her mind for details.

"Amen," Dulce says, pulling out a cigarette and lighting it. "Monaka had plenty of jealous *putas* on her ass. I can't tell you how many of them I had to threaten on a regular basis. I told her she was too damned nice, smiling at everybody all the goddamn time."

"How was your relationship with the victim?" John asks, much to her displeasure. He stays put next to the back door. I think he might be afraid of liking The Honey Spot if he allows himself to get too comfortable.

I'm curious about Dulce's connection to Monaka, too. It sounds like she was more protective of Monaka than any of the other women present.

"Monaka was her bitch," Tiramisu says, sounding more like her mentor, C, than the freshman dancer that she is.

"I'll slit your throat if you call her that again, *mami*. Best believe," Dulce says, blowing smoke straight up in the air.

"Ladies, tempers, please. Especially in front of company," HoneyMama says, cooling the heat in the room as best as she can. As hot as it is outside, it feels ten times worse in here.

When Dulce makes a threat, the person threatened shouldn't take it lightly. Back in the day, Dulce would fight anyone—male or female—at the drop of a dime. She may be a little older, but I doubt her fire's completely died down.

"Dulce and Monaka were in a relationship, John," Drew says, answering for Dulce, who looks like she's plotting Tiramisu's demise. "They lived together in one of the cottages out by the springs."

"I see," John says, shifting his weight from his right cowboy boot to the left. "So when you say a relationship, they were like roommates or . . ."

Before John can finish his query, Dulce sets him straight.

"She was my woman, my wifey, my lover, my best friend," Dulce says, taking a sip of her coffee and visibly choking back tears. *"Tu comprendes, papi?"*

Dulce meets John's stunned gaze and smiles between circular puffs.

"I reckon I do," John says, uncomfortable with Dulce's forthrightness. "In that case, we need to question you down at the station. Spouses—and whatnots—are always the first suspects in a murder investigation."

"Whatnots?" Dulce's smile turns into a scowl. As strippers, we're all too accustomed to being treated like criminals. She sucks her teeth at John, who looks pleased with her response. I can see he's turning out to be as much of an asshole as my boss, Charlie, is.

"Now hold on a minute, John," Drew says, standing up to meet his partner at eye level. "I don't think that's really necessary just yet. We're just talking this morning, getting the lay of the land."

"Detective Drew, don't forget why we're here," John says, as if there's something Drew's not telling us.

"There will be plenty of time for all of that later," Drew says, licking honey from his fingers. "None of these ladies are flight risks."

"The hell they aren't," John says, scanning the room. "Speaking of which, where's the big one?" John asks, noticing C's absence. She is kinda hard to miss.

"What's really going on here, Drew?" HoneyMama asks. "You're here to talk to the girls, so talk."

"Contrary to Detective Drew's nonchalant attitude, we're not here for a walk down memory lane, ladies," John says impatiently. "Seeing as the investigation has no leads, we're gonna have to shut down this house till further notice."

Drew glares hard at his partner, like he wants to take him out back like he'd do anyone who dared get out of line back in the day. Something tells me that if he didn't have that badge on, he and John would've had it out a long time ago.

"What the fuck?" Praline says, jumping out of her seat, as shocked as the rest of us. "HoneyMama, you can't let them fuck with our money like this!"

"Come on. There has to be another way," I say in disbelief.

Drew looks as hurt as the dancers feel. Ultimately, he has no control over the situation. But if there's anything he can do, I know he'll try his damnedest to keep the Spot open.

"If you have anything that can help us come to a resolution more quickly, we'd be much obliged if you'd shed a little light on the subject," John says, completely taking over the conversation.

Drew watches the chaos ensue, powerless to stop it.

"I know y'all need to do your jobs, Detectives. But shutting down my business isn't going to help you find Monaka's murderer any faster," HoneyMama pleads. "None of my girls would do a thing to harm one of our own."

"Are you sure about that, ma'am?" John asks, shooting Dulce the evil eye.

He then glances at Tiramisu, who avoids his gaze. What the hell's that all about?

"This Spanish girl's got quite a temper on her. I'm willing to bet money she knows more about her 'girlfriend's' death than she's saying," John says, using air quotes around "girlfriend's."

"I'm Puerto Rican, you tiny-dick motherfucker. Get it straight. And Monaka was my heart—no fake quotes needed, you racist, sexist, homophobic piece of shit," Dulce says, charging out of her seat toward John, who stands his ground.

HoneyMama and Drew both stop Dulce from committing a serious offense, much to John's disappointment. He looks like he's out for blood, mostly Dulce's.

"*Straight?*" John says, taking a cigarette from behind his ear and placing it between his lips. He scans the kitchen and flicks his copper Zippo lighter open. "Well, isn't that the pot calling the kettle black?"

Dulce disentangles herself from Drew's grasp, swings her left boot in the air, and kicks an empty barstool toward John, who grins at the attempt. It misses by at least a yard, but the wrong cop might consider that move assault, possibly with a deadly weapon because of the pointed heel and steel toe of her couture footwear.

"Drew, do something," I say, begging for him to stop this train wreck before it goes too far.

"Yeah, Drew. Do something," Praline demands. "You're just standing there while your bitch-ass partner's about to close down the Spot and our bank accounts right along with it."

"Believe me, we've been meeting about this all night long. I've done everything I can to try and change our chief's mind, but it's no use," Drew says sadly. "Because we have no immediate suspects in mind, there really is no other choice but to sweep the entire house for fingerprints, items that seem out of place . . . the usual. Anything we may have missed the first time around."

With both their safe haven and their money threatened, all of the dancers will be more than pissed, including HoneyMama, and who can blame them? Bills don't give a shit about murder investigations.

"There has to be a compromise," HoneyMama says, holding

Dulce's hand tightly in an attempt to keep her from lighting John's next cigarette for him. If it weren't for HoneyMama's intervention, John's thick mustache, eyebrows, and judgmental ass would also be up in flames. "I'm determined to keep the Spot going, even if we have to work out of my private side of the residence."

"It's a crime scene, Ms. Thibodeaux. The whole place will be shut down pending further investigation, including your private quarters," John says matter-of-factly, like he's not kicking a person out of her home and snatching her paycheck all before noon.

"That's not really necessary," HoneyMama insists. Her first priority is her dancers. Making sure they can maintain their current lifestyles is one way to keep them safe and out of other clubs that couldn't give a shit about a dancer's well-being.

"The room's a crime scene, not the house," Drew interjects. Sounds like he's already made this argument.

"You heard the chief. We found nothing in the main room. Gotta turn the whole place upside down," John says, glaring at his partner.

"There's also no evidence that the killer ever left the main room," Drew says, raising his voice.

At least I know he's on our side, even if it means going up against his partner and possibly the whole damned department. Those good ole boys run deep.

"We can discuss this later, even if it is a moot point," John says, crossing his arms as if he's already won the battle.

"The hell you can," HoneyMama says, loud enough for Mr. Graves to hear if he's still around back, and anyone else who might happen to still be on the property. "You'll discuss it right here and now in front of us."

"Beg your pardon, ma'am," John says, losing patience. "Drew, give her the warrant. We need to get a move on before the day's completely wasted. We also need to talk to that one down at the station," John says, pointing at Dulce.

Drew reluctantly reaches into his jacket pocket and pulls out a folded piece of paper. "I'll see what we can do," Drew says, handing the paper to HoneyMama.

She unfolds the paper and reads it to herself. "What are we going to do without our business?" HoneyMama asks to no one in particular. Dulce squeezes HoneyMama's hand in support.

"Ma'am, it's a strip club. It can afford a few weeks off, don't you think?" John says smugly. He walks over to Drew and taps him on the shoulder, indicating that it's time to go, and to take Dulce with them.

"Are you fucking kidding me?" Praline says, pacing around the kitchen. I'm sure she's calculating the lost revenue in her head like a psychic abacus. Like most of us, she's all about her money. "Our clients would go crazy if they missed a day of all of this," she says, smacking herself on the ass.

"It seems like one of your clients has already gone crazy, and then some," John says, now helping himself to breakfast. I guess his appetite improves after he gets his way. "Isn't that why we're all here in the first place, unless it was indeed one of your own kind who killed the victim?"

"Stop calling her that!" Dulce screams, tears streaking her reddish-brown cheeks. "I've had enough of your disrespect. Her name is Monaka. Say it: Mo-Na-Ka."

John looks at Dulce like she's lost her mind, and she pretty much has.

"Young lady, I think you ought to calm down and remember your place," John says, devouring his biscuit. "I don't know how they do things where you're from, but insubordination toward a police officer is still a crime here in Butts County."

Dulce starts to mumble all kinds of obscenities in Spanish, and again, HoneyMama intervenes in an attempt to save Dulce from herself.

"Detective, if you need to ask Dulce any questions, I'm sure she'll be completely honest right here and now," HoneyMama says, shaking out of anger, but still composed. "Is it truly necessary to drag her to the police station? We all know she's innocent."

"With all due respect, Ms. Thibodeaux, 'innocent' is the last word I'd use to describe any of your gals," John says, pouring a cup of coffee to go. "This ain't the house of Lot, but I wouldn't be surprised if your heathen ways don't eventually turn all of you into pillars of salt. The Bible warns against fraternizing with Jezebels and such." John glares at his partner, who looks like he wants to choke the shit out of him.

"Do us all a favor and get over your holier-than-thou attitude," Drew says. His chiseled jawline tenses like he's about to throw a punch. I can always tell when Drew's near his bullshit threshold and he's just about crossed that line. "It's not helping any of us–least of all, Monaka."

John narrows his emerald eyes and focuses in on Drew's equally fierce gaze. "Whatever you do on your off time is your business, Detective, unless it interferes with the job," John says, making his way back outside. "Let's go, young lady."

Drew bites his tongue and turns his attention back to Honey-Mama. "I'm sorry to do this, but we need to speak with Dulce privately. She has the right to an attorney," Drew says before putting his hand out for Dulce.

"Is she under arrest?" Praline asks.

"No," Drew says, distressed.

"Not yet," John adds, swinging the screen door open.

HoneyMama remains silent in her indignation, while Tira-misu pulls out her phone to text someone; I have no doubt it's C. Dulce inhales, takes Drew's hand, and rises from her stool.

"I like women and that bothers you, no?" Dulce asks John, who's finally lit his cigarette. Dulce lights a cigarette of her own. "Well, if I can take hell from my mother and judgment from my *abuelita,* I can sure as hell take a little shit from you, and I don't need no damned lawyer to do it. *Vámonos,*" Dulce says, leading Drew outside. "I'll be back in time for the end of practice, *sí?*"

"Let me ask you a question, Ms. Thibodeaux," John says before following his partner and their only suspect so far. "Why would an upstanding, attractive gal such as yourself open a har-lot's den full of lowly hussies on her father's historic property?

I've never understood it. You look like you'd make some man a decent wife, if he'd be willing to tolerate your past indiscretions, of course."

HoneyMama walks over to the back door and stares at John, reading every inch of his strong jawline, bright eyes, and graying blond hair before speaking. "Because I'd rather work with women just like myself for the rest of my natural-born life than submit to an asshole like you any day. And we're *women* to you, always. Never *girls, gals,* or any other terms of endearment *you* might find cute, because you hear *us* call each other those things. You'll *never* be that intimate with another person, I presume."

John looks at his adversary with both lust and disdain. Anyone with good sense can tell this man's feeling her. "Good day, ma'am; ladies," John says, tipping his cowboy hat and exiting the back porch.

HoneyMama walks back inside the kitchen and slams the screen door shut.

Drew leaves Dulce with John and follows behind HoneyMama.

"I'll bring her back as soon as I can," Drew says, reassuringly.

"Here, take these with you." HoneyMama hands him a care package full of biscuits.

"You know I'll do everything in my power to resolve this unnecessary inconvenience as quickly as possible," Drew says, loosening his suit jacket. Drew kisses HoneyMama on the cheek, rubs my shoulder, and takes one last bite of his breakfast before rejoining his partner. That's the thing with all of HoneyMama's treats: even the strongest man can never have enough.

Chapter 10

"WHAT A FUCKING PRICK," PRALINE SAYS, CHARGING DOWN THE long hallway leading toward the back dance stage. "How dare he come up in here acting like our fucking master? Rat bastard."

HoneyMama, Tiramisu, and Praline each peel off the bottom half of their clothing to reveal black boy short panties that show off their rock-solid forms.

"The real question is, how can Drew work with such a dick?" I ask. That man's unending well of patience never ceases to amaze me. The problem is that he always exercises patience with the wrong people.

"And the nerve of him to question my business like that," HoneyMama says, pulling the thick velvet curtains open and allowing the high-noon sun to take over the room and naturally warm the cool space. It can get cold in this old house, no matter the season.

"There are worst things a woman can do for money than take her clothes off," Tiramisu says as she wipes down each of the three rods on the wooden stage. "And most of us are mothers trying to make sure that our children are taken care of. I know that's why I'm dancing."

"How many children do you have?" I ask. Tiramisu looks too fit to have one baby at home, let alone multiple.

"Four," she says, pulling her iPhone out of her bra. "Two girls, and twin boys."

"Cute," I say, admiring her family. The girls look to be about ten and eight years old, and her twins are just toddlers. "They look happy."

"They are happy, because their mama is there when they need me," Tiramisu says, replacing the phone. "And I ain't got to ask nobody for money to take care of 'em, either. The government don't help me, their daddies ain't never been around, and my parents can't help, even if they want to."

"T's a good mother and daughter," HoneyMama says, smiling at Tiramisu, who blushes at the compliment. Like Honey, some of the dancers have their nicknames, too. "She's also good with the other dancers' kids, a true godsend."

"There are a lot of mamas in the business," Tiramisu says, sitting on the floor and beginning a series of yoga poses. She and HoneyMama exchange a look of mutual understanding. Honey-Mama sacrificed a lot for her children, who have since moved on from Indian Springs.

"Even if I ain't got no kids, I still like making my money my way," Praline says, switching legs. Just watching her stretch is making me tired. "Why I do what I do ain't nobody's business, but mine: not the Lord's, my daddy's, or Friar John's."

"I hear that." I wish I had as much confidence as Praline exudes. Unfortunately, the older I get, the more I care about what others think.

"If there's one thing I know about women who strip, it's that they're gonna do it, no matter the club or who judges them," Praline says, walking over to the deejay booth and flipping the light switch on. "Stripping is a calling, just like being a doctor or a teacher or some other type of boring shit like that. Everybody ain't built for this life, but those of us who do are both loved and hated for it."

Praline's always been bold about what she does, as well as loving all of the perks that come along with doing a job well done. She's also the Spot's most dedicated instructor. By the time an introverted Stockbridge housewife is done taking a weekend pole dance course with Praline, she'll become a willing freak with skills on poles of all kinds.

"What I think Praline is getting at is we provide an invaluable service and shouldn't be treated like tramps by those who don't understand what it is that we do," HoneyMama says, now performing some stretches of her own.

"Yeah, but all the clubs ain't like The Honey Spot. Monaka's story ain't rare on the Southside," Tiramisu says, causing me to conjure old thoughts of Mocha. "I don't give a damn how you sugarcoat it. We're still selling our bodies for money. Shit is still shit at the end of the day. All we do is make it pretty."

"Speak for yourself," Praline says, stepping out of the booth and onto the stage with Prince's song "Scandalous" playing in the background. "My body is a fucking masterpiece, and what I can do with it is pure talent worthy of being praised."

Praline takes hold of the pole on the right side of the stage and swings around it like a lynx. She then moves her knees into a figure eight before kicking her left leg up parallel to the rod. After holding the difficult pose a few moments, she brings her extended leg back down and switches sides.

"I'm no fool, Tiramisu. I understand the exchange between the stripper and the game very well," HoneyMama says, joining her girls onstage.

I claim a seat at one of the fifteen tables in the audience and take mental notes on what to follow up on in my later interviews with each of them individually.

"Then you can understand why John feels the way he does about our lifestyle," Tiramisu says, exhaling and sounding a tad bit guilty. "What we do isn't the most noble profession."

"Who gives a fuck about nobility?" Praline says, dropping her backside to the floor and winding her way back up the pole. "This ain't no *Game of Thrones,* trick. This is a strip club, and I, for one, am proud to be here."

"Being proud and being honest are two different things." Tiramisu hit that one on the head. "I can be proud about how I make my money, and honestly say that I don't want my daughters nowhere near this stage when they get old enough to strut."

"That's because you don't understand the power in stripping," Praline says, popping her pussy for the mirror. "You never have. You're too busy feeling bad and sad all the damn time."

"Maybe if you had kids of your own, you'd understand where I'm coming from." Tiramisu shoots Praline a look, and Praline licks her lips in return.

"Ladies, you're both right to a certain degree," HoneyMama says, adding her wisdom to the conversation.

"No, I'm completely right," Tiramisu says, rising from the floor and performing high kicks in the mirror. "There's no power in stripping for me. I always wanted to be a dancer, but I never imagined it'd be like this."

"Oh, honey, you've got to get over this guilt complex and appreciate the gift you've been given," HoneyMama says, touching Tiramisu on the shoulders as the younger woman struggles to fight back tears. I can't wait to get her whole story, as well as C's role in it. Tiramisu seems to possess more of a conscience than I've ever known C to have. Why would she hang around Couverture by choice?

"Can you understand how humiliating it is to submit to these men every night so I can pay my damned rent?" Tiramisu says, keeping up with her kicks. So far, she's done twenty on each leg.

"Yes, I can," HoneyMama says, rotating her midsection and moving through the morning routine exactly the way I remember. "I can also understand the power in submission, the power in knowing where your spot is, and then willingly sharing it with another to enjoy. There's healing in this power."

"Church, preach!" Praline says, winking at Tiramisu, who looks like she's had enough.

"I also know the pain that comes when someone rejects your submission and judges your gift," HoneyMama says, checking Praline's fire. "Whoever did this to Monaka was ashamed of his admiration for her, I guarantee. And anyone who knows Dulce knows that girl doesn't have an ounce of shame in her body, especially not when it comes to her feelings for Monaka."

"Shame's a motherfucker." Tiramisu lifts her right leg and places her slender foot against the pole to the left of the stage.

The very act of stretching is an art form when the right dancers do it.

"Most of the chicks I know who dance do it because they want to," Praline says. "If they gon' strip, anyway, they might as well have a safe, clean, and respectable place to do it. That punk-ass detective can kiss my Black-and-white ass for airing out his bull-shit-ass opinions and leaving them with us to deal with like a silent fart."

Praline's right. Out of all of the dancers I've met in my day, they each have a unique story, but one thing in common is their love for the art form, and the money that comes with it.

"John just needs to do his job and keep his opinions to himself," I say, moving my hips along to Portishead's sensual song without leaving my chair. The music selection at the Spot's always been as diverse as its dancers.

"He should be praising The Honey Spot for being available as an option for strippers and their clients alike. Hell, he looks like he could use a little of our magic to help ease that stick out of his ass," Praline says, making us all laugh.

"As long as an act is empowering, there's nothing wrong with it." HoneyMama acquaints herself with the middle pole like an equestrian to her stallion. "This is one of the oldest forms of entertainment and one of our most influential talents. Embracing it's the first step to reclaiming its power."

"If you say so," Tiramisu says, unconvinced.

"Why don't you pay a visit to Friar John and let him redeem you of all your sins, Mary Magdalene," Praline says, tired of Tiramisu's attitude. "You're such a fucking downer, you know that?"

"All right, ladies. Let's get to work," HoneyMama says, ending the lesson before the drama gets out of hand. "Praline, please lead us through the affirmations."

"'The Honey Spot Creed,'" Praline says, recalling the written document posted in HoneyMama's office from memory. "'Dancing is natural, lucrative, and all in divine order.'"

"Tiramisu, please continue." HoneyMama tightly grips the pole and slowly walks around it.

"'We're not just strippers,'" Tiramisu continues with a hefty eye roll. "'We are talented, intelligent, righteous dancers working what we've got to get to what we want.'"

"Praline," HoneyMama says, leading the breathing exercises as they each exhale the precious words while warming up to their individual rods. If C were here, Tiramisu would have to share a pole with Praline, no doubt: the dancer's hierarchy stays intact, no matter the venue.

"'We control our wombs, our money, and our destinies. And we'll slice anyone who threatens these three things,'" Praline says, taking her index finger and pretending to slit her throat. She looks in the mirror and smiles at her theatrics—once a nut, always a nut.

"And last, but not least, Brandy," HoneyMama says, meeting my eyes in the reflection, "can you please state the last affirmation?"

"Me?" I ask, taken completely off guard by the request.

"Yes, chile. You." HoneyMama looks me in the eye. "I know you remember."

I take a deep breath and recall the words. "'We each have a spot so deep inside that no one can physically touch it without our full submission—this is where our gold is buried, our true honey spot. We will own it and love it for all its worth.'"

"A-woman!" Praline shouts, making HoneyMama smile.

Chapter 11

*P*RALINE MOUNTS THE POLE, SLOWLY OPENS HER LEGS INTO A V FOR-
mation as she spins toward the ceiling. She opens and closes her
strong legs around the pole and continues snaking upward to
every beat of the seductive song. Slowly but surely, she makes
her way to the top, all the while controlling her every movement.

"Okay, sweetheart, that's enough," HoneyMama says, watching her protégé work it. "We need to get through our back exercises before we practice tonight's routines."

"If we leave it up to Papa John, there'll be no dancing
tonight," Praline says. With no hands, she bends backward and
clasps her fingers around the pole underneath her toes. She
then slides down so fast, I have to catch my breath, knowing this
professional won't hit her head against the floor like so many
wannabes have done. About three-quarters of the way down,
Praline stops, opens her legs for the final spin, and lands square
on her feet like an Olympian.

"That's what you call pole art, bitches," Praline says, smiling
victoriously. "We meet every Saturday morning from nine to
eleven in the main dance room. Private lessons available upon
request."

"Show-off," Tiramisu says, smiling in admiration. We may
each have our issues, but can't front when a dancer does her shit
tight, and Praline's got her art on lock.

"Brandy, come hold the other end," HoneyMama says, passing a long bamboo stick to Praline. I dutifully rise from my chair and step onto the stage. "Tiramisu, hit the lights."

"Where's the blindfold?" Praline asks excitedly.

"In the box," HoneyMama says, standing next to the stick between Praline and me. "Tiramisu, would you grab it, please?"

Tiramisu brings the red scarf to center stage and covers HoneyMama's eyes with it. She then ties it snuggly behind HoneyMama's head and backs up.

"Hit the REPEAT button on the stereo remote, Tiramisu. Ladies, hold it right about here." HoneyMama blindly reaches for the stick and lifts it up a few inches, which forces me to hold it tightly near my belly button.

"Get it, Mama," Tiramisu says, smiling at HoneyMama as she winds her shoulders backward, bends at the waist, and lowers her body underneath the limbo stick.

"Scandalous" is HoneyMama's favorite song to dance to and a constant request from her loyal clientele. She makes her way underneath and pops back up like it's nothing.

"Your turn." She passes the blindfold to Tiramisu, who ties it behind her own head before bending back as low as she can.

"Hell yeah," Praline says, clapping her hands as Tiramisu passes underneath the stick. "My turn."

Praline excitedly passes the stick to Tiramisu and claims the blindfold for herself. Effortlessly she does the same thing, but at a much lower level. These girls are more flexible than I ever remember being.

"Brandy," HoneyMama says, claiming my end of the bamboo stick. She must be joking.

"Umm, HoneyMama. You know I love you and will follow almost any direction you give, but there's no way in hell, heaven, or the afterlife in between that I can make it under that stick."

"Girl, here," Praline says, passing the blindfold. "Ain't nobody tripping off your fat-ass thighs. Get under that pole."

When I don't accept the gift, Praline walks over to me and ties the blindfold over my eyes, messing up my hair in the process.

"Now drop it like it's hot," Praline says, smacking my ass.

One of my favorite reggae joints comes on and something tells me it's no coincidence. I used to love dancing to this song, and when Drew was in the deejay booth, he made it a top priority to play it as often as possible.

"'A pimper's paradise, that's all she was,'" HoneyMama sings along to Bob Marley's soothing voice.

I get into the movements and allow the music to hypnotize me, relating to the lyrics as always. I used to be exactly like the sis in the song and would've stayed on that path if it weren't for HoneyMama's intervention. Without realizing how, I've made it under the limbo stick without breaking my back or splitting my dress in two. My mom was right about one thing: miracles do happen when you least expect them.

"There it is!" Praline shouts. "Big girls get it, too."

I remove the blindfold and look at my progress. The pole wasn't as low as it was for everyone else, but that doesn't matter. I can't believe I did it at any level.

"Yes, they do," HoneyMama says, taking the stick and pointing at the three chrome rods. "Opening dance, ladies. Let's see it."

"Oh, no, HoneyMama. I don't know about working the pole," I say, backing away from center stage. "I'm wearing a dress, and it's been way too long."

"Hike up that pretty dress and get your ass up on that pole, Brandy. Now," HoneyMama sternly commands. She's like a czar when it comes to her routines. "We're short a girl and I need to see how the stage looks when Tiramisu and Praline move in sync. Couverture would've been doing her own thing to begin with, anyway. You know that."

"Yes, ma'am," I say, stepping up to the pole on the right side of the stage. I never could say no to her. Unlike the gold titanium pole in the front room, these poles are chrome and allow for a tighter grip for beginning dancers, which is exactly what I feel like.

"Tiramisu, you'll have to be Couverture today," HoneyMama says, pointing at the top of the center pole with her bamboo stick. "Praline, we'll practice you and Dulce's dance when she returns. Follow T's lead."

"Whatever you say, Mama," Praline says, nodding her head in affirmation. She steps to center stage and smiles at her partner.

Tiramisu looks at the top of the pole and then at Honey-Mama, who gives her a gentle smile and nudges her to take control. New girls are always nervous in couple's routines, and rightfully so. One wrong move, you and the dancer underneath could be seriously hurt. And even worse, you could lose all of your hard-earned tips for the night.

Sade's deep, melodic voice creeps eerily through the speakers and into every corner of the room, instantly putting us all into a trance. Our only focus is the center pole and the dancers moving slowly around it.

"'I gave you all the love I got. I gave you more than I could give/Gave you love,'" Sade coos, causing my thoughts and hips to sway to memories of me and Drew. He loved to watch me dance.

"Slow down, Tiramisu. You're making love to Praline, not fucking her," HoneyMama says, directing the ladies as they methodically move in and out of various sensual positions while maintaining total pole control. "Brandy, please show your pole who's boss."

I'm afraid to even walk around it, let alone work it, but I'm more afraid of disappointing HoneyMama. Dancing used to make me feel like I was on top of the world, and not just because of some baller in the audience who was about to break me off—even though that was a big part of it. I felt on top because all eyes were on me. I know I've got mad talent, probably more than the average chick out here dancing. But those days don't come back so easily, once they're gone.

Tiramisu and Praline work their way up the pole in perfect sync. Their legs are strong like the limbs of our ancestors who labored hard all day and night for their survival, much like these sistahs do. Tiramisu expertly folds her body until she's upside down, the tension in her thighs controlling how fast she slides up or down. Praline does a similar move, but with her legs spread apart. Tiramisu's face is now directly in front of Praline's pussy and making me blush.

I walk around the metal rod and reacquaint myself with what used to be my best friend. The fingers on my right hand are the first ones to grip the cool pole, forcing me to quicken my step. I hook my left ankle around the base of the pole and swing my right leg out, allowing myself to spin. Damn, this feels good.

"That's it, Brandy. Ride that pole. Ladies, the fabric," Honey-Mama says, pointing at the satin ribbons tucked inside of Tiramisu's panties.

Tiramisu takes out the orange and yellow strips and slowly waves them up and down before gently moving them across Praline's inner thighs, and then onto her honey spot.

Praline smiles before beginning her descent down the pole. Tiramisu follows, never losing sight of Praline's opened legs. She mimics licking her clit as Praline pretends to come all over the pole. They conclude the dance; HoneyMama looks pleased with their routine.

I'm still curious to see how Couverture would've done it. If they were hot, C would've been on fire.

"Well, now," Drew says from the opened back door, snapping me back to reality. I untangle myself from the pole and straighten out my sundress. I think I came a little myself.

"Back so soon?" HoneyMama says without taking her eyes off the stage. She catches his eye through the mirrored reflection behind the stage and notices his solo entrance. "And where's Dulce?"

"She's being held for resisting arrest, but I doubt it'll stick. She should be out by this evening," Drew says, looking my way. "John's just being an ass, as usual."

"I knew I should've had our attorney meet her down at the station," HoneyMama says, upset.

"It's nothing serious. John asked the judge to show her who's boss, since there's nothing else to hold her on. Her alibi for the night in question checked out."

"As we all knew it would." HoneyMama taps the long bamboo

stick on the floor so hard, it might dent the polished wood. "So, now what?"

"If there's anything that you ladies might be able to tell me about Monaka's associations, it might make things go a little faster with the investigation," Drew says, looking at Tiramisu and Praline. "Even the smallest, seemingly insignificant thing may be just what we need to find this asshole."

"I don't know shit. But if I hear anything, you know I'll holla," Praline says, moving to the pole across from mine. She stretches her left arm along the pole to become parallel with it.

"Tiramisu, I know you're relatively new, but did you and Monaka talk about anything?" Drew says, giving HoneyMama a quick nod before continuing. It's always sensitive when a loved one finds out that they've been lied to. "Maybe she gave you some tips on how to handle clients, especially unruly ones?"

HoneyMama looks from Drew to Tiramisu and nods her head affirmatively. HoneyMama has instructed all of her girls to be careful of whom they trust, especially when it comes to the cops in Butts County. No doubt Drew's one of the only exceptions, and now that he's alone, HoneyMama gives her newest dancer the permission to speak.

"Well, Monaka did mention that one of her regulars started out as a phone sex client," Tiramisu says, wiping down the center pole with a washcloth. All professional dancers carry a personal rag to keep the pole dry and clean. "Monaka recognized his voice when he came into the Spot one night, and he's been a steady patron ever since."

"What's so special about that?" Praline asks. "A lot of my best clients come from outside of the Spot. But once here, they never leave."

Praline circles the pole and hooks her right knee around the center. She spins around twice and then crosses her legs, locking the pole in between. She slowly kicks both legs in the air, flips them over her head, slides down quickly, and lands in a full split. No wonder the broad's body is so tight. Praline has excellent pole control.

"No, this one was *strange* strange," Tiramisu says, replacing the cloth into the back of her left boot. "Monaka just thought he was quiet with a nice smile, but he gave me the creeps."

"Oh, I know the dude you're talking about," Praline says, standing. "That fool became one of Monaka's best clients."

"Yeah, he was," Tiramisu agrees. "She also said that he always desired her full attention, damn-near demanding it some nights, but never got it during the regular shows. That's when she started doing private dances for him and a few other select patrons."

"Monaka rarely did private dances, and when she did, she never did them alone," Praline says. A cunning smile spreads across her violet-colored lips to reveal a crooked top row of badly cared-for teeth, with a gold-and-diamond-encrusted grill covering the bottom. "Ain't that right, Tiramisu?"

Tiramisu shoots daggers at Praline, as if to silence her, but no such luck. She must not know her dance partner very well. Like Dulce, Praline's difficult to intimidate.

"Who'd she dance with?" Drew asks, looking at Tiramisu, who looks scared to answer, but I already know who it was.

"Couverture," HoneyMama says, looking dismayed. "C set up all of our private dances."

No doubt C was pimping the dancers and the clients alike for a nice cut of the private fee. I'm sure she broke HoneyMama off, but I know she kept most of the money to herself. That's just how cold Couverture can be.

"There were always at least two girls in with private clients to keep something like this from happening," HoneyMama says, shaking her head. "I should've never let C take it over."

"It ain't your fault C fell asleep on the job, Mama," Praline says, walking over to give HoneyMama a hug. "Don't blame yourself for this crazy shit."

"Don't even think about this being your fault," Drew says, touching HoneyMama's right shoulder. "And thank you for the information, ladies. I'm going to find out what C knows about Monaka's last client, and why it was a solo dance."

"You can also find out why she's missing in action this morning," HoneyMama says, glancing at the wall clock. "She was supposed to be here over two hours ago."

"I'll definitely see what I can find out," Drew says, also checking the clock.

"So, can we dance tonight or not?" Praline interjects, getting back to business. "Our new dance is the shit, with or without that no-showing heffa, ain't that right, T?"

Tiramisu looks like she wants to spit at Praline, she's so pissed, but she knows better. She chooses to stay silent for the moment. As one of C's chosen protégés, agreeing with one of C's sworn rivals is tantamount to professional suicide for Tiramisu.

"I'm sorry, but the chief's demanding another evidence sweep of the Spot, as well as one of Monaka's apartment, for any clues we might've missed the first time around. It'll happen tomorrow."

HoneyMama looks like she could cry. So do her dancers.

"Drew, we need our money," Praline says, smacking Drew on the hand. "What the fuck are we supposed to do now?"

"Pray that we find the killer soon," Drew says, crossing his ripped arms across his chest. "The chief's not going to reopen the Spot until we do. CSI will be here first thing tomorrow morning."

"Shit," I say, expressing everyone's sentiments. "I knew they'd shut HoneyMama down the first chance they got."

HoneyMama places one hand on her forehead, with the other in the center of her abdomen and inhales deeply. For some people, this stance would indicate stress, but it's one of the ways she prays.

"Keke, you need to be with them tomorrow the entire time," HoneyMama says. "There's a clue there that only you can see. Those jackasses are going to miss it because their minds are closed—no offense, Drew."

"None taken, HoneyMama. And I agree, Keke's always had a keen eye for detail," Drew says. He knows just how thorough I can be.

"Talk about a pimp," Praline says, winking at Drew and walking back to the stage. "Maybe your captain needs to come for a visit, if he hasn't already. He has to know we provide a vital public service, just like the post office. He can't shut us down indefinitely."

"Unfortunately, Captain Jackson has the last word. Not even the sheriff has any say over him," Drew says. "Our best bet's finding out what really happened here, and that starts with finding out C's role in all of this."

I couldn't agree more.

Part Two

Monaka: The Morning Of

*T*HIS MORNING, I FOUND MYSELF IN DAMN-NEAR THE SAME TIRED AND *overwhelmed state that I was when I first arrived at the Spot over ten years ago. Time flies when you're having fun or raising Cain, like my daddy used to say. Back then, I was a professional at doing both—still am, under the right circumstances. The difference these days is that the price is way more than an ass whupping if I miss a step, much like I did last night.*

Like with all of her protégés, HoneyMama wouldn't let me sleep in one of the spare bedrooms inside the main house until I'd bathed in these very same waters. The sulfur springs have been popular around here long before any of the current occupants ever called this place home. The Creek Indians that the town's named for used to come here for everything they needed, from drinking water to washing clothes to taking spiritual baths.

HoneyMama's family maintained this reverence, and so has she. Once she takes a new dancer into the fold, she performs an entire month's worth of ceremonies, including washing as much of our pasts away, as we want, in the powerful springs. She conducts the naming ceremonies here as well, after she gets to know the dancer's true nature, as she calls it. Each protégé has to work as an apprentice under one of the A team dancers, until she's ready to take the pole test and pass with flying stilet-tos. When the mentor says that dancer's ready to take the pole solo, HoneyMama gives the newest dance sister a name and all the love and money that comes with it, just like at any other baptism.

To say that I was a hot mess when I first came to live in Indian Springs would be an understatement. I was downright wretched and didn't know if I was coming or going. I danced wherever I could get onstage, but never stayed long enough to get too close to any of the patrons or the other dancers, until I met C. No matter which club I landed, I've always been on the A team and loved every minute of it. Deep down, I always knew that once they found out who I really was, or who the government says I am, they'd kick me out, and that's if I got away lucky. Most dancers like me—no matter how talented, with or without a pole—eventually end up on the streets or dead, and that's just where I was headed until Honey-Mama found me behind the alley at The Pimp Palace doing hand jobs between dances.

Ever the lady, HoneyMama waited until I finished with my client, slipped me a business card, and asked me to find her after my real shift ended. I didn't know what to say: I'd heard about her, of course. She's a legend when it comes to pole dancing, and a mythical fairy godmother–like figure for those of us who gave up on the Captain-Save-a-Ho version of the fairy tale a long, long time ago. I'd never met anyone like her before and was in awe of the fact that her eyes held absolutely no judgment for me or what she'd witnessed. The only things I saw in those hazel eyes on that humid night in Atlanta were compassion and sadness. I never want her to look at me like that again, and still can't stand the thought of how she'll see me once she finds out what I've been up to with C.

"I can never understand how y'all voluntarily bathe in that stank-ass water," C says, ruining my peace and quiet before the storm rolling in from the south. It looks like it's going to be a strong one, and C's just the dark cloud to usher it in. "You better get that smell off your exotic ass before tonight's show," she says, her thick Kingston accent coating every word with a palpable urgency. "The clients don't want to think of gas when you shake that ass."

"Clever, very. Is that what you came all the way down here to tell me?" I say, staring down at my reflection in the dark water. My sunken eyes indicate that I need some serious sleep and a heavy concealer.

The black rocks lining the riverbed provide the perfect background for the clear water, giving it a sort of onyx-mirror reflection. Dulce loves dark mirrors—I'll have to suggest them for part of our macabre wedding theme. She loves Halloween, and I couldn't say no to the fall date or my happy bride-to-be.

"We have to discuss the terms of tonight's private dance. They've changed," C says, stepping closer to the water's edge. Her modest four-inch heels sink into the gritty sand, creating a crackling sound with every step. "He only wants you there for the after-party this time, not me."

"Not a chance in hell," I say, done with the bath and the unwelcomed chat. So much for a peaceful cleansing.

I charge out of the water, grab my beach towel from the jagged black rocks, and wrap it around the modest one-piece. If I'd known I was going to have an audience, I would've chosen a more revealing swimsuit. Always give them a show, even when you're scared or tired is what I say— never let them see you off your game, and C's a pro at knocking people off center. That's why she came down here, instead of catching me at work in a couple of hours. She knew where I'd be this morning, the same place I am damn-near every Thursday morning since I moved in with Dulce. C wanted to catch me in my most vulnerable state: mission accomplished, bitch.

"That's a cardinal rule, C. Even you know that." I reach inside of the Tory Burch duffel for another towel. "Besides, I don't too much care for the Southern gentleman," I say, drying the ends of my waist-length hair first, before working the T-shirt towel up toward the crown of my head, much to her amusement.

"It's his birthday wish, Monaka. Can you blame him?" she says, coming so close that I can smell her sweet couture perfume of the day. "And you know he's more than generous," she says, running the back of her hand down my right shoulder, giving me goose bumps.

We've already been down that road and quickly realized that we weren't each other's type, but we make one hell of a couple on the pole. Anyone who sees me and C, or me and Dulce, would think we were fucking offstage. And I admit, there's pleasure in the illusion of it all, but nothing about me and Dulce's fake. With C, on the other hand, it's all fog and mirrors, and our clients pay a pretty penny to enjoy the show.

"I'm sure he'll be more than willing to share his birthday loot," she says, too close for comfort. "I won't even take my usual cut. Well, not all of it."

C always thinks she can get her way with that million-dollar smile and cunning, sexy stare, but her tricks don't work on me. Besides, like I said, there's something off about her favorite client. I can't put my finger on it, but I don't trust him, especially not one-on-one.

"Not today, Satan's daughter," I say, done with this conversation and her glitter-covered attempt at seduction. "There's a good reason we never do solo dances. I'm not doing it, no matter how good the bonus might be."

I grab my bag and step in front of C, who takes my right elbow and spins me around so that we're eye-to-eye.

"Let me remind you of who the real boss is if you want your secrets to stay put, you hear?" she says, grabbing my ass with her free hand. "Dis mine, and so is everything else you got, or don't got." She lets out a laugh so fierce that the once-chirping birds hidden in the trees begin to squawk.

"You don't own me or my secrets, fucking cunt," I say between gritted teeth.

"Yes, I fucking do, stupid bitch," she says, reclaiming my arm. "You will do the after-party and the private show after that, or there will be no more Honey Spot for you, and you can kiss your weird-ass wedding good-bye, too. We clear?"

I hate lying to Dulce and HoneyMama, but I need the extra money, and I don't want either of them finding out how I actually came to meet HoneyMama. I push her away from me hard, causing her to slightly lose balance, but she quickly catches herself, just like the expert that she is.

"Yes!" C exclaims, scaring the wildlife again. "That's who I need to see tonight, not that scared trick in the water."

"This wasn't the plan," I say, recalling my dreams to dance on Broadway or somewhere else with my name in lights. I watched Alvin Ailey, Fame, and every other dance show I could get my hands on. My father hated my obsession and let it be known, but my mother indulged my every whim, enrolling me in ballet, ballroom, urban—any dance class they offered in the Southern California area was at my fingertips, even when we couldn't afford it. My mother always found a way to pay for the classes. Even after the cancer took her ability to come to every rehearsal, recital, and audition, she was still my biggest cheerleader, right until the end. Everything changed after her death.

"I don't plan on stripping forever." I smile, remembering the last conversation my father and I had before I packed up my Honda Civic and *drove across country to pursue my dreams. "No time like the present to make a change."*

She wasn't expecting that and, frankly, neither was I. But I've had it with her holding the past over my head. Fuck C and her rich clients if she thinks I'll be under her thumb indefinitely to stay in their good favor.

"I'm done."

Unamused, C steps in front of me and snaps her fingers in front of my face. The flash of her bright green clawlike nails temporarily blind me.

"Everybody can't be the boss, Monaka. But you can be a boss and get this money from these rich white dudes and move on with your life. I don't give a shit if you want to turn into a happy housewife or whatever the fuck you see yourself doing in the future, but right now, you need to wake the hell up and get serious," she says, pushing the center of my forehead with the tip of her nail. "So clean yourself in the waters of Lake Minnetonka and do whatever else it is you need to do to get yourself straight. You better be on that stage tonight with and then without me, or else we'll have a whole heap of other problems to deal with, you hear?"

"After we dance together for his friends, you want me to then entertain that fool by myself?" I say, still in disbelief. "Are you nuts?"

"No, but I am about this cheddar. And if you want to get the last part of your surgery or whatever you said you was going to use the money for, you need to understand one thing in this scenario," C says, removing a vape pen from her bountiful cleavage and taking a hit. "I'm the only boss and you have no say; never have, never will. Ain't no HoneyMama or nobody else in charge of this operation. Just me, and what I say goes."

She blows a cloud of thick cannabis smoke in my face; I wish I could get a secondhand high from the fading vapor, but no such luck.

"But don't you worry your pretty little head about none of that," she says, offering me the pen, which I begrudgingly accept. "At the end of the day, the real boss is the money, and he who holds the purse holds the pussy. Get that through your thick skull. You wanted to be here. I arranged for HoneyMama to find you at just the right place and time to gain her sympathy. Well, you got it. Now deal with it, and get the job done."

"I hate lying to Dulce," I say, more to myself than C. "She'll be so worried when I don't come home at the usual time."

"Well, it's an unusual night, so Dulce's sour ass is just gonna have to

deal with it. Never understood why Honey named her forever-tart ass that. Just goes to show that she's not the all-knowing goddess everyone thinks she is," C says, throwing shade at both HoneyMama and my love, as usual.

I cut her a wicked side eye and she takes a step back. I will fight if pushed too far, and she's damn-near on the edge of pressing all my buttons.

"She'll be fine when she sees the bag you bring home, Monaka. You'll see."

"Dulce's never been all about the money, and you know that. She doesn't like me working with you, and she damn sure wouldn't like it if she knew I was taking on a private dance, especially one arranged by you. That's just something we don't do here, and you know what if HoneyMama finds out . . ."

"Who gives a bloodclaat about HoneyMama finding out shit," C spews with more than a little hate. "Just because she got Mama in her name don't make her mine, and I wish everyone would stop treating her like one, damn hypocrite-ass baddie wannabe." C sucks her teeth hard, snatches the pen from my hands, and hits it.

"I care, and you should, too, as much as she's done for all of us and continues to do. This is how you repay her?"

"Think whatever you want, but I ain't no little girl. Hell, I've never been little. HoneyMama's nothing more than another club owner, a means to an end—that's it. She can keep the life lessons and words of wisdom to her damn self. I'll take an occasional sweet potato biscuit, but that's about all I need from her other than ways to make money for me and my flock," she says, referring to the dancers she takes under her wing for side jobs.

"C, I really don't think you should have those girls out here giving private dances, including me."

"What's the worst thing that can happen? Somebody gets too excited and ends up nuttin' all over the velvet drapes?" She laughs at that, stepping in front of me and back toward the main path. "Stop being such a baby. You worked the streets for a long time before you met me; I know you can handle yourself."

"I don't work there anymore," I say, shuddering at the memory. I was never a fighter unless I had to be. That's why Dulce and I are a perfect match. She'll fight damn-near anyone at the drop of a dime.

"Be careful, Monaka. Keep messing with me and you might end up right back where you started," she says, her words more than an empty threat. *"Get it together and, like I said, I'll see you tonight. Now go turn that frown upside down and let's get to practice. We still have a regular show to do, too, you know."*

Don't I know it. I don't know why I ever allowed C to get in my head like this. If I didn't need surgery, I wouldn't bother with her at all. HoneyMama provides benefits, but Georgia ain't paying for what I need, that's for damn sure. I just have to figure out a way to go home with a straight face and lie to my beautiful, lovely bride for one more night. I swear this is the last dance I'm doing with C.

Nobody knows but HoneyMama and Mr. Graves that Dulce and I already had a private ceremony right here by the river months ago. Honey-Mama united us in holy bliss, until we can make it legal and public. Mr. Graves provided the ambiance, complete with an array of flowers and an opened tent to shield us from the soft rain that fell that cool spring day. It was absolutely perfect.

We've lived together ever since that day and always felt like wife and wife. But now, Dulce wants a big wedding, with rings to match, pledging each other's love for life in front of everyone we love. I just hope she doesn't try and take C out when she finds out what she's got me agreeing to do tonight. I might as well take some extra water home from the springs. I'm sure Dulce's gonna need cooling down once I tell her why we won't be binge-watching our favorites shows after our final set this evening.

Chapter 12

*A*FTER THIS MORNING'S SESSION AT THE SPOT, I HEAD BACK TO AT-lanta for our weekly department meeting at the *Metro Journal.* Charlie's in rare form this afternoon, cussing out everyone for one thing or another, including me. I just walked in and can't wait until the day comes when I can tell him to go straight to hell and take his stale-ass coffee and cigarette breath with him.

"McCoy, what's the haps on the strip club murder? Any juicy leads?"

All eyes are on me, but unlike onstage this morning, it doesn't feel good.

"Not yet, but tomorrow the police are doing a clean sweep of The Honey Spot and the victim's home in search of any missed clues. I'll be with them every step of the way."

"That's great, Keke. But what about the real story. Did this girl have a pimp, a side hustle, something other than the surface story?"

The other dozen reporters nod their heads in either agree-ment with Charlie or sympathy for me; it's hard to tell which is which around here.

"Charlie, there are no pimps. These women are professional dancers, not hoes."

"The hell they're not," Charlie says, raising his voice. "This lit-tle firecracker was definitely no angel." Charlie takes out one of Pete's prints of the crime scene photos and points at Monaka's corpse. "I want this story, Keke. How this naked gal got all twisted and mangled up like this, and who she was dancing for before he strangled her."

"I understand that, Charlie," I begin, attempting to form my response in such a way that it doesn't cause me to lose my job or go back to jail. "But the backstory doesn't necessarily lead to a pimp of any sort," or does it?

I never considered C as a full-fledged pimp, more of a bottom bitch. But women can pimp, too—it's an equal opportunity kind of gig.

"How can you talk about hoes and leave out the pimps?" Charlie asks, missing the point completely. "You need to get in there, Keke. Earn back their trust. Write the real story they're not telling you. Shit, I thought you were our inside girl, our street girl," he says, sounding more than a little racist with his fake *hood* accent.

"I told you to stop calling me that." What little patience I have with this jerk is quickly waning.

"Never, because that's your role. We all have our roles. Andrea's Fulton County courthouse, Tim's Cobb County schools, Pete takes pictures, you catch my drift?" Charlie says, taking the lit cigarette from between his yellowed teeth and pointing it my way. "Start your own damned paper, then you can call yourself whatever the hell you want. Until then, bring me street, McCoy. Gutters, alleys, highways, and byways, you hear? Street, McCoy. That's your beat." He takes a sharp draw and allows the smoke to encircle the air in front of him like a doomsday cloud.

Pete looks from his stack of prints and up at me, then shrugs his shoulders as if to say, *"What the fuck did you expect?"*

"Got it, Charlie: street. I'm on it," I say, anxiously tapping the fancy gel pen onto my scribbled legal pad, ready to get the hell out of here. One good thing about being the *street* reporter is that my place is outside of this toxic office.

"I hope so, Keke. This story's too juicy to mess up, you hear?"

"Loud and clear."

"Good. Get back to me after tomorrow's events with some

good shit, no excuses. Now, Andrea, what the hell's going on with those Black guys who robbed the QT in midtown? Are they getting sentenced to life at the end of the month, or what?" Charlie asks, moving on to other business.

"They're not guys, Charlie. One of the suspects is only fourteen years old, and the other two are sixteen," Andrea says, horrified by Charlie's unsympathetic description. "They're just kids."

She's one of the new hires shadowing Jacob, our City Hall reporter, until her ninety-day probation period is up and she takes over her permanent beat full-time. Charlie's taken a liking to her fresh-out-of-college ideas and body—unfortunately for her. Andrea's driven and conscientious, in a trendy-social-media kind of way. I don't think she cares one way or another if the young men receive life for petty theft. I suspect she just wants to check the old white guy in the room. Being a young white female, she can do just that, as long as she's ready to get checked in return.

"*Kids.* Seriously?" Charlie sneers. "Spare me the bleeding heart and shed some light on the opinion of the impending verdict, would you, please? Fucking idiots, the lot of you!" He sucks the last bit of poison from the cigarette butt and smashes it into an empty Coca-Cola can on the overcrowded conference table that we all take for granted. "Are the Black kids gonna hang or not?"

If I didn't need this job, I'd pimp slap the shit out of Charlie. One day, I'll tell him to fuck off. Until then, I'll grin and bear it, just like most of my other colleagues do, including Andrea, whose ass is on the sneaky link pyre. Better hers than mine.

When I arrive back at my apartment this afternoon, I quickly realize that I am bereft of life's essentials, even for an independent single lady like me: There are no clean clothes or any food in the fridge worth eating. Luckily, Shelley is always around when I need a friend—and some clothes washed free of charge. It's been a long day and I could use some TLC, but Ian's not picking up his cell, as usual. Where's my dick when I need it? Probably laid up with some other pussy, but I don't want to even go there right now.

"I come bearing laundry and wine, just like in the Bible," I say, walking through Shelley's front door and into her massive, messy home. I love coming over here. It's the best birth control a girl could ask for.

"That's my girl," Shelley says, relieving me of two reusable Publix bags full of dirty laundry. "And I think it was fruit and wine back in the holy days."

"Dirty drawers, fruit—it's all the same," I say, giving my girl a hug.

"Whatever, Miss Busy Reporter." Shelley returns the affection and then closes the massive oak door behind her. "Get that beautiful ass in the kitchen."

"Where's the hubby and kids?" I ask, noticing how quiet her house is, which is highly unusual.

"Over his parents' house. I told him to take the kids, even the baby, and give me a minute to hear myself think." Shelley picks up several toys and tosses them onto the couch.

"No visiting the in-laws this time?" I tease, and follow her into the equally unkempt kitchen.

Shelley's in-laws are white and resent her Black-and-beautiful self for being the mother to their only heirs. They love their grandchildren, but can't stand the mama, and the feeling's mutual. They didn't even come to the wedding, hoping that denial would lead to divorce, but Shelley and her man have been happily married for over fifteen years, and keep making beige babies.

"Butts County has made you a funny bitch, I see." She opens a bottle of Pinot Grigio and pours two generous glasses.

I walk into the adjacent washroom and start my load. I only have one, but will probably be here all night. Once me and my girl start drinking and talking, time becomes irrelevant.

"Guess so." I pick up my glass and take a seat next to Shelley at the wraparound bar that separates the kitchen from the family room. When I grow up, I want a house just like this one—minus all the kids.

"What's new at the whorehouse?" Shelley asks, making herself laugh, but after the day I've had defending the Spot, I don't find the comment funny at all.

"Shelley, please," I say in full defense mode. "First it's Charlie; now my best friend. Can a dancer catch a break?"

"Oh, girl, you know I'm just kidding," Shelley says, placing her head on my shoulder. "Damn, when'd you get so sensitive?"

I take a sip of my wine, and then another, until my glass is empty. Shelley dutifully refills it and allows my mood to soften before the interrogation begins. I know she's been waiting to get all of the 411 about my past life.

"So tell me all about this Drew . . . What's his last name?"

"Elijah Drew, but he goes by Drew. He's not really into the biblical name his daddy gave him."

"I see," Shelley says, already feeling the wine as much as I am.

My cell lights up with yet another call from Pete. I silence the call and turn my phone off for the night. I've been avoiding him since our meeting earlier. No doubt, he wants to tag along during tomorrow's investigation, but I've had enough of him, too.

"What's the point of having a phone if it never rings with a date on the other end?"

I toss the cell down on the marble bar top, damn-near cracking the glass back for the third time this year and it's only summer. Something tells me my warranty doesn't include unlimited replacements.

"Hell, I can't even get Ian to answer his phone half the time. Most of our communication's through text or email."

"I see," Shelley says, a goofy smile spreading across her face. "I'm sorry, girl. I'm listening. Can you top me off?"

"Whatever, Shelley."

I pour her the last drops of our first bottle and glance across the spacious room at the full liquor cabinet. The Viognier looks like a good bottle to open after the Cabernet. Shelley is a notorious wine snob—the first Black sommelier of her college class, she loves to brag—and her husband feels the same way about his bourbon.

"Excellent and expensive choice," she says, inspecting the understated bottle of red wine. I'm surprised she didn't insist on staying with white, but I guess she's too tipsy to care. "And I hear you about having a regular man to date. Ian has potential; he just doesn't know how to be your man yet. As Carmen says, we have to identify his obstacles and yours, too."

"Well, tell Carmen that, according to my mother, my obstacles are my weight, my hair, and my mouth, not necessarily in that order," I say, topping off our glasses. Even with the kids around, Shelley insists on real glass for her favorite beverage. "She also says that I should go to church, because that's where all of the good men and the Lord are."

"Has she been to a church in the South lately?" she says, accepting the large pour. "I'd say the pickings were pretty slim at best."

"Every Sunday, and at least twice during the week," I say, saluting with my free hand.

I fill my glass, take a sip to make space, and pour some more.

"Is that right?" Shelley says, surprised. "I would've never guessed you as the daughter of a holy roller."

I never told Shelley about my upbringing, because I didn't think it was relevant before. I know how prudish she can be. But I suppose she needs the backstory in order to understand my deep affection for The Honey Spot.

"There's a lot you wouldn't have guessed about me."

"Oh, please, Keke. I know you like to have your dick and eat it, too," Shelley says, laughing loudly. Thank goodness all of her babies aren't here. We definitely bring out the ratchet in each other.

"I don't miss having a man just for dick's sake," I say, unbuttoning the top portion of my blouse. I changed out of my comfy sundress for my meeting this afternoon and can't wait to get out of these clothes. "I miss the weight of a man on my belly, the smell of him in my sheets. I miss my man, period. Whoever he is, wherever he is. I miss that man."

"Do you regret leaving Drew? Or better yet, do you regret starting something new with Ian when he doesn't seem to know how to give back?"

Ever since Shelley started seeing Carmen, her marriage counselor, twice a week, she thinks she's a goddamned therapist. Next thing I know, she'll be at Emory, for an extra two years, getting a psychology degree that she'll never use.

"When I give, I give all the way," I say, thinking of all the good food I've happily bought and cooked for our dates over the past few months. "I don't look back when the relationship's over, usually, because even after all the drama and bullshit, I'm still happy I had someone to share it with, you know?"

I think my tipsy is catching up to hers.

"And that's wifey material," Shelley says, tuning her iPad to the Goapele station, one of my favorites.

I love that we have a lot in common, no matter how different our lives may be. She streams the melodic vibes throughout the house, creating our own private club atmosphere.

"I just can't open myself up anymore, Shelley. I'm tired of sleeping with a new dude every year or so, because the old dude couldn't lock it down," I say, letting the tears flow freely. "I wish I'd been born a different type of bitch." I know I'm slurring, but still, I'm dead serious.

"And what type of bitch is that?" Shelley's phone buzzes with a text from her husband, on cue. He's checking up on her just as much as he's checking in with her.

"The type that a man wants to marry," I say, claiming her cell as Exhibit A. "The type that a man chooses over his fear of commitment, or change, or whatever his issue is. The type of bitch that makes a man *want* to be her one-and-only dick for life."

"Keke, you are that bitch. Have you ever thought that you're just choosing the wrong men?" Shelley takes a sip, reclaims her phone, and sends a quick text of her own.

"Every man can't be the wrong man, Shelley," I say, lamenting over my many loves lost in the past decade. "Shit, Drew was a good man. Ian's a good man, an excellent writer and photographer, not to mention he's the best lover I've ever had, and he loves my cooking. The dude's already got me twisted, and it's only been a few months since we started dating."

"Them Chicago brothers will do it to you every time," Shelley says, speaking the truth. "And y'all have so much in common. I really think Ian's the one."

"The one to drive me insane." I down the rest of my wine like a shot of one of the smooth bourbons that I wouldn't mind trying next. "He already admitted to me that he chooses not to commit to anyone, but I bet after our relationship's over, he'll be locked down with the very next broad. It's just something about me that keeps a man from committing, but as soon as we're through, he marries the next chick that comes along. My typical life story."

"Yeah, but all of that is his fear talking. Trust me, Keke, stop giving it all up in the beginning and read the bitch books, like I told you to. That's how you'll get Ian whipped so bad that he won't know what to do without you, like my Larry feels about me."

"What you and Larry have is hella unique, Shelley. He's your anchor and you are definitely the ship that keeps your family afloat."

"That's exactly it. Larry helps me bear the storms, because we both know they're coming. When his father was first diagnosed with cancer, and his mother couldn't handle it, I went in and cleaned his bedpan, no matter how many 'nigger bitches' I was in the process. And his mama ain't no better. She still hasn't said a thank-you for all of the times I took her husband to chemo because she had a Rotary Club meeting or some other bullshit commitment," Shelley says.

"I remember that," I say, opening our final bottle.

"I didn't mind doing any of that, because when I chose to be with my husband, I also chose all of his shit. I chose him, for good and bad, better or worse. And he chose me. It took some time, but I had faith in my man. Still do," Shelley says. She looks down at her wet blouse and heads for the kitchen sink, where her breast pump is stationed.

"What the hell, Shelley? Are you spiking the baby's milk now?"

"No, silly. I pumped all day long to make sure he had plenty of milk to last him for two days if necessary. I just need to get this shit out before my titties explode," she says, returning with the pump.

"I know I'm a reporter, but that was way too much information."

"Whatever," Shelley says, pumping the left breast first. "Maybe you need to show Ian some happy couples other than me and my boo. He seemed so into you when we met for dinner last month. Maybe it's time he met your mom. Weren't your parents happily married?"

"Umm, hell no on both accounts."

"Wow. I would've never guessed you didn't come from a happy home."

"Well, I didn't," I say, looking at the family portraits lining her living-room walls. "My parents' marriage was anything but functional. Unfortunately, my daddy channeled most of his frustrations into gambling, and my mom into gardening. When Daddy wanted more kids, my mom said no. When he wanted a dog, she said no. When Daddy wanted to follow his dreams and open his own restaurant—he was an excellent cook—my mom laughed in his face, and then said no. But when he wanted to have sex with the lonely white lady who worked at the post office, that lady said yes."

"Wow," Shelley says. "Your mom must've gone crazy when she found out."

"Nope. She just went to Jesus, and her husband eventually came back to her. Completely broken, but my daddy was home, and that's all that mattered to my mom. It was too late for me to go back by then."

"How'd you become a stripper if your mom was a good, God-fearing woman?" Shelley asks, switching breasts. "I still can't wrap my head around that one."

"Well, I felt like the Whore of Babylon after my mother busted me for having sex the same summer that Daddy left," I say, eyeing her rubbery, dark nipple. "That titty's been through some things."

"Shut up and focus on the story," Shelley says, tossing a throw pillow at my head, and reminding me that I need to take these faux locs down soon, but not till after I leave Indian Springs. The last thing I want to deal with is my hair while working this case.

"As a 'punishment' and to give herself a break from it all, my mom dropped me off at my great-aunt's house for the rest of the summer. While there, I met a stripper, by way of my cousin, who made the life seem so easy, and that's how I felt. Not that all strippers are hoes, but that's how it felt in the beginning, until I found out that they were hustlin' her ass on the side and a couple of other dancers."

"News flash, Keke! All strippers are hoes," Shelley slurs, half evil, half envious. If she weren't my best, and only, friend, I'd cuss her ass out.

"No, they're not, Miss Feminist Studies Minor," I say, throwing a wine cork at her bare chest. "Broads who don't understand the life are too quick to confuse stripping with hoeing. We should have each other's backs and not be so quick to judge."

"Please enlighten me, Keke," Shelley says, throwing the cork right back.

The hard projectile hits me in the cheek. It hurts more than I want to admit.

"What's the difference between taking your clothes off for money and being a hooker?" Shelley stands, hikes up her already-short jean shorts, and pretends to throw money in the air. "They both involve getting naked and spreading your legs so fools can make it rain in the club." Shelley laughs hard at her crass antics, but she's the only one. Finally feeling as stupid as she looks, she stops laughing and sits back down.

I take a deep breath and tell her what I've never told anyone other than HoneyMama, of course—there's not much use in trying to hide shit from her. She always finds out the truth eventually, which is why even though we still can't seem to find C's in-the-wind ass, the broad can't hide forever.

"When I first started dancing, I thought the owner of the neighborhood gym was my friend. He was one of my first clients in the city, and I naively thought that he had my best interest at heart."

Shelley calms down and puts away her drained breasts before pouring us another round. We both take a sip as I continue to relive one of my least favorite memories.

"He'd randomly give me money for books, or to get my car fixed, have my hair and nails done, all the while saying that he admired me for trying to do something with my life other than strip because I always wanted to go to college. And I was so young and stupid that I believed him, that is until one night after I'd finished working out. He demanded payback on the hood of his car behind the gym that he owned," I say, wiping away tears from the corners of my eyes.

I force down a small amount of vomit I can feel bubbling up at the back of my throat. Just the memory alone of that sweaty, beefy, clammy, Southern white man on top of me still makes me sick to my stomach.

"I didn't feel like I could say no, for more reasons than one. HoneyMama unknowingly came to my rescue the very next week, and the rest is history and I never spoke about it after. I knew it wouldn't be the last time, if I didn't find a way out, but home wasn't an option."

Shelley looks stunned at my confession. If she only knew some of the shit I've been through, she'd probably think I was making it all up.

"He thought because I danced that I was for sale in every way he could imagine. After that night, I never went back to that gym. I also clearly understood my limitations, and that my talent—not my body—was how I earned a living."

"I would've never guessed all that about you, Keke. Damn, girl. Fuck the articles, you need to write a memoir. I'd read that shit."

"One day at a time," I say, finishing off my glass before heading into the laundry room. "Right now, I need to finish telling Monaka's story."

"Yeah, but after you find out who murdered her, you need to work on your own story. And I hope it ends with you not being pimped, because right now, that's exactly what you're doing: pimping yourself out to these dudes, and they're happily running shit because you're not," she continues. She stumbles to the kitchen sink and dumps the tainted milk down the drain.

"Put your titties away and stop talking shit," I say, opening the washing machine. I reach across to place the load in the drier and clumsily slam the heavy, too-complicated door shut.

"And the worst part about it is that you're not getting a damned thing in return, except for a good fuck when you can get it," she continues, not heeding my advice. "Stop being so damned nice, Keke. That's all I'm saying."

"Easy to say from your Craftsman-style home, complete with a luxury SUV, husband, and kids."

"A relationship ain't paradise, and nobody should be getting played," she says so seriously that I think she's sobered up a bit. "It's not a game. It's life, and a damned good one from where I'm sitting," she says, pulling the detachable brass faucet from its holder and spraying the oversized farm sink clean. "So, get up, put your big girl bra on, and dig a little deeper. I know you've still got that same bad bitch from college somewhere in there. You just have to let her come out and rule."

"I'd be happy if Ian just ruled for a little while. I'm tired," I say, sitting back down. I turn my phone back on and hope to see a message from him. No such luck. "I just want to be claimed first—then I'll find my bad bitch again. Promise."

"Ian's not going to claim you if you don't claim yourself first. Hang up the pole, Keke, and get a ring. It's time to shit or get off the pot for both of you."

"Deep, Shelley. Real deep." It must be late if Shelley's letting her true country roots show. She's a Grady Baby, straight out of Riverdale.

"It may not be my most profound saying of the night, but it's the truth. The time is now, Keke. Own your shit, and the right man won't be able to help but wife you up."

"From your lips," I say, barely audible.

I'm too tired from the impromptu workout and the rest of the day to argue with Shelley any further. Plus, as usual, she makes some valid points. Hopefully, I'll remember the best ones when I wake up.

Chapter 13

I DON'T SEE HOW SHELLEY WOKE UP THIS MORNING, LET ALONE GOT her kids off to daycare, and the baby to mommy-and-me yoga class. I wish I would try to live her life for one day. I can barely take care of myself, let alone four children and a husband. Just hearing about her day makes me tired.

My arms and legs are covered with bruises, making it difficult to sit still for my morning drive into Indian Springs. I forgot all about the pole kisses and the soreness that comes with dancing, not to mention the headache that comes from drinking too much. Although I sucked down two Motrin, the throbbing in my head still hasn't subsided. Charlie calling and waking me up bright and early didn't help, either. He was up my ass with his whole "Dig deeper, Keke! I smell a Pulitzer!" mantra at the crack of dawn. Does the man ever sleep?

All Charlie wants to hear is the nasty shit he jacks off to, but this murder's about more than lust and jealousy. Last night wasn't the first time I saw Monaka's wide-open eyes in my dreams, and my gut tells me it's a clue to something bigger. I also know that C knows something about it, but she's not going to give up the truth to me or HoneyMama if she can help it. I'm going to ask Drew to focus in on C to get the missing answers. He's always had a way of working the truth out of women, even C's hard ass.

"Good morning, sunshine," Drew says as I put my car in PARK in front of the Spot. "It's nice to see you, as always, Ms. McCoy."

"And you as well." I turn off the ignition and exit my car. I stand still against the car door for a moment and adjust to my all-over body pain.

"What the hell happened to you?" Drew asks, noticing my stiff composure.

"The pole, that's what," I say, exposing the dark bruises on the insides of my biceps. "And way too much wine."

Drew tries to hide his smile, but his pretty whites shine through. "Been a while, huh, Brandy?" Drew offers his arm for support and I gladly accept.

"*A while?*" I say, looping my hand through his elbow and allowing him to lead me up the porch steps. "Shit. I feel like Old Lady Moses."

"Girl, please. When I saw you up on that stage yesterday, I thought I was having a flashback," Drew says, causing my cheeks to flush. He opens the front door and follows me inside of the cool foyer. "You looked good, if I do say so myself."

Drew peeps at me over his shades. I return the attention, imagining which part of his body I want to kiss first. This man's every bit of sexy, and knows it.

"About time you showed up," John says, fucking up the mood. This guy's worse than Charlie, because when an asshole cop is in a bad mood, people's entire lives can get fucked up.

"John," Drew says, removing his shades. "Anything new?"

"Not a damned thing," John says. "Morning, ma'am." John tips his cowboy hat my way.

I nod in recognition and scan the front room for Honey-Mama, who's nowhere to be found. With the Spot now open to public scrutiny, the dancers feel like they're always "on," and I can tell it's taking a toll. The climate in the house is becoming thick with impatience and desperation.

"Flowers and cards are piling up at Monaka's shrine," John says, pointing around the side of the house toward the rose garden. "Seems like the girl had lots of admirers."

"People love HoneyMama and her dancers, whether some

people think they're worthy or not. I need some air," I say, leaving John and Drew to catch up on their morning business.

I knew they wouldn't find anything new. This was all a ploy to shut the Spot down, and to what end? The killer ain't stupid, and the forensic investigators did a very thorough job the first time around. Whatever we're missing isn't in this house.

Choosing the long way around, I step out the side door and onto the veranda, where the intoxicating scent of honeysuckle, jasmine, and roses mingle in the thick summer air. As I make my way down the three extra-wide steps, I stop on the last one and wave to Mr. Graves, who's in the backyard happily tending his duties. What would this place be without his constant care?

HoneyMama outdid herself with Monaka's shrine. It's absolutely gorgeous. There's a collage of various sympathy cards, love notes, printouts of messages from social media, as well as two oversized purple-and-gold Japanese fans, with Monaka's name written in calligraphy. There are also pictures of her dressed in her finest dance costumes, and some with Dulce, where she seems happy and looks very young, even a few without her customary flawless makeup.

From the looks of it, Monaka had many admirers, but only one is here visiting the shrine this morning. We stand in silence for a few minutes out of respect, but also because I can feel her sizing me up, just like I'm doing in return.

"Did you know Monaka well?" I ask the woman I assume to be a fellow dancer, or at least that's what she looks like to me. Who else wears thigh-high boots with six-inch heels and a scarf tied around their neck in this kind of heat? It's cute, but way too hot for that shit.

"I only met her a couple of times, but I admired her work very much," she says with a heavy Southern drawl, her voice almost as raspy as Dulce's—cigarettes, grief, and lack of sleep are hard to hide.

The strange, painfully thin woman cools herself with a pale blue hand fan, like the paper ones church ladies pass out during Sunday service, minus the local advertisements on the back.

Something's odd about this chick; I'm not sure exactly what, but I can usually spot crazy when I see it.

"Really?" I ask, moving closer to her and the shrine. "What part of her performances did you like most?"

"Her attire. Simple, seductive elegance." She takes an embroidered white handkerchief from her small handbag and dabs the corner of one heavily made-up eye, then the other. From where I'm standing, this broad hasn't shed a tear. "Monaka always carried herself like such a lady."

She straightens her expensive glasses and stares at me. I wait for her to say something, but she never does. She just keeps looking at me, attempting to figure me out, I suppose.

"Keke, over here," Drew says, drawing my attention back toward the house.

"Enjoy your day, Keke," the woman says, repeating my name from Drew's call. I don't know why, but I don't like the sound of my name falling from her red-stained lips.

"You too. What did you say your name was?" I ask, extending my hand out of courtesy.

"I didn't, but it's Queenie," the odd admirer says, taking my hand in hers and shaking it firmly.

"Nice to meet you, Queenie." I attempt to reclaim my hand, but she's not ready to let go just yet.

"Likewise, Keke," she says, squeezing my hand tighter than necessary. "See you soon, I hope."

Before I can respond, Queenie releases my hand and heads toward the back of the property.

"Who was that?" Drew asks, watching Queenie walk away as I head back inside.

"One of Monaka's fans," I say, rubbing my right hand. "Does she dance at another club?"

"I don't know, but I'll ask around." Drew closes the screen door behind me. "In my opinion, lady looks like a dude."

"Really?" I say, searching for Queenie, who's already disappeared behind the trees. "How can you tell?"

"Call it a hazard of my profession," Drew says. "I just can."

"So, if I dressed up like a man, you'd be able to tell the difference?"

"Keke, don't take this the wrong way, but you have the type of femininity others try to emulate." Drew looks me over, much like Queenie did a moment ago, but unlike the stranger, Drew's familiar glance gives me a nice tingle.

"Whatever, Drew," I say, rolling my eyes. "Find anything useful?" I follow Drew back to the main room.

"Not a damn thing," Drew sighs. "The rest of the investigators are heading to Monaka's apartment to give it another once over, and John's at the morgue waiting for the autopsy report. It should've been in, this morning, but there seems to be some sort of mix-up with the paperwork."

"Yeah, they're probably wondering 'why bother' with an official investigation," I say, still hoping HoneyMama will grace us with her presence. "As far as the good ole boys of Butts County are concerned, Monaka's just another dead stripper."

"Pessimistic much?" Drew asks, opening the door ahead of me. "Have a little bit of faith in the system, Ms. McCoy. I do."

"That's because, Detective Drew, you're a part of the system."

"Yeah, the best part."

It's a short walk from the Spot to Dulce and Monaka's intimate home. The garage apartment's located behind the detached main house of another rental on the sprawling property. There are four cars in the driveway, and none of them belong to Dulce or Monaka. Dulce's from New York and never saw the need to get a license, but she knows how to drive. And Monaka, born and raised in Orange County, California, loved to drive and had a valid license, but never got around to buying a car.

I claim the small camera out of my bag and remove the lens cap. Taking pictures is supposed to be Pete's job, but Charlie gave him another assignment this morning, much to his disappointment. He gave me explicit instructions on how and what to shoot before loaning me his backup device.

"More flowers," Drew says, noticing another shrine at the bottom of the stairway leading up to the apartment.

"These must've cost a fortune," I say, touching one arrangement before taking several shots. "Lilies, long-stemmed white roses, and Chrysanthemums. Someone must've really loved them some Monaka."

"A lot of people did." Drew notices a card on the most expensive set. "But who's the anonymous admirer?"

"I'm sure a lot of Monaka's clients don't want to be known." I snap shots of the driveway up to the main house and notice plenty of movement through the drawn curtains. They must be tired of visitors on their property, just like HoneyMama.

"Yeah, but this one left a similar arrangement at the Spot and it's very detailed, almost as if he knew her personally." He flips the small white rectangle over and reads the quick note aloud: "'Monaka, so sweet and light. Such a delight.'"

I take the plastic glove and card from Drew to get a closer look at the inscription.

"It's an epitaph," I say, remembering my early days in the newsroom. Like most journalists just starting out, I unwillingly became a master at writing obituaries and epitaphs of all sorts.

"Well, there's another one on the standing bouquet at the Spot," Drew says, making his way into the crowded apartment.

"I need to see it," I say, entering the intimate space after Drew.

I wish we were visiting under better circumstances. Dulce and Monaka have great taste in home décor. The single apartment's decorated in soft hues of yellow, blue, and gold, with green fabric hanging over the lamps, as well as the venetian blinds. It's a cozy space, with the kitchen, bathroom, and bedroom all connected—perfect for two people in love.

"Morning, Sergeant Riley," Drew says to one of the officers busily prying into Monaka and Dulce's belongings.

"Morning, Detective Drew. Haven't come up with anything yet, but we're still looking."

"I can see that," Drew says, doing very little to hide his contempt.

The men continue to rummage through various papers, books, and clothing like they're searching for hidden treasure. When Dulce gets back, I know she's going to raise hell for the careless way they're treating her home.

"May I see that?" I ask one of the investigators, noting what looks like a scarf in the far-left corner of the main room.

"Sure," he says, passing me the cloth he tossed aside.

I take another plastic glove from Drew and inspect the material. "This isn't from the Spot."

"How do you know that?" Drew asks.

"Because it's made of a different fabric, and it's a deeper shade of red than HoneyMama's ever used," I say, recalling yesterday's dance session where both Praline and Tiramisu used identical silk cloths. I rub the soft velvet between my fingers and remember where I've seen something similar. "This makes me think of another murdered dancer in the city who worked at The Pimp Palace."

"You think there might be a connection?" Drew asks, inspecting the scarf for himself.

I snap a few pictures of the cloth and the room, remembering Pete's instructions to pay attention to the details, including the not-so-obvious ones.

"Perhaps, but I'm not sure. Mocha was murdered almost fifteen years ago. Why would the murderer come out of hiding all these years later?"

"Maybe he's always been out, just working under the radar, until now." Drew takes an evidence bag from another inspector and drops the cloth inside. "Let's get this over to forensics immediately. If we're dealing with a serial killer, we've got to get this in the system as soon as possible."

"I'm on it, Detective," the investigator says.

Drew's phone rings and mine vibrates, both with matching text messages.

"HoneyMama wants us back at the Spot once we're done here," he says, echoing my message.

"Yeah, got that," I say. "Has she heard from C?" I know Honey-Mama wants to bite into Miss MIA before we get ahold of her.

"Yes," Drew says, shooting her back a quick text. "She says that C will be there later this afternoon, and I want to be the first one to talk to her. After HoneyMama, of course."

"Of course."

Chapter 14

"*I* CAN'T TAKE IT ANYMORE," HONEYMAMA SAYS, SETTING DOWN her delicate china teacup on the marble countertop harder than necessary. "Drew, where the hell's your partner? We need to come up with a plan to close this case quickly before the Spot is no more." She steps up on her tiptoes, reaches into the liquor cabinet, and removes an unopened bottle of Basil Hayden, one of her favorite bourbons.

"With all due respect, HoneyMama, John's not interested in anything of the sort."

"Well, make him interested. I'm tired of these assholes roaming around my house," she says, removing the wrapper and cork. She takes a long gulp from the top and swallows hard. "Even more than that, they've already affected payroll, and it hasn't even been a full week since Monaka was murdered." Honey-Mama tilts the bottle our way; we both decline. If we weren't on the job, I think we might partake. It's been a hell of a morning, and it's just getting started. "Imagine what'll happen if they shut us down for an entire month or more. My girls will have no choice but to move on to another club—permanently. We can't let that happen."

"I hear you, HoneyMama, but my hands are tied," Drew says, defeated. There's only so far a Black detective will get around here.

"Mine aren't," I say, anxious to help. "What can I do to expe-

dite the investigation?" I ask, anxious to wrap this case up for
Monaka's memory, the Spot's bottom line, and to keep Charlie
as far away from here as possible. They've been through enough.

"Keke, there's not much more you can do that you aren't already doing."

"What do you mean by that, Drew?" HoneyMama asks, taking
another smaller swig before pouring a healthy helping into her
tea. She then replaces the bottle on the top shelf.

"Keke noticed that the cloth accompanying a few of Monaka's
dance clothes didn't come from the Spot. Only a dancer would
know something like that," Drew says, nodding my way.

"You mean *former* dancer," I say, rubbing my sore thighs with
my equally sore hands. The pole demands every ounce of flesh,
and then some.

"Once a dancer, always a dancer, Brandy," HoneyMama says,
taking another sip of her spiked drink. I can smell the liquor
from my seat across the kitchen table. Jambalaya looks tipsy, too,
lying in his owner's lap without a care in the world. "And maybe
it's going to take a dancer to find the missing link to Monaka's
murder. That's why you're here."

"The cloth also reminded me of Mocha's murder," I say, trig-
gering her memory. "It looks like one of the rags they use to
wipe down the poles at The Pimp Palace."

"'The Pimp Palace,'" HoneyMama repeats with a frown.
"What the hell would Monaka be doing at that godforsaken
place?"

"I don't know. Maybe it was Dulce's," I say.

"Perhaps, but either of them working there on the side doesn't
make any sense," HoneyMama says, visibly concerned. "No offense, Drew, but whatever's going on here won't be solved by the
police. This sounds personal, and dancers don't rat each other
or their clients out."

"Agreed, and none taken," Drew says. "So, what do you ladies
suggest we do? John's got the autopsy report and, as suspected,
Monaka died of severe blood loss due to her wounds."

"Her wounds? Don't be so polite about it," HoneyMama says,

taking another large swig of her tea. "Just say it: the girl was butchered in cold blood."

The more HoneyMama sips, the thicker her Southern accent grows.

"I can go undercover," I offer without fully thinking it through.

Both HoneyMama and Drew look shocked.

"*Hell no* you can't, Keke," Drew says emphatically. "There's no more security here, and the other clubs in the city have minimal security guards, if any."

"I'm not sure if you got the memo, but you no longer have a say in what I do."

"Okay, you two," HoneyMama says, stopping us before we go all in. Our fights were epic back in the day. "Drew, Brandy's a big girl and she's a professional." She turns around to pat my folded hands. "Are you sure you want to do this, baby?"

"HoneyMama, you know this is the only way we're going to get to the bottom of this and quickly." I place my hands over hers. "You said it yourself; it's why I'm here. As a dancer, I can get closer to the clients and hopefully work some information out of them."

"It would be a good way to get locker room stories," Honey-Mama says, her eyes narrowing in deep thought. "And I know just the chaperone to help you." She takes a deep breath and lowers her head to Jambalaya, who purrs loudly. She looks up and I can tell she's made up her mind. "It's the only way."

"No," I say, reading her expression.

"You know I'm right, Brandy," HoneyMama says, holding my hand tightly. "C's connected throughout the north and the south. If you masquerade as one of her protégés, no one will suspect a thing."

"Whatever you do, please be careful," Drew says, still acting more like an overprotective boyfriend than a cop. "More than likely, the murderer's someone who saw himself as being teased and never given total satisfaction by the object of his desire. C's girls rarely tease."

"What's that supposed to mean?" HoneyMama asks.

"That means we've always turned a blind eye to C's antics in the past because she services so many powerful individuals," Drew admits. "And by 'service,' I mean she's a *full-service* girl. Unlike you, Brandy."

C's always had a small flock of chicks who'll do anything they're asked, for the right price.

"How long have you known about this?" HoneyMama asks, her voice trembling. She looks at Drew, pissed as hell.

"We've always known about it," Drew says, giving me the side eye.

"Really, Drew?" I say, reclaiming my hand from HoneyMama to smack his.

"We?" HoneyMama says, looking from Drew to me, and then back at Drew, who's tightened his jaw in frustration.

Unlike most, Drew looks his mistakes dead in the eye and owns his shit. I've always respected that about him, even when it hurt like hell to be on the other side.

"You mean to tell me that I'm the only one who doesn't know what's going on in my own club?"

"Not in your club, but possibly through some of your clients," Drew says, matter-of-factly. "Trust me, even C's not crazy enough to pull any illegal activity inside The Honey Spot."

"Where the hell's that girl? She's had an excuse every day for not being here," HoneyMama says, hitting the countertop so hard that Jambalaya leaps from her lap and into the window seat. "Now I know it's because she's been pimping on the side, heffa ass."

"It's not really pimping, technically speaking, if the dancers willingly agreed to allow C to serve as their liaison, in this case." I can tell from the deep furrow in between his well-manicured brows that Drew regrets every single word he's spoken in the last few seconds.

HoneyMama shoots daggers at Drew with her eyes, and he immediately apologizes without saying a word.

"Your partner called this a Jezebel's den, right? Do you know how Jezebel died, Drew?" she says, tapping her modest gel-manicured nails against the hard surface.

I do, and not just because of my biblical upbringing. My mother actually discouraged me from reading the most interesting parts of the Bible. Any stories that mentioned powerful, rebellious women were intentionally overlooked. HoneyMama, on the other hand, made us research all of the names that we were called, Jezebel included, in an effort to empower us when others in the community would try to tear us down. It worked. I would bet that most of the dancers at the Spot—former and current—let name-calling roll off their backs, like water off a duck.

"She was thrown out of a window and left to be eaten by dogs," HoneyMama says, straight to the point. "The point of her story is not about dying for sins or whatever people think. The point is that even though her death was imminent, Jezebel dressed like the queen she was, right before her death, and died like the queen that she was, whether her enemies realized it or not."

"I remember the description from the books in the downstairs library," I say, recalling the first time I stayed up late reading and re-reading the story. The image of her lying in the street being ripped apart, limb by limb, still gives me nightmares.

"Queen Jezebel was among enemies. She was worthy of a dignified death and robbed of that at the very end. Here we are a family of Jezebels, and we watch out for our own. Do you understand?"

"Yes, ma'am," Drew says. I know he must feel like a little boy in HoneyMama's presence.

"Monaka's death will have dignity because her life had meaning," HoneyMama says, tears staining her rosy-pink cheeks. She points toward the main dance room. "Her story will not end at the bottom of that pole for the dogs to feed on."

"You know I'm doing everything I can to make sure this case doesn't go south," Drew says.

"And you know I'm going to honor Monaka's story," I say. "Even if it means working with C."

"Good. Then let's get to it," HoneyMama says, leaving the kitchen to head back down to her office. "See you this evening, Brandy. There's a lot you need to catch up on if we're going to make this work."

"Brandy," Drew says, rising from the table. "I like the sound of that."

"Me too," HoneyMama says from the hallway. "There's just something about brown liquor I can't get enough of," she says, raising her mug.

"Me too," Drew says, making the hairs on the back of my neck stand up.

Oh, the things we used to do full of liquor and biscuits.

John steps inside the warm, bright space and instantly sours the mood. Praline also enters from the side entrance and rolls her eyes at the sight of both men.

"Y'all again," she says, tossing her dance bag down on a chair.

"Hello to you, too, young lady."

Drew laughs at Praline's frankness, but his partner doesn't budge.

"You'll be happy to know that the boss lady can reopen the Spot, but only the back dance room. The front's to remain closed until further notice," John barks like he owns the place.

"Thank God your chief finally came to his senses," Honey-Mama says, reentering the room.

"It wasn't the chief, but one of the local judges. How he got ahold of the case is beyond me," John says, locking eyes with HoneyMama. "I think it's a mistake."

"You would," HoneyMama says, a cunning smile spreading across her face. "Finally some good news."

"Oh, you must be talking about Judge Bobby," Praline says, sucking on a honey stick. She takes another one from the jar on the tray and tucks it between her expertly displayed B cups. "He's a real cool cat."

"How do you know the judge?" John asks.

"You still don't get how this place works, do you?" Praline walks around the kitchen island toward the back door, where

John stands as stoic as a statue. "Judge Bobby is a close, personal friend of mine. He was here last night wondering what the hell was going on."

"That's bribery," John says, his face flushed with embarrassment and rage. "I need to call the chief and tell him about this."

"Not so fast, Friar John. Ain't nobody bribed him. Bobby does what Bobby wants to do, like always." Praline twirls the tip of her tongue around the tip of the amber plastic stick, making John even more visibly uncomfortable.

"We'll just see about that. See you back at the station, Drew. Ma'am," John says, tipping his hat toward HoneyMama and leaving the way he came.

"I don't give a flying fuck what that punk says, HoneyMama. I ain't bribed nobody!" Praline yells out the door to John's back.

"Don't worry about John," Drew says reassuringly.

"If your partner had better sense, he'd know that we don't have to bribe men to get what we want." HoneyMama claps her hands and smiles our way. "Regardless of the bullshit, the Spot's back open for business, which means we have a show to put on. Praline, get on the phone and make sure everyone knows. Keke, you need the practice, so tonight we'll debut you as our new girl."

"Wait, say what?" I ask, shocked. I haven't fully wrapped my head around how this is going to go down. "I thought I was pretending to be a dancer in the city, not a real one here."

"Girl, please. What are you fretting about?" HoneyMama asks as she reaches for the shelves underneath the island, where her baking tools are housed.

"Drew, would you please tell her that in this establishment my place is in the audience with the rest of the investigators, not actually up on the stage?"

"I don't understand," Drew says, giving me a crooked smile. "What'd you mean by 'undercover,' because that's what I understood it to be."

"Not funny, Drew," I say, smacking his arm. "You know good and well I meant staying in the background, maybe a lap dance if absolutely necessary. But never did I mention getting back on that pole."

"I'm with HoneyMama. If you want to be convincing, especially to high rollers, you're going to need to get that fat ass on stage and shake your moneymaker," Praline adds excitedly.

I want to tell her to mind her business, but I'm not in the mood to get cussed out.

"Okay, then, it's settled," HoneyMama says, damn-near giddy. "We'll see you back here later this afternoon. Dress comfortably and wear some high heels, girl. You been walking around here in them flats. I want to see those leg muscles!"

"Yeah, me too," I say.

Praline and HoneyMama get to work in the kitchen, while Drew and I head outside.

"Can I treat you to an early lunch, Brandy?" Drew says, swinging the back screen door open. "We have a few pointers to discuss."

"Sure," I say, following him out. "As long as I'm not on the menu."

"Not yet," Drew says, licking his full lips. "I'll save dessert for later."

Chapter 15

*A*FTER CHOOSING OUR TABLE, WE READ THE MENU AT RED'S CAFÉ, like anything has changed. It looks exactly the same, right down to the yellowed pages with hot sauce–stained corners and all. Drew looks like he's about to speak, but something else has caught his attention. I look over my shoulder, also frozen in place: When a force of nature comes at you, sometimes the only thing you can do is stop and stare.

C's electric blue miniskirt and sheer white halter top can make even the most God-fearing man immediately nut in his pants. She steps one six-inch white platform boot in front of the other until we're eye to crotch.

"Fat Brandy. *Tsk! Tsk!*" She sucks her teeth like a true yardie. "Only back in town for a few days and already sinking your claws back into your ex," C says, making us regret choosing the patio table.

"I thought you weren't coming back until later?" Drew asks, shifting in his seat. I don't think the ancient, wrought-iron chairs are the only thing making him uncomfortable.

"I was, but decided to come back early, instead, Detective Drew," she hisses. "We women can change our minds, ya know."

"Really? After dodging both the police and HoneyMama?" I ask, curious about her true intentions. She's always got another card up her sleeve, fuck the outfit.

"What the hell are you still doing here other than being thirsty?" C's talking to Drew, but asking me.

"Same thing as you, I suppose," Drew says, taking a sip of water. "Working."

"This ain't even your side of town anymore." C shifts her weight from the right side of her body to the left. Walking in high heels of any sort isn't easy on these dirt roads, even for a professional. "Don't you cops have strict jurisdictions or some shit like that?"

For some reason, it seems that C's nervous about Drew's presence in Indian Springs.

"True, but you know the local detectives can't handle a case like this. So naturally I volunteered my services." The right side of Drew's mouth rises slightly into a sexy grin. I could use some of his volunteer work myself right about now.

"Naturally. And your expertise, no doubt," C says, smiling hard at my ex.

Why's she so interested in his business?

"We have work to do, if you don't mind," Drew says, looking past me and signaling the waiter. "Do yourself a favor, C, and stick around. Me and my partner have a few questions, after HoneyMama's done with you, of course."

"For you, I'm an open book, Detective." C licks her lips in my direction and leaves us in peace.

"What a cunt," I say, slamming my menu down onto the table.

"Better a cunt than a dick, like my partner," Drew says, making me smile. "But when it's the right match, they work really well together."

"Is that so, Detective?" I say, returning the smile. Why am I flirting so hard with this soon-to-be-married man? I can't help myself and I'll be damned if I'm going to stop, especially when he's responding so well.

"I know you remember what a good fit feels like."

I do, and as of late, Ian's been the perfect fit when I can get it. I shake my head at Drew and refuse to comment. Instead, I take out my camera and look through the pictures from the crime scene. I delete the least important ones while Drew orders our food.

"Nice camera," Drew says, eyeing the expensive loaner from Pete. "You should take some tester shots of me."

"The last thing I need is more pictures of you."

"And why is that? You don't like my chiseled physique?" he asks, warping his face into a silly grin.

"Stop that!" I laugh and playfully smack his shoulder. "And you know why." The scent of his cologne creeps up my nostrils and excites me, which is the last thing I need right now.

"You know you have the same effect on me, too, right?" Drew's always had a way of reading my body like braille, thoughts included.

"What the hell are you talking about?"

I begin taking pictures of the changes made to the once-ghost-town that is now a thriving tourist community. Luckily, The Honey Spot's off the main road, way back in the woods. The locals that popped up after the Spot was already well established tried to have HoneyMama moved out of town. But she's always been in the town, and without her money, this area would be dead—again.

"You know what I mean," Drew says. "You've always been able to get in my head. No other woman in my life can say that."

"Not even your baby-mamas?" Drew tilts his head down, looking at me as if to say I already know the answer to that question.

Both of Drew's baby-mamas hated me—not because I wanted his trifling ass back, but because they said I always had his heart. What the fuck difference does that make if his dick's steadily courtin' other coochie?

"Come on now, Keke. You know better than that," Drew says, deflated.

I look away from my next shot and up into his dark brown eyes. Maybe if he was wearing his cop uniform, he'd be a little less desirable, but I seriously doubt it. Drew can make my panties wet, no matter how much I hate him at the time. Before we can get too deep in conversation, his cell phone rings.

"Catchy tune," I say, swaying my hips to the reggae rhythm.

"See, you've still got it," Drew says, completely ignoring his cell ringing again. "I don't know why you're so worried about dancing at the Spot."

"And I see you've got jokes," I say, softly swiping his knee with mine. Maybe he is serious about liking what he sees, because his nature is surely rising.

"Aren't you going to get that?" I ask, but Drew's not hearing me or his cell.

"You've always looked beautiful in orange."

My sundress is sticking to my sweaty flesh, outlining my breasts and perky nipples.

Drew moves closer to me. His lips part, he gently touches my face and traces my right cheek all the way down the side of my neck.

"What are you doing?" I ask, placing my now-free hand over his, which is still on my neck. I need to stop him before this goes any further. Back in the day, we fucked anywhere we felt like. But now we both have our careers to think about.

"What I should've done when I first saw you a few days ago," he says, moving his lips close to mine. "You smell so good." I allow him to explore a little more, with my hand as his guide. His touch feels so good.

We just fucked each other in our minds, damn the reality. My panties are soaked, and from the feel of Drew's wet spot, it was good for him, too.

"Drew, what the hell?" a woman's voice shrieks, killing the vibe.

"Corrine," Drew says, nearly jumping out of his seat.

And there she is, walking up the dirt road toward our very own private crime scene. I can barely make out her trim figure until the red dust cloud dissipates. Corrine hasn't changed much. I also see she's holding a toddler on her hip, with his eldest daughter not far behind. I still can't believe he's marrying this woman. She's cute enough, I guess. But her attitude stinks.

"What are you doing out here?" Drew asks, leaving our table and heading toward his soon-to-be-wife and children. I don't know why he's so surprised to see her here. I've known broads to travel cross-country to catch his ass in the act.

"The better question is, why aren't you answering your cell?"

"I couldn't find my earpiece, and you know what they say about cell phones and brain cancer." Damn, he's quick. But his slick answer doesn't keep her from looking over his shoulder and back at me.

I would wave at her hungry-looking ass, but the wrong finger might unintentionally go up. As much as I'd like to lie and say that I've buried the hatchet she placed in my back years ago when she fucked my man, I'm not that big of a woman, and never will be.

"Drew, that mess is all in your head," she says, cutting her eyes my way before planting a kiss on his lips. She drove all the way from Stockbridge to put on a show for all to see, and it's working. All eyes are on them.

"Baby, I'm working," he says, finally free of her heavily glossed lips, but not before she leaves a shiny fuchsia imprint all over his face. "What's so important that you had to come up here?"

"I need a credit card to pay for the cruise," she says, putting her hand out like a twelve-year-old asking her father for her allowance. Drew's always been a sucker for a begging broad.

"I thought the cruise was already paid for, Corrine." Drew takes a paper napkin from the holder and wipes his face clean.

"Well, I don't have the money to cover it. I'll pay you back as soon as I get paid, baby. You know I'm good for it," she says, shamelessly rubbing up against him.

"Corrine, what the hell? All you had to do was come up with your part—that's it."

"Baby, I didn't mean to make you upset," she says, walking off in the same direction she blew in from. Drew looks after her and his children, knowing he has to follow. Before leaving, he heads my way.

"Sorry about that," he says, looking as if he wants to pick up where we left off, but I'm already reabsorbed in the details of my article. "Can I take you out for drinks later?"

My first instinct is to decline, but his pleading eyes, full lips, and smooth complexion compel me to say otherwise.

"Sure, why not?"

Corrine doubles back and looks our way. This time, I do wave, just to piss her off. She's definitely holding his balls tightly and I don't blame her. His women are always threatened by my presence. Mostly, I assume, it's because they know I used to dance. Even now, when I feel like I have so many rolls to spare that I can sell them at Kroger, this trick is giving me the evil eye. I guess HoneyMama was right: Once a dancer, always a dancer, and in this case, that's not such a bad thing.

Chapter 16

*T*HANKS TO DREW'S EARLY DEPARTURE, I TOOK HIS LUNCH AND the rest of mine back to my cabin, and then changed clothes before returning to the Spot for rehearsal. HoneyMama's still in her office, giving C the third degree, and Tiramisu's not here yet. I'm not sure if Dulce's up for dancing, especially since they just let her out of jail this morning. That just leaves me and Praline. It's the perfect time to get her take on what happened to Monaka.

"Are you ready to get back at it, girl?" Praline asks, putting the last of the client packages together. She and HoneyMama went overboard preparing for tonight's show.

"Honestly, I'm terrified of dancing onstage in front of an audience. It used to come so naturally."

"It's just like riding a bike, Brandy. Once you get out there, it'll all come pouring back, just like honey."

"From your lips," I say, taking the large orange wicker basket full of sweets from the kitchen counter and placing it on the table near the entrance. "Do you mind if we get our interview out of the way?"

"Sure," Praline says, taking a seat across the table from where I'm seated. She reaches into the oversized gym bag and trades her house slippers for dance boots. "I've got nothing to hide."

I make myself comfortable at the table, pull out my recorder and writing pad, and press RECORD. "Where were you the night Monaka was murdered?"

"I was giving a private dance of my own in Buckhead. I have three clients who like for me to come to their business meetings. It gives it more of a social vibe when discussing big shit-like mergers and hostile takeovers, you know what I'm saying?" Praline's huge smile tells me she's being truthful.

"Do a lot of business outside of the Spot?" I ask, jotting down a note to check on her uptown clients.

"Not really. Like I said, my personal clients keep me pretty busy, but I do like my downtime." She flashes her fresh nail set filed into points that should be illegal. "Self-care's essential to my bottom line and my sanity," she says, twirling her curly blond wig—today's choice. She's good at keeping the client guessing. She looks me over once, then again. "You could use a beauty day yourself, hon. Come with me next time. It'll be fun."

I know she means well, but the truth still hurts. "Maybe once we solve this case, I'll take you up on that. In the meantime, do you know if Monaka had a lot of private clients?"

Praline looks out of the window and shakes her head from side to side. "She was a wanted woman, both in person and on the hotlines."

"The hotlines?" I repeat, taking more notes.

"Yeah. That's what they call their Lovers Only site. She and a couple of C's protégés have quite a following. I think they also meet a few of the clients in person. Some even became regulars at the Spot. They have personal cells just for that side of the business and everything. C's all about the money, you know."

"Yeah, I know."

"Can I ask you a question?" Praline asks, kicking her feet up on the chair next to mine.

"Sure." I reach to pause the recorder, but on second thought, I'll let it run. If she can lay it all out, so can I.

"Why'd you write that article about dancers being powerless and shit? I mean, you're one of HoneyMama's girls, not some pimping-ass nigga's bitch on the Southside."

"I didn't mean for it to shed a negative light on the profession," I say, defensive. I've been justifying that article more in the past few days than I have in years. "I just wanted to tell my truth. I did come from a pimping-ass nigga on the Southside before HoneyMama found me, and at the time, I was still healing from that experience. Still am."

"Me too," Praline says, relaxing her stance a bit. "Did you know that I was a child sex slave, or at least that's what the social worker called me during the hearing? I never heard the term before then," Praline says, a little too rationally for someone who lived it.

"No, I didn't know that. I knew that you were abandoned by your parents, a ward of the state until you aged out," I say, recalling the brief meeting when Praline was introduced to all of the dancers as a new hire.

Physically, she looked like she'd had a rough life. Draped from head-to-toe in Gucci and Balenciaga equally, you'd never know she arrived at HoneyMama's home with the clothes on her back and a bag full of not much. Praline is one of a few dancers who still chooses to live in the main house rather than rent a place of her own. I think she likes the feeling of being in a real home with other people.

"Yup, I was pimped out by my own crackhead-ass parents when I was twelve years old. But it wasn't all bad at first," Praline says, taking a tea cake from the center of the table to snack on. "I was a military brat until they got strung out, and an only child. I had it pretty good for a while." She takes a bite of the treat and smiles at a private memory.

"How long were you on the streets?" I know that my line of questioning has nothing to do with the case, but I can't help but feel for Praline's lost childhood even if she seems to be mentally and emotionally well-adjusted. According to Charlie, sympathy's my biggest flaw as a reporter.

"Four years. Never got any money from it, just a few unwanted pregnancies and an array of venereal diseases."

"Were you ever afraid for your life?"

"Not really, but there were some mean motherfuckers out there," she says, taking a sip from her water bottle. "One time, I got my teeth kicked out by my pimp after I threatened to call the cops on him for keeping my parents high all the time. After that, I was left with him indefinitely to work off their debt. He was the meanest of all the niggas I ever dealt with."

"How'd you get away from him?"

Praline looks like she wants to cry at the thought, but holds it in. "I don't really remember how it all went down, but ATF busted the house wide open. I was turning a trick in the back, and my parents were getting high in the living room, as usual. My pimp was outside handling business, but didn't realize he was selling to an undercover agent. Next thing I knew, it was smoke everywhere. I passed out and woke up in a juvenile detention center infirmary, and the rest, as they say, is history."

"Damn, Praline. Ever thought about writing a memoir?" I review the page full of notes I've taken in the few minutes we've been here and can only imagine how much more she could share.

"Hell no," Praline says, helping herself to another tea cake. "I barely want to remember the shit I went through, let alone write it down for all eternity."

Makes perfect sense. Wish I could forget some of my writings, but I'll keep that admission to myself. Don't need her telling the world that I regret my article, because I really don't. Just wish I'd done a better job with the delivery.

"Did you find out what ever happened to your parents?"

"Don't know and don't give a flying fuck," Praline says, again staring out into the rose garden.

I keep expecting to see Mr. Graves round the corner with gardening tools or a paintbrush or something, but I haven't seen him since this morning.

"Hope they got clean, but I seriously doubt it. Hell, they could be dead, for all I know."

"I'm sure Drew could help you find out if you ever wanted to," I say, making a note to ask him about it later. No matter how awful Praline's parents were, I'm sure she at least wants to know if they're dead or alive.

Praline looks at me and blinks back more tears. "I don't need closure, but thanks, Iyanla. I'm good."

I smile at the reference, remembering our days of watching the show on our breaks. She helped several of us have break-throughs in one way or another. "Okay, but if you change your mind—"

"I said I don't give a shit, Brandy. Drop it, Nancy Drew. Seriously."

I touch Praline's hand and hold it tightly. No matter how much she tries to deny it, I know deep down she still cares about them and the little girl she used to be. Finally she allows a single tear to drop from her right eye before she wipes it clean.

"On my eighteenth birthday, I went to work at The Kitty Kat, by the airport, and that's where I met HoneyMama," Praline says, checking her eye makeup in her cell phone reflection. "My life changed from that moment on, and I've never looked back. The first thing HoneyMama did was buy me a new grill to re-place the broken one my pimp left me with," she says, smiling wide.

"They still look good."

"I know, right? HoneyMama takes good cares of us," Praline says, rising from her seat ready to work. "You should've told *that* story."

"That's why I'm here," I say, tapping the recorder. "And that's the story I plan on telling."

"Good. Because HoneyMama's my only mama, got it? And she deserves better than to be crucified for something she didn't have no part of. C's the one you need to be going after. I bet my left titty that the bitch knows more about Monaka's death than she's saying."

"I couldn't agree more."

Chapter 17

I TURN OFF MY RECORDER AND JOT DOWN A FEW MORE NOTES, ANX-iously waiting for rehearsal to begin. I'm going to need a few drinks in me to even think about getting up on that stage in front of an audience. I also want to see what's up with C, and why she's been avoiding Indian Springs.

Tiramisu and HoneyMama enter the kitchen at the same time, but from different doors.

"Are we ready to get to work, ladies?" HoneyMama says, strutting across the floor as her expensive heels tap loudly against the tile. "Vacation is over."

"Where's C?" Praline asks, just as excited as I am to see her.

"She went back to the city for the night," HoneyMama says, visibly worn. A conversation with the Devil's apprentice will do that to anyone. "She needs to collect herself before coming back to work."

"Who's going to take her place?" Tiramisu asks, replacing her flats with thigh-high boots. "We've got to get this money, and she's a moneymaker. Fuck the bullshit!"

"Brandy is going to dance with you and Praline this evening," HoneyMama says. "Hopefully, Dulce will be up to dancing, too. The rest of the girls will arrive at their usual time."

"Brandy? The same Brandy who thinks dancing is tantamount to hoeing?" Tiramisu asks, looking dead at me. "Uh-uh. I don't think so. Men can smell a prude in disguise a mile away, and their money won't flow the way we need it to."

"I don't think that dancers are hoes," I say, taking a cookie for myself.

"That's not what you wrote down for all of Atlanta to read," Tiramisu says, zipping up her left boot, and then the right. "And aren't you supposed to be investigating Monaka's murder, not trying to recapture your youth?"

"This is a no judgment zone, Tiramisu, or have you forgotten our rules of engagement?" HoneyMama asks, pointing to the wall.

"No judgment intended, HoneyMama," Tiramisu says, tossing her oversized gym bag down on the floor and taking a seat next to Praline. "It's just that when I read Brandy's article, it made me think of why women become strippers in the first place."

"And why is that Tiramisu?" HoneyMama asks, exasperated. She's had it, but still makes time to hold space for her dancers when needed.

I turn my recorder back on, just in case something valuable comes out of this conversation. Otherwise, I'm going to take it all personally.

"To get paid," Praline says, playfully pushing her shoulder against Tiramisu's.

"Yeah, but we don't even get the lion's share of the money at a typical club," Tiramisu continues. "It's mostly men who finance the industry. The women simply hustle and do the best they can in any given situation, more than likely trying to raise kids, like me."

"Damn straight," Praline concurs, even though she has none of her own.

"And then we have to pay the city for a fucking permit to strip. Once you get linked up with a fucking club, they hold your license hostage so you can't work at multiple spots without their consent, pimping asses. What kind of bullshit is that?" Tiramisu says, raising a question that's been on the minds of many dancers. But Georgia is a right-to-work state, and without organized unions, dancers will always be at the mercy of club owners.

"Agreed," HoneyMama says, allowing Tiramisu to vent, while

HoneyMama checks the time. She's patient, but time is money, and too much of both have been lost lately.

"Seeing all the baby-mamas at the county office earlier today makes me wonder how many of those sistahs are strippers," Tiramisu continues as she takes a sip of Praline's tea. "And I wonder how many of them have pimp niggas that'll pay for them to get weaves and pedicures, but won't help with their childcare."

"Amen, sistah!" Praline screams like she's in church.

"That's why we started the childcare center here at the Spot," HoneyMama says, pouring four shot glasses full of honey whiskey at the miniature bar next to the stove. "Any employer in her right mind knows a mama can't focus on work if her babies aren't taken care of first."

"Right?" Tiramisu says, taking a shot straight to the head. "It's a wicked experience to give up all your info to the government for some goddamn food stamps. Ain't it some shit how they make us bark like dogs to take care of our children? But when these same children become basketball legends, there's no reparation for the years his single mama had to stand in the county line, lay on her back, shake her ass, and do whatever else to get him there."

She may be generalizing for the sake of conversation, but Tiramisu's talking about her own experience. Both her daughters attend private school and have extracurricular sports activities afterward. Tiramisu's parents are as supportive as they can be, but she's the youngest of eleven, and they're getting up in age.

"That's true, Tiramisu. But there are some women who love to strip for the art of it, and enjoy handling their business while doing it," HoneyMama says, refilling our glasses with another one of her favorite liquors.

"Hell yeah we do," Praline says, sipping her drink. "My last daddy took me to Vegas. When I saw them girls in those shows, I felt like I did when I was a little girl and saw the Alvin Ailey dancers on television—like that could be me someday up there, dancing on top of the world, all eyes on me," Praline says, reliving the moment.

"I hate Vegas," Tiramisu slurs, letting the whiskey do its job. "The dance scene is way too competitive."

"Well, I wanted to do more than take off my panties onstage and have niggas throw dollar bills at me. I wanted to get dudes to break off that real cash. When I told my pimp, he laughed so hard, he almost choked on his lobster tail," Praline says, shaking her head. "Then he sent me upstairs to fuck some nigga he said was a producer. He made me dance for him first, even offered me a part in one of his music videos, which I promptly declined before putting his dick in my mouth while my pimp watched from the other room."

"Why did he watch you?" I ask, unable to take my reporter hat off. This is the story I need to tell, not the one Charlie wants to read.

"To make sure I did it right," Praline says, taking a pack of cigarettes from her bra and placing one in her mouth. "I'm so glad HoneyMama found me when she did. I was about to kill a motherfucker if I had to keep living like that for much longer."

HoneyMama walks over to Praline and kisses her on the cheek.

"My babies' daddy saw me reading the ad for a job at The Honey Spot and slapped my eyes right off the page," Tiramisu says. "Even if I looked like I was thinking about leaving him, I got beat like a runaway slave. I was his solid gold dancer—that's what he used to call me."

"What did he do for a living?" I ask, standing up and stretching like HoneyMama. We only have a couple of hours to warm up. I still can't believe they've got me dancing tonight, but it's too late to turn back now.

"He was a stockbroker. I was well kept, and he wanted me to dance only for him. I was his deal sealer. He took me all over the place, making me do private dances for his clients to close the deals," Tiramisu says, swallowing the bitter memory with her last shot. "He did business with some of the top moneymakers around the world until he got busted by the Feds for insider trading. He went away for a long time, and I finally found my way to the Spot."

"And we're so glad you did, my dear." HoneyMama playfully

smacks Tiramisu on the ass and puts a smile on her face. "All right, ladies. We have titties to shake and asses to bounce before our clients arrive. Let's get to it."

"All right, y'all," Praline seconds. "I been ready."

"Brandy, a word," HoneyMama says, holding me back while Tiramisu and Praline enter the hallway.

"What's up?" I ask. I hope she's changed her mind about me actually dancing while undercover.

"The truth is, C's being a bit difficult about cooperating."

"No shit," I say. "Isn't that her middle name?"

HoneyMama smiles and then gets serious. "You may have to go to her to get her side of the story, and to convince her that it's in her best interest to let you pose as one of her newbies. In the meantime, I'm going to pair you up with Praline. I know she has a few connections in the city as well. She can help you get in."

"Whatever it takes," I say, slightly relieved. I'd rather work with Praline any day over C.

Chapter 18

I FOLLOW HONEYMAMA INTO THE BACK DANCE ROOM, WHERE TIRA-misu and Praline are already warming up with a few leg stretches. Praline works in several twerks and Tiramisu follows suit.

"Places, ladies," HoneyMama says, directing each of us to a pole. "Tiramisu, you're backstage. Praline and Brandy, you'll come together in the center at the end of the opening act."

"That's what I'm talking about," Dulce says, surprising us.

We heard she'd be released today, but weren't given a definite time.

"Dulce, I'm so glad you're here," HoneyMama says, welcoming her into the sacred space.

"I need to work like everyone else," Dulce says, looking and smelling like the liquor she's more than likely been steadily drinking since Monaka's death. "Besides, I can't sit up in that apartment by myself any longer. Hurts too much, and the fucking cops ripped the place apart, fucking *putas*."

"Sorry about that," I say, taking my place at the back of the stage with Tiramisu. Dulce's the senior dancer in the room, and we all adjust to her presence.

"It wasn't your fault, *mija*. I know how pigs work." Dulce removes her oversized T-shirt to reveal a sheer black bodysuit that fits her classic hourglass shape like a glove. Even through her grief, the girl still looks damn good.

"Don't we all," HoneyMama says, removing her skirt. "But at

the end of the day, men are men. We have to kill their stupidity with kindness like only we can."

"Whatever," Praline says, claiming the pole to the left of the stage. "I don't work for none of those dudes, no matter how much they break off."

"That may be true. However, something happens when a client enters the room," HoneyMama says, taking a seat at the table closest to the stage. "There's an unsaid shift that occurs when the money exchanges hands. He doesn't need or want to have to say it: he paid to be serviced by you. Therefore, the client shouldn't have to say that he wants you crotch-out or titties bare. It's your job to anticipate his needs, no matter who he or she is," Honey Mama says, lifting her right leg to reveal one of her perfect black stilettos. She's serious about her Choos. "That's why Monaka was so good at her job. She knew what her clients wanted before they knew themselves, and she worked it to her advantage."

"She was a'ight," C says, walking in through the side entrance.

If another surprise walks in, I'm done for the rest of the day.

"What the hell are you doing here?" Dulce asks, moving from her pole to the edge of the stage.

We're all unhappy to see her.

"C, I thought we agreed you'd go back to the city and get your head on straight before stepping foot back in my establishment," HoneyMama says, looking from C to Dulce, who looks ready to pounce.

"We did," C says, tossing her large Louis Vuitton tote onto an empty chair next to HoneyMama. "But then I thought about the fact that you asked me to text my contacts and let them know the Spot's back in business tonight, and then I had a second thought: why should I pass up all that cheddar when everybody knows I'm the big cheese up in this bitch?"

"Because your fucking ass is guilty as sin, you evil *puta!*" Dulce's so mad, she spits all over the stage.

"Damn, Dulce. You'd think your ass would be grateful," C says, approaching the bottom of the stage steps. "Top-shelf liquor cost money that you barely have."

Dulce lunges offstage and straight for C's throat.

"You fucking bitch! I'll kill you for what you did to Monaka!" Dulce screams as she and C struggle to the floor.

"Ladies, please!" HoneyMama screams, pulling Dulce off of C, who's getting a kick out of the catfight. Some broads live for drama. "That's enough."

"Dulce, you act like you don't know how I roll." C's statement is loaded with innuendos that pass right over HoneyMama's head. "And for the record, I didn't do shit to Monaka she didn't want done."

I look at Tiramisu, whose brown cheeks turn red at the mention of C's work habits. What are they really talking about? HoneyMama was right: If I'm going to find out the truth, I need to get on C's team.

"Can you bitches calm the fuck down?" Praline says, twirling around her pole like this is the norm for The Honey Spot, which couldn't be further from the truth. "We have work to make up for. I, for one, need to get my hustle on, not watch you two heffas go at it."

"Agreed," Tiramisu says, walking over to the deejay booth and dimming the lights.

"Y'all can have at it. I'm out." Dulce grabs her things and heads for the door, damn the T-shirt she's leaving behind.

"That's it, Dulce. Run like the little scared bitch that you are," C says after her, taking center stage.

Dulce drops her things and starts toward C again, her heels tapping the floor at a quick pace.

"Don't do it," I say, meeting her at the bottom of the steps.

"She needs a good beatdown, and I'm just the bitch to do it," Dulce says, taking her earrings off.

HoneyMama's ready to intervene, but knows that if two grown women want to fight, they will. Smart bystanders, like us, stay out of the way so we don't get hurt in the process.

"She's not worth it," I whisper in Dulce's ear. "You just got out of jail over nothing. Imagine what Friar John will do if he's called to the scene of a brawl you're involved in?" I say, using her description of Drew's partner.

That seems to get Dulce's attention; she calms her stance.

"Fine," Dulce says, replacing the gold hoops. "But if you fucking come near me, C, or mention my girlfriend's name again, your ass is mine. ¿*Comprendes?*"

"Yeah, I understand," C says, still smiling at the heat emanating from Dulce's tongue. "Do you understand that you shouldn't bite the hand that feeds you?"

HoneyMama looks at them both, bewildered.

"I feed my damn self." Dulce flips C off and finally walks out, choosing the path of least resistance.

"What the hell is she talking about, C?" HoneyMama asks.

"Oh, I just meant that she shouldn't start no shit at the Spot when she needs to get paid, like we all do." C's quick with her bull, but I'm not convinced.

"Okay, C. If you're going to be here, cooperate," HoneyMama says, pissed. Her eyes narrow at C's denial and quick save—she's not falling for it. "We have a lot of ground to cover."

"Yes, ma'am," C says, taking hold of her pole and expertly wrapping herself around it. "You know I'm always professional about my shit."

"That's just it," HoneyMama says, climbing the steps, one expensive pump at a time. "This ain't your shit. This here," she says, gesturing around the opened space, "is my shit, and you'd better not fuck it up any more than you already have, are we clear?"

C wipes the smug smile from her flawlessly made-up face. Everyone knows better than to mess with HoneyMama, especially not when she's this hot. This is the South and she's not against exercising her Second Amendment rights, even if it's not really made for *us* to use.

"Tiramisu, we're going to open with Usher tonight. Brandy, you and C will share the center pole."

"Hold on a fucking minute," C says indignantly. "I have to share center stage with Miss Piggy? And mess up my cash flow?"

"Watch yourself," I say, ready to slap C my damn self.

"You have two choices, Couverture," HoneyMama says, stepping back offstage and reclaiming her seat. "You can do what I say or get the fuck out. Brandy, are you ready?"

C looks at me spitefully before moving her hands so that I can take my position.

"Yes, ma'am."

Tiramisu starts the soft yet heavy music, and then takes her position at the pole across from Praline's.

"Try to keep up," C says, leading me through the routine.

"Don't worry about me," I say, removing my shirt and tossing it offstage. "I'm not the one with something to hide."

C stares me down as the music heightens and sweeps us up in its rhythm. She knows I've got her card. And when the time comes, I'm definitely going to pull it.

Chapter 19

*I*T'S ONLY BEEN TWO HOURS, BUT I FEEL LIKE I JUST RAN AN ALL-DAY marathon. Every part of my body is sore. I'm so glad Honey-Mama's giving us a five-minute break. I know it's been a while since I had a good workout, but damn. I could barely catch my breath while I struggled to keep up with C's merciless ass.

"Great job, girls," HoneyMama says, tossing dry towels onto the stage. "Brandy, you've got nothing to worry about. A few nights onstage and you'll look like you never left."

"Ha!" C says, letting out a hearty laugh. "Fat bitch was panting like a dog in heat the whole time."

"Fuck you, C," I say, tired of her shit. I might be breathless and damn-near a heart attack, but she's still out of pocket. "Your sideways comments are about to get you pimp slapped by this fat bitch right here."

"You want come when I slap that big ass of yours, nah?" C says in her thick Jamaican *patwa*.

I'm with Dulce. C needs to be checked—the sooner, the better, and safer for us all.

"Girls, please," HoneyMama says, directing us to wipe down the poles with the clean towels. Accidents can be costly for the dancers and the business. "We had a wonderful session. Let's not ruin it."

"Hell yeah we did," Praline says, high off endorphins. She finishes wiping down her pole and steps offstage. "Monaka would be proud."

I look at C for some sort of reaction, but she's as cold as ever. "Were you and Monaka good together that night?" I ask, knowing they danced together on several occasions, much to Dulce's dislike.

"I was where I was at," C says, following Praline into the audience.

The lack of information does little to mask her shady behavior.

"Good evening, ladies," Drew says, stepping inside from the back door.

The setting sun illuminates his partner's grimace in its shadow. Has the good detective ever chilled?

"Gentlemen," HoneyMama says, rising to greet our unexpected guests. Practice sessions are always private, unless invited by HoneyMama herself. "Please tell me you have some good news, like a suspect in custody?"

"I wish we could, Ms. Thibodeaux." John looks around the room of half-naked women and shakes his head—I can't tell if it's out of disgust, shame, guilt, or a combination of all three.

"We looked through Monaka's phone records to get an idea of who she was in contact with before she died," Drew says, holding up the blinged-out iPhone. "We've decided it might be a good idea to invite them back to the Spot for a free pole dance, and introduce them to the "new" dancer, Brandy."

"Brandy," I repeat, letting it sink in. The soreness, the heat, the expectations, the murderer.

Drew taps the back of the phone anxiously and holds my gaze, sharing my fear. Disappointed clients are nothing to play with on a regular day. Adding a killer to the mix is a whole other level of crazy.

"Why the hell are we giving away dances?" C says, like she's our unofficial union rep. "Uh-uh. That shit is contagious."

"No, your STDs are," Dulce says, entering the room more tilted than before.

She'd better watch out. Friar John would love to take another crack at her.

"Ran out of vodka, I see," C says, amused by Dulce's vitriol.

"How are you holding up, Dulce?" Drew asks sympathetically.

We all attempt to ignore C, but I know her presence pisses everyone off, mainly Dulce, and rightfully so. I can only imagine how it feels to have the love of your life ripped away from you so violently, and in the space you both shared with the person suspected to be responsible for her death, no less.

"As well as can be expected, no thanks to y'all," Dulce slurs. "Got tired of cleaning up the mess you and your associates made in our apartment, so here I am."

"It's a crime scene, ma'am. We were just doing our jobs," John says, almost grinning at her distress.

"Dulce, honey. Why don't you go clean yourself up so you can join the rest of us for rehearsal," HoneyMama interrupts, and right on time. Dulce's bloodshot glare might as well be considered assault. "The other girls will be arriving shortly. Detectives, we'll help in any way we can," she continues. "Let's go back to the original plan. C, you'll be Brandy's mentor here and in the city. Introduce her to all of your clients, and make sure they want to see her again."

"I don't work for free, HoneyMama," C says, sucking her teeth. "Whatever I do, whenever I do it, is paid for in full at the time services are rendered."

John looks like he wants to say something, but Drew silences him with one look. The last thing we need is John and C going at it.

"How much do you think you'll get when they close us down permanently because they can't wrap up this case?" HoneyMama says poignantly.

C thinks about it for a moment, looking me over like a piece of meat. "Fine, but you're not getting any special treatment. You do what I say to who I say, ya heard?"

"Heard," I reply through gritted teeth. The things I'll do to get a good story.

"It's settled. C, go with the detectives and assist with Monaka's client list. We'll invite them to tonight's show. Brandy, you need to become completely acclimated to that pole. Give me fifty spins, top to bottom, right now," HoneyMama says, tapping her left heel on the floor. "We can't have you rough around the edges for our top clients."

C smiles at the command and follows Drew outside, while John stays put at the entrance. He lights a cigarette and takes a long, deep draw. I hope he chokes.

"I got you, *mami*," Dulce says, mounting the stage. I could use a refresher myself. She wraps one ankle and then the other around the pole parallel to mine and begins to count as she spins.

I join her in the rotation—still sore from my earlier go-around, my counts a bit slower than hers. She, being the compassionate partner that she is, slows down the pace so that I can catch up.

"Ten, eleven, twelve . . ." We continue to count in unison. It feels good to be in sync.

"All right now," Praline says. "We've got ourselves a show."

"Fifteen, sixteen, seventeen . . ." Dulce leads, breathing harder as we pick up the pace.

"I knew that girl was into some kinky shit, but damn," C exclaims from the porch.

"What's that?" HoneyMama says out the screen door.

"There were some, let's say, sexy pictures on Monaka's cell sent to an unknown caller," Drew says, bringing the phone back inside to HoneyMama.

"Well, well, well. The plot thickens," HoneyMama says, scrolling through the photos.

"Anyone else have experience with this side of the business?" John asks, releasing the toxic smoke over his shoulder into the evening air. "And don't bother lying. I can sniff out a liar a mile away, and then we'll have to take you to the station, and, well, you know the rest. Ain't that right, Dulce?"

"I hate you, twenty-seven, twenty-eight . . ." Dulce counts without missing a beat. She looks mad enough to kick the shit out of the detective, but restrains herself for the time being.

Tiramisu looks from HoneyMama to John, her eyes wide. "I

already told you that I do sometimes. C hooked me and Monaka up with the gig."

"You little snitch," C says from the back porch. "I didn't make her or Monaka do a damn thing they didn't want to."

"No one's saying you did, C," Drew says, attempting to calm her down. "Tiramisu, have you ever been threatened by any of those clients?"

Dulce stops at fifty and I'm right behind her. Without my recorder handy, my memory will have to do. Charlie wants a rough draft at tomorrow's meeting, and this is just the type of info I need to fill in the blanks.

"I've run into some trouble with certain men who can't get enough over the phone, but nothing major."

"Do you know you gals are playing with fire?" John asks, sounding more like a preacher than an officer of the law. "Nobody likes a tease, least of all a paying client."

"And you know this how?" C asks, standing behind both men.

"I just do." John turns around and meets C at eye level. If they come to blows, my money's on C. I don't think John knows who he's dealing with, but C's used to cops. "And you're the infamous Couverture, right?"

"That's right," C says, stepping close enough to John that his body has no choice but to respond. "And you are?"

"The man who's been waiting to meet you," John says.

"Get in line," C says, licking her plum-colored lips.

"C, do you know this number?" Drew says, stepping in between them and reading the number aloud. "It appears in her call list several times the day before Monaka's murder."

"That's Dylan and Ryan Peterson down at the funeral home," HoneyMama says, recognizing the number. "They're regulars."

"They're also fans of Monaka's. We'll go down there and have a little chat with them," Drew says, tapping his partner on the shoulder. "We'll let you ladies get back to work. Call us if anything else comes to mind."

"Oh, I'm sure something will jog their memories before we have to come back down here," John says. He's talking to all of us, but looking at C.

"You don't have to make up excuses to visit," C says, stepping back inside and reclaiming her pole. "The Spot is open to all."

"Yeah, and therein lies the problem."

"Good night, Detective Miller," HoneyMama says, fed up with his unprovoked slights. "We'll let you know if any of our guests have something to share."

"You do that," John says, following.

We all breathe a sigh of relief that the interrogation is over, for the moment. C flips her middle fingers at Tiramisu as Praline turns the music back up. I'm sure Drew and John will question C at the station tomorrow. Until then, I'll play her game and let her think she is leading the way.

Chapter 20

WHEN I FIRST CAME OUT ONSTAGE LAST NIGHT, I WAS BEYOND scared. But as soon as the music began, all of the dancers came into sync, including me. I was swept up in the routine. We all got along, finished to a standing ovation, and collected our bags. Each of us cleared about a stack in tips last night—cold, hard cash. I haven't touched this much money since I left stripping. One night's work is about half my monthly salary after taxes, which makes me wonder why I ever left dancing in the first place to come and sit on my ass all day and get yelled at while writing about shit that I don't want to.

"The Lovers Only site is a good angle, but your story ain't juicy enough, Keke," Charlie says, choosing to degrade me first this morning.

My good vibes from last night's haul are officially wearing off in this toxic environment.

"In my opinion, that's the story the readers want to read because it's the truth."

"Thankfully, no one gives a shit about your opinion," Charlie says, turning his iPad toward me. "This isn't a feature. Readers of the *Metro Journal* expect hard-core reporting, not a persuasive fucking essay. You should've learned all of that by now, Miss Magna Cum Laude in Journalism, or whatever the fuck you were. Your feelings are irrelevant on every street except Sesame, got it?"

My colleagues think he's funny, but I've had about all I can take of Charlie's belittling.

"I was thinking we could do an exposé on the club's owner, this HoneyMama broad," he says. "You know she is as much to blame as the murderer is for that girl's death, if you ask me."

"Good thing no one asked you." I cross my feet at the ankles, one burgundy pump over the other. "And it was summa cum laude. A good reporter always gets her facts straight."

My coworkers look at me like I've lost my mind, but after conquering the pole last night, I feel like a fucking gladiator. I've got half a mind to tell this punk to kiss my Black ass, but my money ain't there quite yet.

"Touchy, touchy," Charlie says, chewing on his cigarette butt, slightly amused.

He knows me about as well as I think I know him—we can go on like this for hours, but today's not the day. The Spot doesn't have that kind of time and I don't want to waste any more arguing with this prick.

"Look, it's only been a few days," I say. "It could take months to solve this case."

"Exactly. In the meantime, we can dig into the backstory."

"If there's a backstory, it has nothing to do with Honey-Mama." I carefully eye each reporter present, making it crystal clear that anyone looking to make a name for themselves off of HoneyMama or the Spot will have hell to pay.

"To the contrary, Ms. McCoy. That lady is very interesting." Charlie pulls out a file from underneath the stack of papers on his desk and opens it. "Josephine Thibodeaux. Daughter of Joseph Thibodeaux and one of his many, many mistresses, Ms. Betty, who also happened to be a whore. That sounds like a good story just waiting to be told. Good job, Margeaux."

"I'm there to report on a murder, that's it," I say impatiently. I will not let him crucify HoneyMama.

"No, Keke. That's where you're wrong," Charlie says, his obtuse pink face turning crimson. "Shit, I could've sent Pete down there just to write about a simple murder," Charlie says, gesturing toward Pete, who looks like he doesn't want to be involved in this debate. "I sent you to Butts County because you used to be one of them. I sent you, Ms. McCoy, to get behind the scenes, but you're too busy reminiscing about your life as a former Jezebel or dancing call girl, or whatever you gals do down there, to write the real story. I think you're too damn close to get the grit, Keke. Maybe Margeaux can do a better job. Hell, she found all of this out in just one day," he says, shaking the thick file toward the young intern.

"I didn't have to dig too deep. It was public record," Margeaux says, attempting humility, but I can see straight through her innocent act. She's obviously batting for my job and she can have it when I'm done. But not yet. Not yet.

"Hey, Keke. How's this for a title," Charlie says, flicking at a yellow sticky note on the desktop calendar. With all the different-colored Post-its, it looks like a dysfunctional rainbow. "'Female Strip Club Owner: Mama or Madame?' We can expose her for the real lady pimp that she is. Yeah, I like the sound of that."

"I'm outta here," Pete says, shaking his head at the freak show, presumably as disgusted as I feel. "Keke, call me if you need more shots. The ones you took by yourself are pretty good, but the lighting could be better."

"Thanks," I say, flattered. After doing his job for a day, I admit he's pretty skilled. I think Pete is missing being in Indian Springs, too.

"No more naked broads till we finish with that Alpharetta homicide," Charlie says, moving a purple sticky note from one side of the calendar to the other. "Make sure to get a pic of the head by itself," Charlie says to Pete. "It's not every day a preacher gets decapitated by his wife. We need that one for the archives."

"Sure thing, boss." Pete rolls his eyes, picks up the camera bag, and leaves the office.

"That's what I like to hear. Now, about the strippers . . ."

I'm with Pete: it's time to get out of here.

"Charlie, as of last night I'm working undercover as a dancer," I say, interrupting his tirade. "The lead dancer is making sure I get in good with all of the clients Monaka worked with. I'll get the story."

Everyone becomes silent, except for Charlie, who gets a good laugh at my expense.

"You, a stripper?" he says, giving me a slow once-over, along with the majority of my colleagues. I'm pretty sure this qualifies as mass sexual harassment. "Who's going to pay to see your big ass dance anymore?" Charlie barks.

"My clients," I say, removing a hefty roll of bills from my bag and tossing it onto the table. "And that's only half of what I got."

"Damn, Keke," Charlie says, eyeing the cash. "Impressive. Didn't think you had it in you."

"Me neither. But I do, and I'll write my article my way, truth included." I look dead at Margeaux to let her know I'm onto her ass. She can have my position when I'm ready to leave, but in the meantime, she needs to back the hell up and let me do my job. If she is smart, she'll learn a thing or two and stay out of my way.

"Let me know if you need any more help," Margeaux offers, still not taking the hint.

"I didn't need any, to begin with," I say, glancing down at the overstuffed file on HoneyMama and her family businesses.

Margeaux opens her mouth to say something, but stops short.

"Competition. I love it!" Charlie says, looking at the only two women in the room, like he's about to witness a mud fight. "It's good for morale."

"Whatever you say, Charlie. I have a meeting to get to. Later." I reclaim my earnings, stuff them back in the bag, and head out.

C's meeting me at The Pimp Palace this evening and I want to be there before she arrives. I need to see her walk in. Her demeanor will tell me whether or not she's truly going to help with the investigation, or if she's trying to play us. My money's on the latter, but even a succubus deserves the benefit of the doubt.

Chapter 21

"W ELL, IF IT ISN'T MISS FAST ASS HERSELF!" SHELLEY SAYS, ushering me inside.

Doesn't look like she's cleaned up much since the last time I was here, poor thing. Think I'll use part of my extra earnings to gift my bestie with a housekeeper for a couple of weeks. Mommy needs a break.

"Tell your mama to use her nice words," I say, kissing the resting baby on her shoulder. "Where's the rest of the brood?"

"Outside playing with the neighbors' kids," Shelley says, closing the door behind us. "How was the meeting?"

"Shitty, as always." I stretch out across the cluttered couch and accidentally kick a rattle onto the hardwood floor.

The baby doesn't budge at the loud, clattering sound the hard plastic makes. Guess that's one advantage to having a houseful of kids: they get used to sleeping under noisy conditions.

"And last night?" she says, moving the baby to her lap and making herself comfortable.

"I promise, I've never been this sore in my entire life."

"Sliding up and down a pole will do that to you," Shelley says, tossing clean laundry over the baby's head and into a full hamper next to her on the couch. "It'll also give you cooties."

"Cooties, Shelley. Really?" I take a pillow and toss it at her. "I think you've been around the little people way too long. You need to get out more."

"And you need to keep your clothes on when you work."

I glare at Shelley's judgmental ass and smile. Sometimes how we ever became friends is a mystery to us both.

"Shut up and let me catch up on my social media before I have to meet this chick," I say, taking the laptop from my workbag and flipping it open.

Files from the case pop up, including a few photos of the detectives.

"How's Drew?" Shelley says, noticing my stare.

"Sexy as ever." I click AUTOSAVE and log into my Facebook account. "I should send him a friend request."

"I think not," Shelley says, putting the still-sleeping baby down in the bassinet next to the couch and joining me.

From what I've witnessed, newborns are the easiest to handle. It's the older ones that are a handful. I bet she wishes they could stay this small forever. That's probably why she keeps popping them out.

"And where are we in the Ian countdown this time?" Shelley says, already knowing the drill with his habit of disappearing.

"Thirteen days and counting."

"Damn, Keke. I would've slit that fool's tires by now."

"I can't," I say, envisioning his black Audi coupe pull into my visitor's parking space. "I think I love that car more than I love him."

"Whatever, Keke," she says, working her way through the laundry. "Thankfully, you have a career to keep you busy. Speaking of, how's the story coming?"

"Slow and excruciatingly painful," I say, touching my face. If I don't get this whisker out of my chin, it's going to be a bad day. "I swear Butts County has it out for the Spot."

"Hell, you already knew that shit," Shelley says, slapping my hand. "Stop scratching."

"I'm not scratching. I have a chin hair."

"I got it." Shelley locates the whisker and pulls it out with her nails. "I feel you on writing bullshit, because I don't want to read it. Writing for the *Metro Journal* is only temporary. Your time is coming, just wait and see."

"That's what you said when you set me up on that blind date last year without my knowledge."

"Girl, when are you going to get over that?" Shelley opens the ottoman that doubles as storage and pulls out her weed box. "My bad for wanting you to meet someone."

"I don't want just anyone. I want *the* one. The one who's supposed to make me forget about Drew."

Shelley lights the small joint and passes it to me.

"You know all this is going to do is give me the munchies," I say, taking a hit.

"Nothing wrong with that," she says, inhaling deeply.

I scan through several profiles matching Elijah Drew, but none of them are my Drew.

"Keke, you'll never forget about Drew. The best you can do is stop comparing other men to him. Maybe then you can move on and up to bigger and better."

"Whatever. I'm still mad that you turned me onto those bitch books, which, by the way, made me not call my man for almost two weeks and counting." I rarely check Ian's page, because he doesn't post often, but I just want to make sure the brother is alive and well. "I could kill you and the bitch who wrote them. She was obviously not a Black woman dealing with Black men."

"He'll call, Keke."

"When? When will Ian realize he's missing out on all of this and call?"

"Keke, I like Ian, but even I, the hopeless romantic that I am, will admit that this might not be the right man for you, or at least not right now. You're worth so much more than this brother is putting out," she says, the philosophical side of her becoming more apparent with each puff. "You do everything for a man from jump, which is the opposite of the bitch books' advice, by the way." Shelley takes one more hit and puts her contraband back in its place.

"I can usually tell right when the moment comes that he realizes it's getting too close. He stops calling and his texts become curt, nothing like the cute words that made me wet when we first started dating." I type in Ian's name and wait for the page to load.

"That's why you haven't met and kept the one, because you think you need to. When are you going to realize that it's you who needs to be kept?"

I stare at Shelley and feel the high go straight to my head. When the page finally loads, I scroll through his most recent posts and notice dozens of hearts and flower emojis, along with well-wishes.

"Oh, shit," I say, reading Ian's latest update. "Ian was in a biking accident."

"Damn," Shelley says, reading the post for herself. "And you had to find out about it online? That's cold."

"Shelley, that's not important right now. I hope he's okay," I say, calling him, but there's no answer, as usual. I send a quick text, instead of leaving a message.

"Isn't he always?" Shelley says curtly.

My cell vibrates with Ian's response.

"What did he say?"

"He says he is fine," I say, summarizing the message.

"Did you ask him why the hell he couldn't pick up the phone and let his girlfriend know he was okay before posting it for all the world to see? And who was he biking with?"

"I won't phrase it quite like that, but I'll ask." Ian hates it when I ask too many questions, but in this case, I think some answers are in order.

"You're too damned nice, Keke. When are you going to realize that the mean bitch gets the man?"

Before I can respond to Shelley's insanity, Ian replies. I reread the nine words until tears pour down my hot cheeks.

"What's wrong?" Shelley asks, taking the phone from me and reading the message aloud.

"'I just can't do this anymore, Keke. I'm sorry,'" Shelley reads aloud, and then tosses the cell phone onto the ottoman.

And just like that, Ian's gone—again.

Chapter 22

I THOUGHT BY NOW THAT I'D BE NUMB TO IAN'S VANISHING ACTS, but instead each time turns out to be more painful than the last. What's not numb is my headache, one of the few memories from yesterday's impromptu pity party with Shelley. Our day drinking and smoking turned into night drinking and smoking. Luckily, the hangover look works well for today's assignment.

C requested that I dress like I'm trying out for a job at The Pimp Palace if I want to get behind the scenes. I searched my closet for the most provocative outfit I could find, but had nothing near what the girls who work there would wear. The closest I could come was a shape-hugging black dress that shows just enough leg and way too much cleavage. With my matching open-toed high heels, it works well enough to get me inside. There's nowhere to hide a recorder or even an ink pen. I pray that my headache quiets down so I can recall what I need to, later on.

I can't believe I ever worked here. Unlike at The Honey Spot, there's nothing supple about this club. The cold, smoke-filled room is dark and musty—the perfect breeding ground for bacteria and indecent encounters. There are several new flat-screen televisions and pool tables, but everything else is the same, including the full bar and bartender.

"Can I help you?" Loretta says with a snarl across her permanently sunburned face.

The average-height white woman could easily pass for Honey-

Mama's run-down aunt. She went from dancer to bartender after her fifth child, if I remember correctly. We weren't close at all, and I wasn't memorable enough back then to be recognizable today. Lucky for her, the last baby was with the owner's nephew. She's got job security if nothing else. Once a family business, always a family business.

"Yes. Can I get a vodka gimlet straight up?" I ask, grateful she doesn't recognize me, not that she would. I'm sure she's seen at least a hundred girls come and go in the twenty-plus years she's been around.

"It's on the house, Loretta," an older man says, approaching the bar, grinning hard through his few remaining front teeth, half of which are capped in gold. "I'm Jimmy King, but folks around here just call me Big Jim. And you are?"

"Keke," I say, shaking his extended hand. This man's pinky rings could cover my rent for an entire year.

"Keke. I hope you don't mind me saying so," he says, licking one of the diamond-encrusted gold incisors, "but you're the classiest piece of ass I've seen come through here in a long time, even if you do have a few years on you. The juiciest too. Ain't that right, Loretta?"

"If you say so." Loretta looks unimpressed by me and the conversation.

"That's no surprise," I say, accepting my free drink. "Anyone can tell the pussy is a bit stale up in here."

Loretta stops wiping the smudged countertop and gives me an evil look, but she can't say shit. She knows I'm right.

"Ha!" Jimmy says, getting a kick out of the uninvited observation. "I like this girl, Loretta. Gimme a Woodford on the rocks." He taps my glass, signaling for a refill. "I have a feeling we're going to have a good night."

Loretta gives her ocean-blue eyes a hard roll at no one in particular and proceeds to pull down the liquor bottles from the sparse top shelf.

"Actually, I'm saving this seat for a friend." After yesterday's drunk fest, a little hair of the dog is just what I need to get straight, but not too much. The last thing I want to do is entertain this old fool or get too drunk to do my job.

"My heart!" He grabs his chest, feigning pain. "Big Jim's the bestest friend you could ever have," he says, biting the tip of his lit cigar.

"Is that right?" I sip my drink and allow him to lead the conversation.

"Absolutely," he says, blowing the foul smoke over my head. "You see, I'm the new co-owner of this here fine establishment. Like I said, best friend."

"Isn't that a coincidence," I say, crossing one bare bronzed leg over the other. "I'm waiting for C, one of your dancers. She said that she's the only friend I need."

"C, huh?" Jimmy says, winking at Loretta, pleased. "You one of her girls?"

Jimmy and Loretta both sense my hesitation.

"I'm new to the scene, looking for my first break," I say, remembering what HoneyMama said about me needing to act the part. A pole virgin it is.

"She told me you'd be stopping by, said your name was Brandy." Jimmy looks at my toes, calves, and finally my breasts.

Loretta places a bottle of brown liquor on the bar and another drink in front of me, without looking up.

"Brandy. My favorite," he says, eyeing his crystal shot glass. Unlike my cheap martini glass, his shit's the real thing. "Get your permit yet? If not, we can easily sponsor a pretty, thick girl like yourself."

"I'm working on it." I begin sipping my second drink, hoping that my alleged chaperone will show up before it becomes obvious that I'm avoiding a third.

"Well, you should consider working on it here," he says, taking his drink to the head.

Loretta refills the tall shot glass without missing a beat.

"You ain't gon' find a better club in all the Southeast. I even take my girls down there to them fancy spots in Miami Beach to make a little extra money on the side, know what I'm saying? Big Jim's all about opportunities."

"I see." I suck on the tiny black drink straw to avoid laughing in his snaggletoothed face. "I'd appreciate that very much," I say, playing along to the script C already set in motion. Where the hell is she?

"I knew you would," Jimmy says, puffing his chest, but the beer gut will not be outdone. "And who knows? Maybe you'll become one of my girls, too."

"Why would I do that?" I ask, fed up with his bullshit. Jimmy's a welcome distraction from Ian's ass, but I'm not in the mood to fight off a horny pimp. I wouldn't be in this uncomfortable situation at all if C's ass was here to handle him.

"Because I take care of all of my girls, long as they act right." His phone buzzes on the counter and he smiles. "This one of my young tenders right here. She wants me to come over, but I ain't driving all the way to Douglasville tonight."

"Can't find a side piece in the city?" I say, grateful that he has someone else to focus on.

"This is just one of them. When a man gets to be my age, you can't waste a hard-on. So I keep several asses on deck."

Jimmy looks at me like he wants to eat me alive and have whoever is on the phone as an appetizer.

"I'd better check on C." I pull out my cell and send her a quick message.

"This one likes to send pictures of my pussy," Jimmy says, showing me the girl's dark lips and clit.

What the fuck?

"No thanks," I say, pushing the cell away. "I know what pussy looks like." I'm going to kill C for leaving me with this pervert. "Does Ms. Douglasville know you're showing her private pics to another woman?"

"She can't say shit about who I show them to," Jimmy says, staring at his cell. "They're mine now."

"If that was your wife, would you have a little more respect for her privacy?"

Loretta audibly sucks in air and holds it. They both seem taken aback by the mention.

"I do have a wife at home," Jimmy grunts. "And if she sent me pictures like this bitch right here, I wouldn't have these to show off in the first place. Bottom bitch, my ass," he says, not sharing that memory, but Loretta's exhale tells me she gets it.

"Big Daddy," another dancer says, greeting Jimmy tits first.

"Hey, baby." Jimmy slightly rises from the barstool to kiss the young woman, barely eighteen if that. "Lap dance took a little longer than usual, don't you think?" He eyes the older gentleman seated at a corner table across the dimly lit space.

"Had to take my time with that one, but I finally worked it out of him," she says, passing her earnings to Jimmy. "He's coming back tomorrow."

The customer stands, adjusts his pants, and heads for the front door.

"That a girl," Jimmy says, smacking her naked, glittered backside. He pockets the majority of the cash and then gives the rest back to her. "You can take five, baby."

She sits down on the empty stool beside him and happily kicks up her feet, grateful for the break.

Loretta and I exchange a familiar look. Like her, I'm so glad I'm not in that life anymore.

"Uniqua's another girl who'll do anything I say," Jimmy says, scanning the room. "Nearly half the girls who work here are mine, including C."

I wish C were here to hear him say that shit. She belongs to no one, especially not a pimp like Jimmy. He may not know it, but she's running game on him, too, no doubt.

"So, how 'bout it, Keke? Want to become one of Big Jim's girls?"

"I'm not sure," I say, beginning my escape from the bar. If C's not going to rescue me, then I'll have to save myself. This situation's about to go downhill fast when Jimmy sees that I'm not down for another free drink or what he expects to happen afterward. "I don't have the money to pay the city right now."

"Consider this an advance toward your permit," Jimmy says, placing several hundred-dollar bills under my martini glass. "Bring it straight to me when you get it and you can start dancing immediately."

I stare at the money on the cluttered, moist bar and consider taking it to show good faith, but think twice about being indebted to a pimp.

Uniqua and Loretta look at me like I'm a leper. No broke-ass chick's going to pass up money, especially not when it's considered an opportunity to make more. Damn C for putting me in this position.

"Thank you," I say, reluctantly accepting the advance. I'll have to call Charlie to report this exchange as soon as I get out of here. It's one thing to earn money on the side, but another to accept a loan from a known hustler.

"Uh-uh," Jimmy says, taking the bills from my hand and placing them in between my overflowing breasts—Rihanna sure can make a good bra. "Keep Big Jim close to your heart," he says, smacking Uniqua on the ass.

My cell vibrates loudly on the bar. C finally returns my text, but not with an ETA.

"I knew Jimmy'd like your thick ass. Remember who put you on. I'm done," the quick message reads.

This bitch set me up. What the hell was she thinking, leaving me to the wolves like this?

"It's C. I have to meet her outside," I say, only half-lying. The sooner I get out of this place, the better.

"Tell her I said thank you and the check is in the mail."

Big Jim laughs as I walk away from the bar and out of the seedy environment. Fuck C and her trifling-ass tricks. The next time I see her, she'll have more than money coming her way.

I step outside, grateful for the fresh air, even if it's thick with heat and smoke from the many different things burning in the bustling parking lot. There's always at least one patron with a barbeque pit or two, not to mention the weed, cigarette, and cigars burning alongside the incense for sale. There are also a few women with racks of sparkly, mostly spandex clothing, with complementary jewelry, makeup, and wigs, just to name a few of the hot items for sale on a nightly basis.

I hot-tail it to my car, on the side of the club, away from the main crowd, where the dancers usually park. The last thing anyone wants after a long, hard shift is to be hassled into buying shit they don't need.

My cell vibrates again, but it's not C calling to apologize, as if that would ever happen.

"What an asshole," Shelley says, picking up right where we left off a few hours ago. What are best friends for, if not to relive your worst moments with you until you learn better?

"I assume you're talking about Ian?" I say, thinking of the asshole that I just left inside, and the one who left me yet again via text. "There are a lot of assholes to go around lately."

I look out into the main parking lot as the ballers pull up for the night shift, also known as the A team. Once I get my license cleared, I'll be able to pick up some shifts and get in good with C's clients. I'm not sure exactly what Drew and Friar John think, but her shady behavior alone makes her suspect number one in my book.

"Don't be funny, Keke. This is serious."

"I know that, Shelley. I was the one sleeping with him," I say, tugging at my tight dress and the gear underneath. These Spanx are about done for the night. "When it's the best sex ever, you know it's about to be the end of some shit."

"It's not just about the sex, Keke," Shelley says, lowering her voice. Guess she's got ears around. "This is about the time you've spent investing in a man who you thought would be your partner, maybe for life."

"Spoken like a true married woman. The end, Shelley," I say, tired of her preaching. "I fucked him, fed him, rolled his blunts, and he still left me. Another day, another dollar, right?"

I unlock the car, plop down onto the cloth-covered seats, and lock the driver's-side door. Luckily, my apartment's less than fifteen minutes away from the club. My body can't take the long drive back to Indian Springs tonight.

"I'm sorry it didn't work out, Keke," she says, genuinely feeling my angst.

"Maybe I should try calling him. He might be hurt more than he's letting on," I say, feeling the loss all over again. Even this controlled underwear contraption underneath my too-small dress doesn't hurt as much as Ian's absence.

"Why? He was in an accident and didn't bother to inform you personally, girl. He's not going to answer," Shelley says, making a valid point. We both know his ways too well, but only one of us takes them to heart.

"But I miss him so much, Shelley. I can't take it anymore."

"Keke, don't call!" she shouts into my ear. "There's no sense waiting in vain for one man when there are so many more to choose from."

"Obviously, you haven't been in the dating scene in a while," I say, shuddering at the thought of some nasty old man showing naked pictures of me to another girl he's trying to fuck. "Ugh!"

"Let's learn the lesson from this relationship so we can move on to a healthier, happier solution the next time around."

Shelley's been reading too many damned relationship books and drinking too much rosé this evening, I can tell. In what little downtime she has, my girl loves to study for the family counseling degree she wants to gain in the future and uses me as her guinea pig until then.

"You act like you're the single one, Shelley."

"As long as you're out there looking, then so am I," Shelley says, making me smile even though I feel like shit. "Just be still for a while, Keke. He'll come. I promise."

"Good night, Shelley."

It's time to go home and I really miss Ian. He left one shirt at my apartment, and I'll wear it to sleep. I thought him leaving clothes behind meant that he was ready to move forward. It actually just meant more laundry. Silly me.

"Night, girl. Call me if you need to."

"Okay," I say, trying to hold off the tears until I get home.

I'm tired of crying over dudes. Sometimes I cry so hard that I don't even know who I'm crying for. Maybe I'm crying for my first love, lost by suicide. Maybe I'm crying because I know that I need to let go of Drew completely if I'm ever going to breathe again. Being wide open is no longer an option in relationships for me. From now on, a man is going to have to prove himself in several ways before I give it my all. Fuck being the bitch: I'm going to be the freaking Virgin Mary herself—if Mary was a ho, but still.

Chapter 23

*J*IMMY, OR BIG JIM AS HE SIGNS EACH MESSAGE, HAS CALLED AND texted multiple times this morning about my dancer's permit. He's not going to let up until I text him proof of an appointment with the licensing board, or give him his money back. After last night's meeting and subsequent conversation, I don't have the energy to entertain anything extra today, including his paranoia. Once I confront C about exactly what the hell's up with her leaving me hanging, I'll deal with Jimmy.

"Missed you yesterday," Drew says as I enter the rear side door of the Spot. I'm a few minutes late and couldn't give a shit less. I'm tired from the inside out and no amount of coffee or chiseled ebony cheekbones will make me feel better. "How'd it go last night with C?"

"It didn't," I say, still upset about C's setup, not to mention that I didn't get much sleep worrying about Ian. I stared at the phone for hours, waiting to hear his ringtone, before finally giving up and falling asleep.

"What the hell do you mean 'it didn't'?" HoneyMama asks, overhearing us from her stance at the kitchen sink.

The teacups and other delicate dishes are stacked high in the sink, with most spilling over onto the countertop. Every single tray of biscuits is gone—there's usually a couple dozen left over in the morning. Looks like they had a good, busy night.

"C never had any intention of showing me around herself, but she did hook me up with one of the owners, Big Jim," I say, displaying the missed calls and messages. "I spent the morning applying for my dancer's permit. Should have it in a few days."

"Excellent work, Brandy." HoneyMama nods in approval, but the crackle in her voice says she's still pissed about C. "Who knows? You may want to use it to come back to work here, part-time, of course."

"You never know," I say, the vision of the snaggletoothed pimp stuffing money between my breasts still fresh in my mind. I shake off the thought and settle into the sweet smell of Honey-Mama's kitchen. Being here on a more regular basis wouldn't be such a bad thing.

"We checked out the funeral home," John says, creating a dark cloud over the inviting space, like the shadow Drew didn't request. "Both owners admit to being admirers of Monaka's, but have good alibis for the night in question."

"Solid alibis?" HoneyMama asks, keeping her eyes on the sink full of water and suds.

She's just about had it with the detectives, their theories, and John's presence. Drew, she loves and will happily welcome him home, once the case is over. But John's been adversarial since the first day he stepped foot on HoneyMama's property, when she's been more than hospitable. Knowing HoneyMama, I'm sure she can't wait to tell him the many different ways he can kiss her ass on the way out the door.

"They were processing a body up in Macon. At least two officers can collaborate their stories," John says, tossing his cigarette over the porch railing and fully entering the room. "We're waiting for more information on an unidentified number Monaka regularly received calls from, see if that leads anywhere."

"Once that info comes back, we'll run the name against the database to see if there's a match in the system," Drew says, unbuttoning the sleeves on his crisp gray business shirt and rolling them elbow high, one by one. "The owners did say that they've had unusually large requests for elaborate floral arrangements from one person in particular: Walter Adams." Drew claims the broom leaning up against the island and begins to sweep.

"The mayor's bastard son," John adds, sounding like the well-known neighborhood moniker is the man's birth name. "That boy's a strange one; he always has been. Lives a few miles out with his mama." He watches Drew help clean and crinkles his angular nose in disgust.

"We know Walter and, yeah, he's crazy. Monaka used to talk about how he gave her the creeps, leaving strange haikus and shit in her locker," Dulce says, rinsing the dishes that Honey-Mama hands her. "He wanted Monaka to teach him how to move like she did or some shit—fucking psychopath."

"From what I experienced last night with Jimmy, C doesn't give two shits about the safety of the dancers or the mental stability of the clients," I say, still shook at how close I came to choosing between my safety and my story. As long as C got her cut, she'd definitely leave Monaka alone and vulnerable with someone capable of murder—just like she did.

"We know from the way the crime scene was cleaned and the position of the body that the perpetrator's psychologically disturbed on more than one level," Drew says.

He places the copper dustpan on the hardwood floor, perches his foot underneath the handle, and angles it just right to catch the broom's debris. That's one trick of several I learned from him that I still use to this day.

"He likes strippers, but may be ashamed of his affinity for them," John offers without immediately recognizing the irony in his statement.

HoneyMama looks at John, who turns red at the unspoken accusation.

"If there's something there, we'll find it," Drew says, replacing the broom and empty dustpan and leading the way out. "We're going to talk to him now. Wanna tag along?" Drew asks like it's a date, and not a murder investigation.

"Yes, she does," HoneyMama insists before I can agree. "Don't forget you're onstage with Dulce tonight, Brandy," she says with a smirk. She enjoys using my dance name way too much.

"Yes, ma'am." I look over my shades and blow a kiss to Honey-Mama and then another to Dulce, who smiles at the gesture.

I'm actually excited about dancing tonight. The extra cash is quite nice, even if it's temporary. Technically, the paper doesn't bar journalists from having side gigs, but I'm not up for a return to the stage long-term. These past couple of days have shown me that I don't have the stamina for dancing, but who knows? If anyone asked me a month ago if I'd ever strip again, I would've laughed in their face. But now, being back onstage with my old dance family is just what the therapist ordered.

When we arrive at the unimpressive shotgun house a few miles outside of Indian Springs, the first things I notice are the stunning floral arrangements that line the living-room window spanning the entire length of the modest home. A spread like this probably cost more than my monthly salary.

"These are similar to the arrangement at Monaka's shrine," Drew says, noticing the same thing.

John takes a step to the left and checks the side of the house, while Drew checks the right. It's a modest, well-kept home, with modern amenities. Unlike the surrounding homes, most of which are a step away from being condemned, this one has central air, city sewage hook, and a two-car garage.

"I also remember expensive flowers appearing for several days after Mocha's body was discovered," I say, looking over the porch swing toward the immaculately pruned garden and recognize the tall white lilies similar to those found at both crime scenes. "I just brushed them off as a nice gesture."

"Clear," John says, returning his focus to the shut front door. "We may have a serial killer on our hands, after all. Stay back." He and Drew approach the front door while I watch from the garden. John removes his gun from its waist holster and uses the butt to knock on the door.

John and Drew hold their weapons low, but steady, ready for

what—or who—comes next. The detectives exchange a knowing look and signal for me to take several steps back. Before they're forced to make a move, we can hear hurried steps approach the front door.

"Who's there, please?" a woman's voice calls from somewhere near the back of the house.

"Butts County Police, ma'am," Drew says, tightening his grip. "We're looking for Walter Adams. Just need to ask him a few questions."

"Just a second," the gentle voice calls.

An elderly lady with all salt, and no pepper, short, loose curls unlocks the weathered storm door, but not the security screen. I don't blame her. No need letting cool air out and mosquitoes in if it can be avoided.

"You do have to understand, my eyes and my ears don't work so well these days," she says, taking the cheetah-patterned reading glasses from the multicolored beaded chain around her neck and placing them over her eyes. "You said you were cops?"

"That's right, ma'am," John says, removing the badge from his vest pocket and holding it up for her to read. "Just need to have a quick chat with Mr. Adams, if you'd be so kind to let him know we're here."

John tips his cowboy hat at just the right angle to highlight his tanned features. Walter's mother, Ms. Adams, equally captivated, allows her glasses to fall to her flat chest and steps aside to allow us to see indoors.

"Walter," she yells toward the back of the house. "Company!"

"Who is it, Mama? I'm busy," Walter says, stepping into the front room, wearing a smoking jacket only James Bond would look normal in, slacks, and an expensive pair of sunglasses.

"It's the police," his mother says, speaking over her right shoulder. "For you."

Walter joins his mother and unlocks the screen door.

"It's all right, Mama. I've got this," he says, joining us on the porch. "What's this all about?"

"The murder of Monaka, a dancer at The Honey Spot," John says, holding up Monaka's professional dance picture. "Recognize this woman?"

"Of course, I do." Walter looks back to check for his mother, who's disappeared down the long corridor. "Monaka and I were in love, but had to keep our relationship a secret because of her girlfriend's jealousy," he whispers. "I finally broke it off a couple of months ago. Monaka's lovely, but Dulce's too crazy for me."

"Is that right?" John says, unconvinced. "Dulce claims that the relationship was all in your head."

"Dulce's a lying whore," Walter says, a little too salty for my taste. "If it weren't for that bitch, Monaka and I'd still be together."

"Where were you the night Monaka was killed, Mr. Adams?" Drew asks, stepping closer to Walter.

We can see straight through this psycho's bull.

"I was here watching a movie with Mama," he says. *Dirty Dancing*. Our favorite."

His mother appears in the doorway behind him.

"I just love me some Patrick Swayze, and my boy here's sweet enough to pull up all his movies for me whenever I ask. Isn't that right, Walter?" she says, backing her son's alibi.

Instead of standing down, Walter straightens up as tall as Drew. He takes another step closer, nearly touching Drew's lips with his own.

Unflinching, Drew clenches his jaw and tightens the grip on his weapon.

"You need to take a step back," Drew says to Walter, who's also standing his ground.

"It's the station," John says, answering his cell and saving Walter from the beatdown he so deserves.

Drew takes his handcuffs out, anticipating that the prints and the phone number are matches for Walter. I hope so. We may not be able to prove it yet, but I know we've got the murderer standing right in front of us.

"My son ain't have nothing to do with those harlots," Miss Adams says. "He's a good, God-fearing boy."

"Let's go," John says, rushing back to the truck parked in front of the garage a few feet away. "The suspect's at the Spot."

Drew looks at Walter and returns his handcuffs to their holder. "Don't leave town, Mr. Adams."

"Wouldn't dream of it," Walter says, his stance now less defiant and more comparable to, dare I say, Monaka's posture? She had a real presence about her, and her statuesque frame was the beginning and end of it. I think Walter knows this all too well.

The three of us hop back into the Ford truck and John speeds down the road toward Indian Springs. When we arrive at the Spot, HoneyMama's already well into protesting Mr. Graves's impending arrest. And, as usual, Mr. Graves appears unbothered by the chaos, even though for the first time, he's the main character in the faux story.

"As I've already stated repeatedly to Ms. Thibodeaux, Mr. Graves's fingerprints are the only ones present at every site," Officer Cannon says, explaining the new results to the detectives. "They were in the main dance room, on the porch railing, and on the flowers delivered at both locations."

"He's the groundskeeper," HoneyMama says, her voice quaking with anger. "Of course, his prints are all over the place! It's his place to take care of."

"Also, the mystery number on Monaka's cell belongs to one, Mr. Paul Graves," Officer Cannon continues. "Can you explain why the victim would call the groundskeeper on several occasions outside regular business hours?"

"Regular business hours," HoneyMama scoffs. "What are those?"

"Mr. Graves is known to help out anyone who needs it, day or night, especially the dancers at the Spot," Drew says, vouching for Mr. Graves's character. It's never too early to start mounting a defense, especially if the defendant is a Black man.

"He's always there when you need him," I say, recalling a few calls of my own. "Looks like he still was for Monaka."

"He'll have an opportunity to tell his side of the story down at the station." Officer Cannon unclips the handcuffs from his holster, just like Drew did less than twenty minutes ago to arrest the *actual* murderer. We just have to prove that Walter Adams is the only viable suspect.

"She was always so nice to me, to everyone," Mr. Graves says, sweeping his way up the back porch steps. "Monaka was one of the kindest, most honest girls I'd ever known to come through here. Y'all ain't doing her no justice, if you ask me."

"Paul, stop talking right now," HoneyMama pleads. She walks toward him and removes the broom from his hand, hoping the stillness will shut him up.

"I will not," he says, indignant. "I never harmed a person in my life, including that old bastard of a captain y'all got to answer to. You know, he beat my brother and me mercilessly many moons ago when he first put that damned badge on. That's why my right eye twitches now."

"Mr. Graves, you do have the right to remain silent," Drew begins, unofficially Mirandizing our longtime friend.

"I know that. And I also have the right to speak. I didn't hurt Monaka. We were just friends. She was interested in the honey-making business and would come down to the cabins to get some peace. That's all."

"Sweep the cabins," Detective Miller says to Officer Cannon. "And, in the meantime, get this man in the back of the squad car."

"Paul would never do something like this. Never," Honey-Mama says, hugging Mr. Graves. "I'll get your wife. Please don't say anything else until we get there."

This can't be happening.

"You've only got circumstantial evidence, from what you've stated," I say, taking out my recorder to document part of the arrest. "Mark my words; you'll regret arresting an innocent man."

"That's what they all say, ma'am." Officer Cannon reads Paul his full Miranda rights as John cuffs his hands behind his back. They lead Mr. Graves toward one of three squad cars parked at the front of the property.

What a fucking nightmare. HoneyMama's already halfway to the cabins, ahead of the remaining officers, to alert Mrs. Graves that her husband has been arrested. Knowing the police around here, I'm sure they're already considering this an open-and-shut case, now that they have a suspect in custody. They've got the wrong man, and I have a strong feeling that we're the only ones who can prove it.

Chapter 24

*I*T'S NICE TO SIT UNDER THE COOL CEILING FAN AT RED'S CAFÉ, ESPE-cially after a long afternoon of dealing with trifling-ass cops who are convinced of Mr. Graves's guilt. For a minute, I thought Drew was going to come to blows with a few of the cops—seeing Mr. Graves hauled off this afternoon was a lot for us to swallow. Drew did what he could to make the process as easy on him as possible, which isn't saying much.

"There's a difference between chosen dedication and blind allegiance," I say, gripping the cold olive between my teeth be-fore tossing the bare toothpick back into the glass. The only martini they make is a dry one, and it's damn strong. We're both well on our way to being tossed.

"What's that supposed to mean?" Drew takes a sip of his sec-ond drink and loosens his necktie after a long day.

"It means that you're so blinded by the perfect vision of what you want that you can't appreciate the gift you have right in front of you. Never did."

"Who says I don't appreciate my gift?"

Drew takes the tip of the plastic toothpick and drags it down my throat and into the center of my breasts. I knew I should've worn something that didn't show so much cleavage.

"I do," I say, stopping his hand before it goes too far. There was a time when nothing could keep us from touching. "You've always taken me for granted, and we both know it."

"Truthfully, Keke, I always thought that you and I'd end up

married. We were together for as long as Corrine and I have been engaged," Drew says, continuing to plead his case about moving slowly with Corrine, but I'm not hearing it.

"Like that fucking matters!" I laugh, brushing off his excuse. "You're committed to the psychotic, needy wench, for only Lord knows why, and that's that. I want no part of that drama."

"After seeing you again, I'm not so sure that Corrine's the one I want to marry."

"Drew, don't do this."

Ignoring my plea, Drew leans in and kisses me hard—damn the witnesses.

"Here we are," the waiter says, interrupting us. He places my turkey sandwich in front of Drew and his baby back ribs in front of me by mistake.

"This is my plate," I say, reaching for the sandwich as Drew eagerly claims his extra-large platter.

"Yeah, okay," the pimpled-faced punk says under his breath while placing our side dishes on the table.

"Did you have something to say?" Drew asks, putting the young boy in his place.

Embarrassed, the waiter looks at me, shakes his head from side to side, and dashes off toward the kitchen.

"You look beautiful, Brandy. You really do," Drew says, spreading the white paper napkin across his lap before lowering his head to say grace. I hope he's praying for the same thing I'm praying for: us together in every way imaginable without consequence. Aren't fantasies worth praying for, too?

"Amen." I guess God didn't hear my prayer, because his cell's ringing . . . again. It could be work, but Corrine's called every hour, on the hour, since finding out I'm on the case with him. That's what the broad gets for cheating with him when we were together.

"Damn it," Drew says, placing his utensils down on the table. He snatches his cell out of its holder and reads the message. "It's the station. New evidence has surfaced that might further link Mr. Graves to Monaka's murder. I'd better get down there."

"I don't care what the evidence says. Everyone knows Mr. Graves didn't kill Monaka. It's a setup, and I'd bet my right pinky toe that Walter is the puppet master."

"Agreed." Drew takes a forkful of his mashed potatoes and wipes his face clean with his napkin. I guess I'll be eating by myself, as usual.

"Are you sure you can drive?"

"John's still at the Spot. I'll catch a ride with him," he says, downing the rest of his drink. "Can I get a rain check on dinner?" Drew takes another bite of his ribs, takes a large gulp from his glass of water, and stands.

"Maybe," I say, accepting his lips to my left cheek.

I watch him disappear around the corner and back toward HoneyMama's property. Before I can get into the second half of my sandwich, my phone vibrates on the table with a call from Drew.

"Yes?"

"I miss your voice, Brandy," Drew says, breathing heavy like he's paying for this call.

"And I miss yours." I return my sandwich to the plate and sigh. Why am I allowing this man to get back in my head? It took me years to get him out from under my skin. Every time we're around each other, it feels like we never broke up.

"I don't want to lose you in my life, girl—never again," he says, closer to the Spot—I can hear his partner in the background telling him to hurry up.

"We'll have to see what happens, Drew," I say, finishing off the remainder of my martini. "Be safe and please let me know how it goes."

"You know I will."

I end the call and signal the waiter for another drink. Luckily, my cottage is right across the street. Most people walk everywhere they need to go in the village—visitors included.

The waiter places a new overflowing martini glass down on the full table and removes the empty one. I wish he would say something else to me about my food choices, alcohol consumption, or my weight. There's enough vodka in my system to allow a few expletives to escape freely from my Southern tongue.

The calendar on my phone beeps, reminding me of the interview tomorrow morning with Dulce. I'm glad we've come to an understanding about my infamous article. If I'd known that it was her girlfriend who was murdered, I would've been more compassionate toward her from the beginning.

I hope Monaka knew how lucky she was to have a loyal chick like Dulce in her corner. Dulce letting anyone into her inner circle is a rarity. Her being devoted to one person—man, woman, or anyone in between—is a fucking wonder. Tomorrow I'll see just how much Dulce and Monaka meant to each other, and if Dulce has a clue about who'd want to kill her beloved. I can't wait to pick her brain about Drew and Corrine, too. It may be my imagination, but their relationship seems to be on the rocks. I want to know if it's always been like that, or just since my arrival. Either way, I'm not adverse to a second chance, as long as it's on the right terms.

Chapter 25

BETWEEN THE LIQUOR AND THE HEAT, IT WAS TOUGH GETTING comfortable in the cozy cottage room, but I eventually drifted off. I slept a little better last night, but the repeated sight of Monaka's body lying on the stage disturbed my otherwise-peaceful rest. The last place I want to be is back at the crime scene, especially in my sleep. In this dream, her eyes were wide open, with her bloodied hands holding the scarf wrapped tightly around her neck. Every time I thought I shook the vision, there it was again, only in a different position.

The usual crowd of nosey investigators, including local newspaper and television reporters, is already present at the Spot. Tongues have been wagging for twenty-four hours about how Mr. Graves was everything from a rapist to a child molester. Yesterday half the town didn't know much about Mr. Graves at all, other than he was HoneyMama's groundskeeper and that he was raised not far from Indian Springs. Poor Mr. Graves. Hopefully, we can shed some light on the facts soon and get him released.

I ignore the crowd outside while I wait for Dulce, who is a few minutes late, but I can't blame her. Getting dressed and walking up the road was more than a struggle. I retrieve the usual tools and place them on the table, ready to get to work.

"Look at that sexy ass," Dulce says, walking in through the side entrance. "You know we should be practicing."

I rise from my seat at the table closest to the stage and meet her halfway. I'm not sure when HoneyMama will be able to open the main stage again, even though the cleaning crew did an excellent job in here. It's almost as if Monaka's murder never happened—almost.

"There'll be plenty of time for that later, but thanks for agreeing to chat on your off time," I say, embracing her tightly. I'm glad we're finally making amends.

"You're almost back to your old self onstage, Brandy. All of that jelly looks good on you. Your waist is so small, highlighting all of this good stuff," she says, jiggling my breasts with hers.

"Thanks for the love," I say. "I could use some more of that right now."

I glance around the vast room and notice two men staring at us. Were they hoping for a free show or something? When they realize that we're not here for that, they back out without looking away, just in case.

"I assume the reunion between you and Drew's not going all that well," she says. I lead her to the table already set up for our interview. "I heard about the scene with his baby-mama the other day. Sorry, hon. They've always been like that," she says, retrieving a silver flask from her oversized Prada bag and taking a swig. "I would've come to your defense, but I was almost to the end of my vodka bottle, and I didn't want to be a quitter."

I know this shit show has been really hard on her, no matter how tough she tries to appear.

"Dulce, you know you're too much sometimes," I say, laughing at her silly self.

"As *mi abuelita* would say, God rest her soul, 'There can never be enough truth,' and I'm telling it like I see it, *mami*." Dulce cracks a smile and reveals several gold teeth. "Drew wants to be with you, and his wifey knows it."

I roll my eyes at the thought of the drama between Drew and Corrine.

"He wants to be friends again, maybe more," I say, not necessarily to Dulce. Just saying the words aloud makes me want to vomit all over the freshly cleaned floor.

"Friends. Okay, *mami*," Dulce says, lighting a cigarette and blowing circles of smoke up into the conditioned air. "They all want to be friends at the beginning. And you may start off with the best of intentions. But then, somehow his dick ends up in your mouth and your panties on the floor. After that, you're no longer just friends, no matter what he may want to call it."

Dulce takes another sip of her truth potion, hurting my ego in the process. She's as real as it gets, with a grandmother's sweetness to back it up. That's why HoneyMama gave her the name she did: Dulce befits her perfectly.

"He's trying to think of another subtitle for us at the moment," I say, ready to get to work and stop talking about Drew.

Since our interrupted dinner last night, I've been feeling very uneasy. What if Drew's partner hadn't called and we kept drinking and eating, reminiscing about what used to be? With my room only a few steps from the café, who knows what else we'd both be recovering from this morning?

"I loved you and Drew together, but he's a man on lockdown, and that's not fair to you, *chica*," she says, patting my hand. "Friends with benefits, lovers, side chick, whatever. You'd basically be his ho, and he's pimping you for next to nothing if you're not smart enough to get paid for your talents, love. That's why this stage is so important. I mean, look at it," Dulce says, looking at the stage where she last saw her lover's body, alive and then dead. "Doesn't it remind you of a shrine?"

"I honestly never thought about it like that," I say, taking notes. I would turn on the recorder, but I don't want to interrupt her flow, nor do I want to capture the personal portions of our conversation on the recorder. Charlie would have a field day if he knew that I was out here getting reacquainted with my ex, too.

"*Mira, mami,*" she says, pointing her cigarette at the gold pole. "We're at the top, looking down on these men worshiping at our feet, throwing their sacrificial offering of money on our altar," she says, making it rain gray ashes—fuck the clean floor. "We seduce the prayer out of them. I never take advantage of that power, unlike some. We're their religion, and they know it."

Dulce's waist-length, blond-streaked, curly brown hair's pulled back into a slick ponytail at the nape of her neck, giving her a façade of innocence, even though she's the oldest dancer here, after HoneyMama, of course.

"I feel you, girl," I say, tapping my pen against the legal pad, anxious to get back on topic. "But still, you have to admit that some dancers pimp right back. Clients do get mad at that shit sometimes."

"I don't pimp a *papi*. Never that. I let him think that he's the pimp, of course," she laughs. If the clients could hear our conversation, I doubt they'd laugh along.

"That's also part of the game, Brandy," Dulce continues, ignoring the men constantly moving in and out of the room. "We stroke their egos the way their wives won't. I don't give a damn if the man left his dirty drawers on the floor, took out the trash, or if he paid the bills on time. As long as he's throwing money on that stage, I'll make him think that he's my king, and I'm dancing just for him. That's real power," she says, bringing it down a notch. "That was Monaka's mantra, and she knew what the fuck she was talking about, too."

I turn on my recorder and prepare myself to listen. "Dulce, tell me what really happened to Monaka."

"The same thing that happens to all of the good ones. She got strung out on pussy power." Dulce looks from the stage to me, her eyes swollen from days of crying, not sleeping, and drinking. "That's what happened to her, to us." She empties the contents of the flask into her mouth before replacing it in the bag hanging on the back of her chair.

"What exactly are you talking about?"

"Pussy power. Those girls sucking dick in those pornos have nothing on me, *mami*. I know I get daddy sprung off my head game."

I don't need to record this part of the interview, but I'm equally fascinated, nonetheless.

"It's nothing for me to give head because I love sucking

dick—probably more than I love eating pussy. Most women can't say that. I love it when I can get a *papi* to spread his legs wide like a bitch. I really feel like I'm doing my job properly when I can get his ass up in the air."

Dulce laughs at my obvious discomfort. I guess this is the power she's referring to. If Monaka was anything like her girlfriend, I can see how someone might want more than she was willing to give.

"What does any of this have to do with Monaka's death?"

"It has everything to do with it, Brandy. Aren't you listening?" Dulce says, almost yelling. "Monaka gave up control; she started doing shit she didn't want to, and it got her killed. But dancing for the Devil, as she called working with C, made her feel powerful in a way she'd never felt before—like a real, bad-ass bitch, she said."

"Is that what happened? She made one of her clients mad?" I ask, checking the time on my cell. I need to keep Dulce on track.

Dulce grunts. "Monaka never angered anyone with her skills, especially not Mr. Graves. He always watched out for us."

Two more detectives enter the room from the foyer and point toward the stage. One of the men takes out a small camera and begins shooting pictures, as if enough of that hasn't been done in the past week.

"She was a *papi*'s dream girl: proper on the outside, a freak on the in," Dulce continues. "She was too good." Dulce looks off into the haze of her smoke, remembering something that I can't see. "I know me and Monaka didn't seem like we were always happy. But she made me smile more than I've ever done before. I miss her. The Spot will miss her."

I reach across the table for Dulce's free hand and squeeze it tightly. Dulce looks down at the cigarette burning in between her index and middle finger before tapping it in the ashtray. She looks up at me, teary-eyed.

"It's strange, being in a position where women want to be you and men want you. It's lovely, but powerful, which can also be depleting." Dulce pauses, puffs, and then continues. "I'd tell Monaka all of the time that she wasn't getting the right exchange value fucking with C."

It's almost noon and the afternoon crowd's approaching the back of the house. The dancers will be onstage soon, including Dulce.

"Once you allow someone to control your reality, your true power is up in the air," Dulce says. "If you remember nothing else, *chica,* remember this." She moves closer, takes my head in her hands, and brings her forehead to meet mine. "Control your head, or they'll control yours."

With that last drop of stripper's wisdom, Dulce releases her grip, puts out her cigarette, and exits the room, stage right.

Part Three

Monaka: High Noon

*W*HEN I RETURNED FROM THE SPRINGS THIS MORNING, DULCE WAS AL-
ready well into her morning routine. She made a fresh pot of Café Bus-
telo, although we have a Keurig, did the laundry, and made enough
pollo, beans, and rice to last us a week. I convinced her to take a bath
with me and added some of the spring water for added patience, but no
such luck. Once Dulce's hot, nothing much will cool her off. When we
first met, there was just something about our energy that aligned perfectly. I don't believe much in the moon and stars, but Dulce does and
swears we were twins in another life because of how easy we are together.
Right now, our identical energy's more at war than the peace we usually
enjoy.

"I know she's holding something over your head," Dulce says, pacing
back and forth across the intimate living area. "Please tell me it's not
what I think it is."

"Don't go there with me today," I say, nervously tidying up the place.
That's one of many things that we have in common: we love a neat
home.

"Go where? To your job tonight, because I'm coming with you," Dulce
says, tossing a throw pillow from one end of the couch, which doubles as
our bed, to the other. "Hope C's got room for one more in the private
show." She plops down onto the long side of the L-shaped furniture and
folds her arms across her chest like a stubborn teen.

I stop dusting and stare at my love. She's been worried about me, her
sick mother back in New York, and her brother on Rikers Island, but I'm

the one person she can touch at the moment. The dark circles framing her usually joyful eyes look distant and panicked, like she knows something that I don't.

"What's wrong, Dulce?" I say, sitting down on the couch next to her. I take her feet into my lap and gently massage them, going straight to her spot. "What aren't you telling me?"

"Nothing you don't already know," she says, softening a bit with each rub. "You can't trust that bitch as far as you can throw her. And if you haven't noticed, she's a solid piece of ass."

"I don't trust her, not necessarily," I say, realizing how wrong that sounds. Under any circumstances, not trusting the person in charge isn't a good look.

"Then what the fuck are you doing working with her after hours again?" Dulce says, snatching her feet from my lap to resume her pacing. "You said the last time would be the last time, Monaka. Seriously! I'm sure if you ask HoneyMama she can give you some extra shifts or find some other way," Dulce says, but I can't have her involving Honey-Mama in C's shit. That won't bode well for anyone.

"Dulce, stop! Just stop, please," I say, standing to meet her. I look down at my wife's soft brown eyes and wish she'd stop worrying, for her own good. "Every problem isn't yours to solve, or HoneyMama's to know about."

"You know she doesn't judge, Monaka. Get off your high horse and tell her what's really going on. She'll be happy to help in any way she can."

"She's already done so much for me," I say, recalling all the ways HoneyMama's changed my life for the better over the years.

If it weren't for her, I doubt I'd be alive today. And as long as C keeps her mouth shut, HoneyMama will never find out the reality of how I came to meet her. She loves me like a daughter, and I love her like the second mother I didn't know I needed. The last thing I want to do is cause HoneyMama pain.

"I have to do this for myself, by myself. I don't want anyone else involved," I say, shaking my head at the thought of another botched surgery.

The last surgery was stopped prematurely due to a complication that I still don't fully understand. What I did comprehend was that there are *no refunds if the first procedure doesn't take. Now instead of one surgery remaining, I have to pay for two out of pocket, not to mention the medications and follow-up visits. There's no way I'm asking HoneyMama for that kind of money.*

"I'll find a second job to help you pay for the surgery," Dulce says, still not getting it. "You don't have to do this, baby."

"Damn it, Dulce. Enough! I want to be proud of me, of us, but I can't when I feel so broken. Please let me have this," I say, kissing her on the nose, then her glossy lips. "After our shift at the Spot, I'm going to a job with C. And like always, I'll be back before you wake up."

"Promise, mi corazón," Dulce says, returning the affection. She is still upset, but coming to terms with my decision.

"I promise," I agree. We keep kissing until we fall onto the couch and into a relaxed lovemaking session before the first shift.

Of course, I'm coming home. There's no place else I'd rather be.

Chapter 26

AFTER DULCE LEFT FOR REHEARSAL, I STUCK AROUND TO CATCH up on my notes. There are lots of pieces to the puzzle, but there's still something we're all missing. This murder feels personal, and not just where Monaka's concerned. I think whoever did this—Walter included—wanted to ultimately hurt HoneyMama, and Monaka was a convenient means to an end, just like Mocha. I want to catch up with her before I head out for the day.

HoneyMama has been solemn since Mr. Graves's arrest, and I want to make sure she's okay. No one believes Monaka was Mr. Graves's girlfriend, least of all HoneyMama. She's made sure to vocalize her opinion to everyone, including the Butts County Police, where she has been all morning. I wanted to also brief her on my interview with Dulce.

My phone buzzes with a call. Thankfully, it's not Jimmy again. I told him that C had helped me secure my license, so he'd get off my back a bit. We'll see how long that lie holds him off.

"What's up, Shelley?"

"I know you're glad they caught the murderer," Shelley says enthusiastically. "Now you can come home. How about a small dinner party to celebrate?"

"Not so fast," I say, walking up the porch steps toward the back dance room. It's too damn hot to wait outside. "Don't believe everything you hear. Mr. Graves didn't kill anybody."

"The cops sure do seem to think so," Shelley says, her constant companion cooing in the background. "And what the hell kind of hillbilly town are you in? It looked like a blast from a redneck's past on the news."

"Shelley, I've got to go. There's still a killer on the loose and I have a story to finish," I say impatiently.

I've been defending Mr. Graves since last night. The last person I should have to convince of the innocence of one of my oldest friends is my current BFF.

"Yeah, okay. But pictures don't lie. His mug shot is quite menacing."

"I have to go." I end the call. Public opinion can be swift and delusional, including Shelley's. She needs external drama in her life to keep it spicy.

"How are you, HoneyMama?" I say, entering the house. Last night's performance wore me out, but I feel stronger than I have in years.

"I'm okay, baby," HoneyMama says, looking more tired than usual. "I wish those motherfuckers outside would leave us the hell alone."

"Well, damn. That's not very Southern of you." I pick up her coffee mug and sniff for alcohol. "Nope, you're not drunk," I say, joining her at the kitchen island and pouring a cup of my own.

"I don't need to be drunk to be fed up." HoneyMama stands to hand me the creamer.

"You can't let these folks get to you," I say, pouring the sweet creamer into my cup. "They're like vultures, and, unfortunately, they're going to be here until the last ounce of flesh has been eaten." I taste the hot liquid and allow it to warm my already-boiling blood.

"I know, Keke," HoneyMama says mournfully. We both look out of the window to where Mr. Graves would normally tend to his morning duties. "First they mislabel Monaka as some whore who got what she deserved. And now they're crucifying the most loyal man I've ever known. Paul Graves wouldn't hurt a fly, let alone one of us."

"And we'll make sure they know they've got the wrong person." I needed coffee this morning. These late nights are becoming a challenge.

"HoneyMama, Keke," Drew says, greeting each of us with a kiss on the cheek.

He looks as tossed as I feel. Guess we both need a caffeine jolt.

"How's Paul?" HoneyMama asks, looking hopeful. She pours him a cupful from the antique carafe, which he happily accepts.

"Thank you. He's holding up," he says, taking his coffee all black. "Unfortunately, it's not the first time he's seen the inside of Butts County Jail."

"No, it's not, but let's pray it's the last," HoneyMama says.

"I'm sorry about all of this," he says, locking his eyes with mine.

He looks apologetic, like we have unfinished business to tend to when this is all over. I couldn't agree more.

"I don't know why. Ain't none of this your fault, Elijah. If it weren't for you, they would've closed the Spot down when they had the chance."

"I know, HoneyMama," he says, breaking our link to focus on the matter at hand. "But still, I can't help feeling that I'm missing something important that'll lead us right to the real killer, not this fabricated bull they keep coming up with, fucking cowards." Drew is as frustrated as we are. "Now they're down there trying to dig something up in the cabins."

"We already know who the real killer is," I say, reminding everyone that we still have another number one suspect, and a damn good one. "Walter's not innocent. I know it."

"Yeah, I feel you. But we need proof linking him to the murder scene, and with his mama providing an alibi, we have little probable cause to issue a search warrant," Drew says, helping himself to a sweet potato biscuit on the countertop. "Trust me, I've already tried."

"Detective Drew, a word," Officer Cannon says through the screen door, the same jerk of a cop who couldn't keep his eyes off of Monaka's dead body.

Drew walks over to the back porch with his pastry and coffee in tow.

"What is it?"

"We found the scarf used to choke the hooker to death. It was down in one of the cabins used to make honey, right next to the main suspect's home."

Drew grabs the cop by the collar, like he wants to shake the shit out of him. "She wasn't a hooker."

"Okay, okay, Detective," the officer says apologetically. "Back off."

Drew releases him, but not before tightening his grip one more time. "Get the scarf to the lab and tell forensics to put a rush on it."

"Whatever you say, Detective." The officer straightens out his shirt collar and walks away.

Drew looks around as bewildered by the news as HoneyMama and I are.

"Mr. Graves didn't do this, and you know it," I say, reassuring both him and HoneyMama, who is close to tears herself.

"Of course not. But whoever did has done an outstanding job making it look like he did." HoneyMama grabs a bottle of honey whiskey from the lower cabinet, pours a healthy shot into her coffee, and leaves the kitchen.

"So, now what?"

"I guess someone has to tell his wife that Paul needs a good lawyer. A very good one. The sooner, the better," Drew says, looking out toward the cabins. "Mr. Graves can't take much more of this, and neither can HoneyMama."

"I'll tell his wife," I say, claiming a biscuit and heading to the back door. "You go on to the station."

"Tell Mrs. Graves that we'll get her husband home as soon as we can," Drew says, following me outside with a to-go sweet of his own. "And, Keke, still on for the rain check for last night?"

"We'll see, Drew," I say, heading toward the cabins. "Let's get through this mess first before creating another."

"Life's always messy," Drew says. His smile wakes up my everything, all the time. "Thought you would've learned that by now."

"Me too."

Why Mr. Graves and his wife chose to stay in Georgia rather than move to Mississippi where she's from, and apparently inherited quite a bit of land, used to be a common source of gossip around Indian Springs. People used to comment on how much they resembled one another, and the fact that they never had family around for the holidays or went home to visit her kinfolk we knew of. One thing is for certain, though. Paul and Paula Graves are still fiercely loyal to each other. When they fight, they fight hard, but they always forgive each other the next day.

"Keke, it's nice to see you. Paul said you were back in town," Mrs. Graves says, welcoming me inside the quaint home. "What brings you by?"

"Unfortunately, I have some bad news." I accept the Mason jar full of cool water she hands me, grateful for her hospitality. My memories of her, way back when, aren't so pleasant. "It looks like Mr. Graves won't be coming home as soon as we thought. But Detective Drew is doing his absolute best to make sure that the real killer is found so that we can get your husband out of jail as soon as possible."

Her eyes swell, but she doesn't let a single tear drop. "But Detective Drew assured me that the matter would be cleared up this morning. We have Bible study this afternoon, and Paul's the presiding elder."

"It's going to take a little while longer, ma'am." I pat Mrs. Graves on the hand. She doesn't need to hear about the scarf near the honey cabins right now, and not from me. "Do you know of an attorney you can call? If not, I'm sure HoneyMama will be glad to help."

Mrs. Graves shoots daggers at me for mentioning Honey-

Mama's name. She's never been fond of her husband's employer, and I'm sure she sees this incident as her fault.

"I've known Paul all my life. It wasn't until we were already in love that we realized we weren't supposed to get married, under the law," she says, tears gradually making their way down her smooth, almond-toned face. "It wasn't our fault that we shared the same great-grandmother. Didn't find out about it until we were already engaged to be married. As far as we were concerned, our union was divinely blessed, still is."

I guess the town was right about them having something to hide.

"I know what they're saying about us out there, what they've always said," she continues, pointing at the front door, which sits between two yellow-wallpapered walls lined with family pictures. "He may have been kind to the Devil's daughters, but he never cheated on me, and he never would. I was his first and have remained his only woman. That's the way the good Lord intended it. My husband's innocence will be revealed."

Like HoneyMama said, couples go through thick and thin. And from what Paula Graves just shared, she and her husband have been through much worse.

"For the record, I know Mr. Graves is innocent."

She wipes her face dry and forces a thin smile. "Honey, those rednecks have had it out for my husband for decades. I know he didn't do it, but that ain't proof. Find the real killer and bring my man home to me where he belongs."

"Yes, ma'am." I look past Mrs. Graves to see police officers and crime scene investigators moving in and out of the honey cabin nearby. "Who'll tend to the bees?" Making and selling pure honey, creamed honey, and honey wine's their family side business.

"I will," Mrs. Graves says, pointing to the two netted hats perched on the coatrack behind the front door. "We are partners in every way, Keke. Now, if you'll excuse me. I have some housework to do and Bible verses to study. I guess I'll have to lead the study today."

"Have a good day, Mrs. Graves. And again, if you need help finding an attorney—" I begin, but she cuts me off.

"We'll be just fine. I'm sure the church has a lawyer we can call upon. Please tell Detective Drew thank you for all he's doing for my husband," she says, taking the glass from my hand and ushering me toward the front door. "I'll be by to bring him something to eat later on."

"I'll let him know."

Chapter 27

SPEAKING WITH MRS. GRAVES SHOOK ME MORE THAN I CARE TO admit. She reminds me too much of my righteous, judgmental mother. I hurry through the screen door back into the welcoming kitchen and allow the oversized ceiling fans and air-conditioning to calm my nerves.

"Drew still here?" I ask HoneyMama, who's baking for tonight's show. I can tell from the furrow between her brows that she's still upset.

"He went back to the station," HoneyMama says, beating the dough harder than necessary. "Said he wanted to make sure the other officers treated Paul right when they get him in the interrogation room, whatever the hell that means."

"Shit." I'm trying to process it all, but it makes no sense. How did Mr. Graves end up taking the fall, and how are we going to fix it?

My phone vibrates in my pocket. Charlie has been blowing up my phone all damn day. Apparently dumb-ass Margeaux went out with the story this morning about Mr. Graves being arrested, and Charlie's tickled pink. I hope she likes sucking his dick, because after I expose the truth, she's going to be on her knees for a very long time.

"What's the matter?"

"Nothing I can't handle," I say, sending Charlie a quick reply. "I wanted to tell Drew that Mrs. Graves sends her gratitude."

"Does she, now?" HoneyMama says sarcastically. "Did she hire an attorney yet?"

"She said she'd look into it."

"What the hell's taking her so long? She hasn't even gone down there once to check on her husband since his booking," HoneyMama says, dropping the biscuits onto the baking sheet. "That woman is a piece of work."

"At least they're faithful to each other," I say, thinking about Ian's scary ass. "It's more than I can say for a lot of relationships."

"Whatever," HoneyMama says. I sense that the issues between her and Mrs. Graves run deep.

"Well, she's prepping a care basket to take to the jail in a little while," I say, attempting to reassure HoneyMama that his wife ain't all bad. "She knows he didn't do this, too. I'm sure of it."

"Hola, mamis," Dulce says, looking like she's going to the club rather than rehearsal.

It's nice to see her acting more like her old self, Gucci shades with the oversized bag to match and all, even if she hasn't had a chance yet to fully grieve.

"Good morning, sunshine," HoneyMama says, returning the two kisses on both cheeks that Dulce planted on her.

"Hey, sis," I say, hugging Dulce.

"You seem a little off today, *chica.* What gives?" Dulce joins us at the counter and pours herself a cup of coffee.

"I was just thinking about my ex-boyfriend. We broke up a couple of days ago."

"You have a boyfriend?" HoneyMama asks. "Please dish. We need a distraction from all of this," she says, wildly gesturing her hands above her head. I don't know if she's more surprised that I had one, or that I didn't tell her the whole story.

"And all this time I thought you were being deprived," Dulce says, touching my thigh. "You've been getting it in, girl. I'm proud of you."

"Well, I was deprived," I say, thinking about all of the times Ian would disappear for no apparent reason. "But I had a boyfriend or lover or whatever you want to call him for a while."

"How were you deprived if he had all of those titles?" Honey-Mama asks, taking a tray of biscuits out of the oven and placing them on the counter before putting the other in. I hope she didn't beat the hell out of all the batter, or we won't have any soft ones to serve at tonight's show.

"He's a professional at playing the disappearing act, and I miss my lover."

"Don't call him that, because the word 'lover' is definitely a verb, and your dude sounds lazy as fuck," HoneyMama says, taking all of the shade she's feeling for Mrs. Graves, Butts County, and every other enemy of the Spot and throwing it all on Ian. "Every person you fuck shouldn't be given that title."

"That's the truth," I agree. HoneyMama hit that one on the head.

"In my opinion, sex with a man is never about love," Dulce says. "Your father fucked your mother, plain and simple. Where do you think the term motherfucker came from? Look it up if you don't believe me."

"Dulce, do you know how crazy you really are?" I ask, grateful for a little comic relief.

"*Sí, mami,*" she says, nodding. "But I'm still right."

"Brandy, there'll come a time when you will absolutely re-claim your honey spot. When you do, never let it go again, you hear?" HoneyMama says, joining us at the counter. "Remember, child, it's that spot only you can touch. When you choose to share it, give it freely and reap the benefits thereof. Otherwise, keep that shit close to the chest." She quickly pats her full bosom, leaving a red indentation in the center of her bare chest.

Dulce and I both nod in agreement while devouring the hot biscuits with fresh honey drizzled on top. HoneyMama always knows how to say what she wants us to know for sure.

"In all honesty, I thought Ian was the one," I say, my throat full of tears. "After this experience, I think that I'm ready to give up on love altogether."

Dulce looks like she wants to agree with me, but stops herself. I know it's different when you've lost the love of your life rather than some fool just up and leaving again.

"You can't run from love, Brandy. You just have to learn to sleep in the bed you've made, and also recognize when it's time to change the sheets."

"Hallelujah!" Dulce yells loud enough for the nosey neighbors and other outsiders still roaming out front to hear.

Jambalaya looks up from his comfy window perch and then falls right back to sleep, used to Dulce's loud ass.

"I don't know why men want other pussy, and I say this, having been *other pussy* on more than one occasion." In full confession mode. The kitchen's always had that effect on us.

"Don't feel bad, *chica,*" Dulce says, pulling out her flask full of courage, not that she needs it. With or without liquor, Dulce's always been good at speaking her mind. "Trust, you're either the main bitch, or the other bitch—there's never just one for too long. For whatever reason, men need both."

"Dulce, not all men cheat," HoneyMama says, smiling at her silliest dancer. "Look at Paul Graves, an honorable man if there ever was one."

Dulce offers us both a shot of rum and we happily oblige: it's five o'clock somewhere.

"I don't mean no disrespect, HoneyMama, but yes they do. You're one or the other every time." Dulce takes a big swig and continues.

"I just wish I knew why men lie. And they lie about the smallest shit possible," I say, recalling some of Drew's stupid-ass lies during our relationship. "But even more than that, I wish I knew why we can't live without their bullshit. We could live like fucking goddesses if it weren't for that damned dick."

"I hear you, baby girl. That's why I like it here," Dulce says, rising from her barstool and pointing at the logo on the back wall. "This place is the most realistic shit ever, in my book. Here men cannot lie. Here daddies don't have to say a word to speak the truth. It's all over their drawers by the time they leave." Dulce drops her ass to the floor and winds back up, grinding up against HoneyMama's leg, who's getting a kick out of the impromptu show.

"Hey, y'all," one of the dancers from the B team says, entering through the back door.

"Good afternoon, Caramel," HoneyMama says. "I don't know if you've met Brandy yet. I told you about her, one of our best dancers."

"Hello," I say, shaking her hand. "Caramel befits you perfectly."

"Thank you," she says shyly. "And I remember. Nice to meet you, Brandy."

HoneyMama smiles and directs her to take a seat. "Doesn't her name suit her? She's the color of caramel, sweet as ever, and she sticks to our guests like a true hostess."

"Okay, so what's she doing here?" Dulce asks, unimpressed. "Morning rehearsals are for team A dancers only."

"Dulce, play nice." HoneyMama gently checks our tipsy girl. "Caramel's training for a promotion."

We all fall silent, remembering the Spot's down a permanent dancer on the A team.

"And we may have to promote another dancer if C keeps playing games."

"Amen to that, HoneyMama," Dulce agrees.

I haven't asked the B and C team dancers about C, because I know the lower teams don't interest her much. There'd be limited interaction, if any. But maybe this chick knows something, since she's next in line for a promotion. C's like a vampire when it comes to new stripper blood.

"Caramel, has C ever approached you about working outside of the Spot?" I ask.

"Yes, but she seems shady to me—no offense, HoneyMama."

"None taken," HoneyMama says, smirking. "What gave you that impression, Caramel?"

She looks around nervously before continuing. "I overheard C on the phone the night before the murder making a deal with a client to leave him alone with another dancer for the evening, but I didn't know which dancer it was."

"Why didn't you say something before?" HoneyMama jumps to her bare feet, pissed all over again.

"Because I ain't no snitch, and no one asked," Caramel says matter-of-factly. "Besides, she's always doing that shit. She even approached me about entertaining some private VIP client, but I told her I'm not interested in her or her little side tricks."

"Good for you, little *mami*," Dulce says, offering Caramel a drink, but she declines.

"Is there anything else about C's private client that we need to know?" I ask, taking my notepad out of my purse.

Caramel checks the wall clock, reminding us all that it's still a workday. "Later that day, a large bouquet of flowers was delivered to C with several hundred-dollar bills and a thank-you note attached. As usual, I tried my best to ignore her. She's always bragging about receiving nice gifts from clients."

"Brandy, enough's enough," HoneyMama says, slapping the marble countertop so hard that the cups, spoons, and other dishes rattle. "Meet C on her own turf and trap that bitch. That way, she's got nowhere to run."

Neither will I, but I'm over it, too. C's been running game on us and the cops for long enough. It's time for me to woman up and force her to tell me the truth. If that means I have to go to the bitch's den, then so be it.

Chapter 28

*A*FTER TODAY'S EXCITEMENT, I DECIDED TO TAKE THE NIGHT OFF at the Spot and drive back to Atlanta to spend the night in my own bed. I needed a break from the murder scene, the pole, Drew, and Mr. Graves's arrest. Charlie has been after me to finish the story, since as far as he's concerned, the murderer has been apprehended. As far as I'm concerned, there's no story until I interview C. Something tells me that she has the missing link that'll make everything about this case fall into place.

My phone vibrates with a call from Shelley. I would let the call go to voicemail, but knowing her, she'll just call right back.

"You didn't call me back, trick," Shelley says into my ear. After our last conversation, I really didn't feel like entertaining another one of her housewife theories.

"Because I've been working, Shelley," I say, considering what to wear for tomorrow's interview with C. "Ever heard of it?"

"As a matter of fact, I have. I'm doing it right now as I change one baby's diaper and cook dinner for the rest of the herd," Shelley snaps back. She's a fierce defender of the working-house-mom movement. "How goes it?"

"Honestly, it's been a shitty day, and I can't get past Ian dumping me through a text message."

"At least it wasn't a Post-it note and his name's not Berger," Shelley says, recalling one of our favorite *Sex and the City* episodes. "Besides, you're a hot piece of ass. All you have to do is get back out there and find another man to help you get over the jackass."

"Girl, please. The last thing I feel is attractive."

I move through the motley crew of hangers and clothes, some I can fit into, most I can't. I need something that says boss bitch without appearing to try too hard. C knows how to tear a person down from the bottom up, and I want to make sure that I'm confident about every piece of my outfit before our encounter.

"Keke, how many memes do I have to send?" she says, referring to the dozens of forwards I receive from her on a daily basis. "The power of attraction is in your thoughts. How you see yourself is all in your head, girl."

"Was that from the book club, or straight from Oprah's mouth?"

I reach the back of the closet and stop at the worn Atlanta Braves T-shirt: Ian's.

"Shut up, hater," Shelley says, only half-playing. She's serious about her self-help collection. "You know you want to be just like her when you grow up. Speaking of child's play, have you heard from the jackass? Can't believe he had us fooled into thinking he might be the one."

"Actually, yeah," I say, putting the phone on speaker so that I can read her the text. I love how she's always on my side in any situation no matter what. We've been ride-or-die through many relationships, jobs, and other life events and I don't see that changing anytime soon. "He sent a message earlier saying how much he misses my company."

"And what did you say? Shit!" she mutters. The sound of pots clashing with metal utensils in the background grows louder. Sounds like she's cooking a feast.

"I said I want my fountain pen back. I left it at his house weeks ago and he still hasn't returned it."

"Seriously, Keke?" Shelley asks.

"Hell yes," I say, removing the soft red cotton T-shirt off the hanger and bringing it to my nose. Damn, I miss his scent. "You're not a writer, Shelley. You wouldn't understand."

"You can always buy another pen, Keke. Just admit that you want to see the brother."

Leave it to my best friend to call me out for being the weak broad that I am. It's almost as if she can see me sniffing the man's clothes.

"That's the one thing I'm going to miss most about being with Ian: writing was our strongest link, other than excellent sex," I groan, my body responding to the memory of his touch. If I'm not careful, I'm going to end up in Sandy Springs knocking on his apartment door. I replace the T-shirt and close the closet door.

When I step back into the small dining area, someone's brights are shining straight through my blinds. I peek outside to check the parking lot below, where I notice a familiar black Audi parked in the visitor's spot.

"Speak of the devil," I say aloud, but not to Shelley in particular. Talk about power of attraction.

"Keke, what is it?" she asks, concerned. I can hear the kitchen timer beeping in the background.

"I'll get it, Mom," one of her boys says. Having four kids under four is more than a notion.

"Ian's here," I whisper, as if he can hear me from downstairs. I don't think tinted windows come with supersonic hearing.

"Are you okay with seeing Ian so soon after he pulled that disappearing shit . . . again?" she whispers back. Her spies are within earshot.

"I don't know," I say, glancing in the mirror hanging between the door and the window. I look as tired as I feel. "I gave him the option of mailing the pen, but I guess he decided to drop it off, instead."

"Yeah. That, and a little something else," Shelley says, cracking up at her own joke. "But, seriously, please don't give in to the dick." She knows me too well.

"No, no more sex until I'm sure it'll be the last penis that I see, promise." I don't even believe that, but I'm going to try to be strong. It's been a minute since we last connected, and seeing Drew on a daily basis hasn't helped calm me down one bit.

"Yeah, right. Wait until you have a son," Shelley says, ignoring the fact that I don't want children, and she knows it. "Then you'll see more penis than you ever wanted to."

I can't imagine raising a kid. With my track record, I'd most likely be a single mom. My mother would have a field day calling me all kinds of biblical synonyms for a slut—her favorite being Jezebel, which became my nickname after the incident—and I'm not ready to relive those flashbacks.

"I've had a long day and need an equally long shower, alone. I'll call you tomorrow, girl."

"Be strong, Keke. You're too good for the shit he's put you through. Demand better, no matter how horny you are."

As soon as I hang up with Shelley, my phone rings with Coltrane's melodic rhythm. God, I've missed his ringtone.

"Ian."

"What's up?" Ian asks pensively. The car door shuts behind him.

"I don't know." I remove my shoes and head straight for the bathroom. I have to at least get a quick washup in before he sees me. "You tell me."

"Keke, don't treat me like one of your interviews," he says, walking up the single flight of stairs, one by one. Unlike his usual quick trot, he's taking his time this evening.

"I can't help it when I know there's more to the story." I prop the cell between my right shoulder and ear, reach underneath my shirt, and unclasp my bra. The last thing I want is for him to hear our echo in the hallway. Luckily, most of my neighbors keep to themselves and ignore outside conversations.

"I'm at your front door," he says, his footsteps coming to a halt. "Are you going to let me in?"

"I wasn't expecting company. I'll need a minute," I say, removing the rest of my work clothes and opting for a short sundress hanging on the back of the bathroom door. He usually doesn't care what I wear, as long as I'm not wearing a bra.

A few minutes later, I open my front door and bypass our

usual polite greeting. Ian walks past me and into my small dining room.

"How are you?"

"Good, you?" I don't know if I should be relieved to see a man who puts me through so many changes, but I am happy he's here.

I watch him fall back into his comfy pattern, as if the breakup text never happened. Ian takes off his loafers and puts them in the usual spot near the front door, where his house shoes still sit.

He walks into the kitchen, stands behind me, and wraps his toned arms around my waist. "Better now."

"Whatever," I say, refusing to return the affection, no matter how much my body wants to betray me and my promise to Shelley. She's right: I do deserve better.

"I've missed you. Can't you tell?" Ian rubs his protruding manhood against my ass. I can't help but get excited at the prospect of having all of that inside me, but I need to hold out if I truly want more.

"Not really," I say, pushing him away. "It's been a long day, Ian. Other than my pen, I don't want anything from you."

"Look, I know I said that I didn't want to be in a relationship, but these past few days have given me some time to think," he says, turning me around and pulling me into him. "We're on a whole other level now, Keke. I know that."

"So the next time you have a near-death experience, I won't have to find out about it on Facebook?"

"I don't think that'll happen again." He smiles big, showcasing his single sexy dimple.

"You know what I mean, Ian. A real relationship has full disclosure."

"Whatever you need," Ian says, kissing my forehead, and then my nose.

I can't help but melt into his solid embrace, even if I know it's a lie. "Whatever I need?"

"Yes," he says between pecks. "Whatever you need."

"I need a real kiss, Ian." We rarely kiss deeply, unless we're in bed. I look into his hazel eyes, begging him to tell me the truth, not just what I want to hear. "Can you do that?"

"Close your eyes."

I obey and allow Ian to run the show. Like Dulce said, let them think they're in control.

"Open your mouth."

He kisses me deep and slow at first. Then all of the passion we've been holding in takes over. We fall to the floor and tear at each other's clothes. Ian enters me, and the text, C's punk ass, and Drew's beautiful smile all fade into the background as Ian eliminates my worries, one stroke at a time.

Chapter 29

A GOOD FUCK THE NIGHT BEFORE ALWAYS PUTS ME IN A CHEERFUL mood the next morning, even if I know that part of the day will be spent alone with C. Ian stayed long enough for a quick breakfast and then we went our separate ways; me back to Indian Springs, and him back to work, freelancing. Ian promised to call this evening and gave me every assurance that things will be different this time around. I want to believe him, but can't help the familiar doubt setting in. Dulce may be crazy, but she was on point. We're either the woman, or the other woman, and I'm still not sure where I stand with Ian.

Drew called while I was on the way back down I-75 and asked me to meet him at the coroner's office first thing. I hope he can't tell that I got tuned up last night. That's not a conversation I want to have with him. Even if he goes home to another woman every night, Drew's always been a bit possessive.

"Morning, Ms. McCoy," John says from inside the coroner's office. "Detective Drew should be back any moment. He went to go see about Paul Graves."

"Is Mr. Graves okay?" I ask, taking a seat in front of the neatly organized but packed reception desk.

"Yeah, just ran into a little something with one of the sheriff's boys during the interrogation," John says, like it's nothing.

Sounds like police brutality to me. With my recorder in hand, I turn it on and begin my own line of questioning, just in case.

"Tell me about the relationship between the sheriff and the police captain?"

"It's actually a threesome, with the two of them and the mayor," John says, taking a seat on the bench next to mine. "They were all real tight growing up, right here in Flovilla."

"There's something that Mrs. Graves said that's been bothering me," I say, shuffling through my legal pad until I get to the right page. "She said that they've been after Paul for a while. What's that all about?"

"Oh, just kid stuff," John says, shifting uncomfortably in his seat. "Like I said, they all grew up together. Just a little friendly hazing, nothing more." John sounds like he's trying to convince himself of the lie more than he's trying to sell it to me.

"Doesn't seem like Mr. Graves thought the hazing was too friendly."

John stares at me hard for a few moments, without blinking. I stare back just as fierce. He's not the only one who can play word games.

"Sorry about that," Drew says, interrupting our quiet standoff. "I took Mr. Graves some food. He hasn't eaten since last night."

"What the hell happened to three meals a day?" I ask, still recording. "I know we're in the Deep South, but human rights are still in order."

"Mr. Graves doesn't like the food down at the station," John says, looping his thumbs through the belt loops on his pants. "You could say he's on his own hunger strike, of sorts."

"Don't worry, Keke." Drew shows me a container full of fried fish, hush puppies, fries, and coleslaw. "Mrs. Graves and Honey-Mama have been keeping him well fed—me too."

John looks disapprovingly at the full platter. "I'm due in court on that drug bust. Let me know if the coroner finds anything new."

"Will do," Drew says, switching places with his partner.

"Ms. McCoy."

"Detective Miller." I turn my recorder off and join Drew on the other side of the short hallway.

"So they all know what happened to Mr. Graves back in the day, including your partner?" I ask, stealing a thick fry from Drew's plate.

"Of course. Hell, they were all probably there that night," Drew says, dipping the catfish in tartar sauce and taking a bite. "All of these good ole boys roll deep like that."

"I have a feeling that the mayor put pressure on the sheriff and the captain to wrap this case up quickly, but why?" I ask, stealing another fry. "He doesn't give a damn about Honey-Mama or Monaka."

"Which means they've got bigger fish to fry," he says, cracking a smile.

I forgot how corny he can be.

"Drew, that sounded so country, and you know I'm country."

"It was too easy not to pass up. Had to give it a shot. Speaking of," he says, leaning in for a kiss.

Before I can sidestep his advance—two men in twelve hours is too much for me to deal with—the single door that leads from the waiting area into the back of the building opens and scares me half to death.

"Detective Drew, the sheriff said you wanted to see me," a scrawny old white man dressed in a white lab coat says. "I'm Dr. Hunt."

"Yes. We have a few more questions about the dancer who was slain at the Spot last week," Drew says, closing the container and standing to meet the odd-looking man, eye-to-eye.

Neither of them extends a hand toward the other. A hazard of their professions, I presume.

"What can I do for you? I am quite busy," he says, rubbing his partially bald head with the tip of a pen.

"Aren't we all," Drew says, dabbing the corners of his mouth with a paper napkin. "Wondered if there was anything unusual about the body we may have missed the first time around?"

"More unusual than what I already shared with your department?" the coroner says, more irritated than curious.

"Yes. For example, did she have anything on her person that might've stood out, like a new tattoo, or an unusual scar?"

The coroner places the ink pen in the lab coat's chest pocket. "Gonna shoot straight with you, Detective. Strippers and such don't hold much interest around here," the coroner says, checking the wall clock. "There were a lot of unusual things about her, if you know what I mean," he says, seemingly alluding to a secret that I'm not privy to.

"We don't mean to waste your time, but this is important," I say sarcastically. These judgmental bastards have worked my last nerve. "Can you remember anything out of the ordinary?"

The coroner glares at us, clearly out of what little patience he had. "You've got my official report. Everything's in there," he says, removing his thick medical goggles and wiping them clean on his coat. "We've got more important things to look into than a freak that met her fate, and not a moment too soon, if you ask me. If there's nothing else I can help you with, I need to get back to work." The coroner walks back down the hall and leaves us in the waiting area.

Before either of us can protest the rude departure, Drew's phone rings.

"Detective Drew," he says, pointing to my bag on the floor.

I pick up my work brief and prepare to leave.

"We have to go," Drew says, hurrying toward the double doors. "There's been another attack."

"What? Who?" I say, following behind.

"Tiramisu was just admitted to County General," he says, still listening to the caller as he opens the door and we exit the stark building. Something tells me there's more to the coroner's story, but we'll revisit that topic later. "Luckily, she's still alive."

"Does HoneyMama know?"

"She's already on her way," Drew says, disconnecting the call.

"At least we can prove that it wasn't Mr. Graves," I say, following Drew to his squad car.

He unlocks the car doors.

"Maybe, maybe not." Drew starts the engine and backs out onto the main road. I have a feeling that we're going to make it to the hospital in record time, with or without a siren. "Things have a way of sticking around here, even when anybody with good sense knows they shouldn't."

When we arrive at the hospital, reporters and curious bystanders are crowding the opening, each throwing around their bullshit theories about what happened this time. HoneyMama must be beside herself. Two of her girls hurt in less than two weeks—it is more than even she can bear.

"She's in the ICU," Drew says, leading the way through the crowded corridor.

When we get to Tiramisu's floor, HoneyMama is at the nurses' station talking to the staff. She signals for us to join her.

"Our girl is going to need surgery," she says, reaching for our hands.

"Several surgeries, ma'am," one of the white coats adds. "If you'd like to speak with her, I suggest you do so soon. She'll be out for a while, once the sedatives kick in."

"We hear you, Doctor," Drew says, thankful for the opening. "This is Keke McCoy. She's helping us with the case."

"You've got two minutes, then we need to take her back," another doctor says, pointing to a room several feet away.

"I'll wait here," HoneyMama says, her voice shaken. "She can't take too much excitement."

We walk through the heavy curtains and stand beside the hospital bed, careful not to disturb the tubes and other equipment occupying the tight space. It's painful to look at her once-lovely face, now battered beyond recognition.

"Who did this to you, T?" I ask.

"I don't know," she mutters, barely able to open her gauze-filled jaws.

"Was it a man, a woman, tall or short?" Drew asks, standing as close to the bed as he can without touching it. He holds back his emotion in an attempt to stay professional, but the tears are there and ready to fall. "Anything you can remember would be helpful, T."

"Tall, thin. Couldn't tell if it was a man or a woman," Tiramisu mutters, gently moving her head from side to side. "All I re-member is someone approaching me from behind and grab-bing me by the throat."

"You couldn't tell if the hands belonged to a man or a woman?" Drew presses.

"It felt like a man's chokehold, but I remember seeing bright, lavender-painted toenails in a bad-ass pair of peekaboo heels be-fore I passed out."

HoneyMama follows the doctor back inside, ending the brief interview.

"That's enough for now," the doctor says, checking Tiramisu's chart. "The nurse will be in soon to prep you for surgery, young lady."

"Okay, Doctor," Drew says, patting Tiramisu on the foot. "We'll check on you tomorrow."

"Drew, wait," Tiramisu says, slightly raising her voice. "I need to tell you something."

The doctor looks at us impatiently and leaves the room. I turn around to follow him out, but Drew grabs my hand, urging me to stay.

"We're listening," Drew says, pulling me closer.

Tiramisu hesitates before speaking. I know she's not my biggest fan, but this is bigger than C's petty drama. We need to catch the monster that did this, and as a survivor, she's our biggest lead yet.

"It was a private client," Tiramisu whispers, her voice barely audible above the loud drip of the IV. "I didn't want to dance for him, but C gave me the key. I didn't have a choice."

"The key?" Drew asks.

"It can't be," I say, remembering the phrase from my days at The Pimp Palace. Mocha was the last one to hold the key, right before she was murdered.

"What do you know about it?" T asks, attempting to sneer, but her mouth's too badly hurt to be much of a smart-ass, and the drugs are kicking in.

"Enough to know that it's nothing to play with."

"What's this about a key?" Drew asks, making note of the mention.

"There are different keys for different masters and mistresses. Depends on the client's request," T says, taking a deep breath before she continues. "C holds the master key for all of the rooms, belts, and cuffs. She's the pole mistress."

"'Rooms, belts, and cuffs'?" Drew repeats, baffled by Tiramisu's confession.

"Yes. I had the key to my master's room last night. When the girls came to dress me, I was gagged and my hands were tied behind my back—that wasn't unusual, but when I was escorted to my master's room, he was a she. I told C a long time ago that I don't fuck with women, but there was something strange about this chick."

"In what way?" Drew says.

T starts to breathe heavily. "She had grayish-blue eyes, so pale they were almost white." Without warning, her eyes roll to the back of her head. She passes out.

"Help!" Drew yells as he rushes to T's side. He checks for a pulse, but the buzzing flat line from the heart monitor beats him to it.

I back up next to the door to make room.

"Shit," Drew says. He tilts her head back and begins CPR.

The hospital staff rushes inside and pushes Drew out of the way.

"Damn it. Get the crash cart!" the doctor yells out of the opened door. "Nurse, call the OR and tell them we're on our way up. You two, out."

Drew and I step out into the hall and stare at Tiramisu's limp body as the doctor attempts to shock her back to life. I know Drew won't be able to fathom what I have to tell him about my last few weeks working at The Pimp Palace, but he'll have to get a grip. I thought C was done with all of that mistress bullshit, but I guess it's hard to teach an old bitch new tricks, even when she has a teacher like HoneyMama around to guide her.

"Here," HoneyMama says, handing Drew a small plastic bag as

we watch the staff hard at work saving T's life. "This was at her feet when they found her last night."

"'Light as a feather/Nobody does it better. Tiramisu,'" Drew says, reading the note aloud.

I take the bag from Drew and immediately recognize it as another epitaph. "This can't be a coincidence."

"What is it?" Drew asks.

"'Thick and sweet/Just like homemade fudge. Mocha,'" I say, recalling a similar note left at Mocha's crime scene years before. "He's leaving epitaphs for his victims."

"*Victims,* as in more than the two that we know of?"

"Yeah," I say, looking at them both. "I wasn't sure before, but now I'm almost certain this is the same person who killed Monaka and possibly Mocha."

HoneyMama turns pale at the mention of Mocha's name. Drew never knew her, but HoneyMama always considered Mocha one of the dancers she could've saved.

"I'll have to do some research when I get back to Atlanta. I know we have more information in the *Metro Journal*'s archives."

HoneyMama looks at Tiramisu and then back at me. "Let us know what you find out, Brandy. And by all means, dig deep with C. We have to get to the bottom of this before anyone else gets hurt."

Chapter 30

*O*UT OF PROFESSIONAL COURTESY, I SEND C A TEXT INFORMING her that I'll be late, but not why. If she doesn't know about Tiramisu, I'm not going to be the one to tell her. I left the hospital and came straight here, but stayed in my car to process what's happened. I'm sure Drew will be questioning C soon enough about both attacks at the Spot. Hopefully, she's smart enough to cooperate, even if it's just for protection. If I were the killer, C'd be next on the list.

I hate her, I really do. I know it sounds cruel, but there are just some people that should've never been born. HoneyMama took sympathy on C and her daughter and has been paying for that good deed ever since. Now I have to go and talk to this woman with my professional hat on. I'm not usually one to let a broad fuck with my head or my money, but if anyone can make me switch hats, it's C.

When I arrive at C's apartment complex, I instantly remember why I hate coming out this way. It's located smack-dab in the middle of the hood and way too crowded. I park in front of her building and exhale deeply before exiting my car. Before I make it up the flight of stairs, I instantly begin to sweat. It's too hot for this shit.

"'Bout time you showed up," C says, holding the apartment door open. Most people would get dressed before their company arrives, but not C. She always prefers an audience for her show. "Some of us have busy schedules, you know."

How can she have such a foul attitude so early in the day?

"Hello to you, too, C," I say, entering the cool, dark apartment. Her apartment's loud and whorish, just like her.

"You can do away with the bullshit formalities, Brandy," she says, closing the door and leading the way into her living room, which she's turned into a bedroom, complete with a stripper's pole in the middle of the messy space. "Honey said you wanted to talk, and like I told her, I don't have shit to say."

"I know you don't give a damn about me, but you can show HoneyMama some respect and call her by her full name." We sit across from each other at her dining-room table, ready for the confrontation I've been anticipating since coming back to the Spot.

"I'm a grown-ass woman. What I'm gon' look like, calling another woman who ain't my mother mama?" C says, getting up from her chair to fumble through the pile of clothes on the floor.

"The same way you look calling a grown-ass man daddy," I say, clearing a space on the cluttered table to make room for my writing pad and recorder. You'd think with all of the money C's supposedly making, she could afford a housekeeper.

"That shit don't fly with me, I don't care if she is the owner," Couverture says, sucking her teeth like only a true Jamaican can. She's the only person I know who truly loathes HoneyMama, which means that there's something seriously wrong with C.

"When I first started dancing there, she made it perfectly clear that we were all partial owners: stocks, bonds, all that shit." She takes out a cigarette and lights it before sitting back down. "If it weren't for the benefits, I would've been up out that bitch long time ago, but you know how it is out here. You got to get your hustle on wherever it comes. And my game's tight right where it is, you feel me?" she says, blowing the minty smoke into the stale air.

"This job's more than a hustle, C," I say, waving smoke out of my face. "HoneyMama gives you way more opportunities than you'd normally have stripping at another club."

"Can she give me Stripper of the Year?" she says, slapping her curvy hips. "No, I don't think so, because she won't allow us to enter those types of contests on behalf of The Honey Spot."

"That's not what I'm talking about." It's a wonder she didn't become a model, as stunning as she is, but the bitch's a bit on the raunchy side.

"Then, what exactly are we talking about? I know you're on some other shit and you think all niggas and bitches are your friends and shit, but that's what fucked your shit up in the first place," she says, stubbing her cigarette into the full coconut shell doubling as an ashtray. "Look at you. You used to be kind of cute and thick. Now you just look tired and fat."

"C, I know we've had our differences in the past, but this isn't a personal visit," I say, trying to maintain my professionalism and stay on point.

"Don't try and be all sweet and shit to me. I know you're looking to gain 'reporter of the year' or some other fancy-ass title, just like me. So, what the fuck do you really want, Brandy? And, more importantly, what do I get in return?"

There's the C I know and hate. It's time to cut this interview short and get to the point.

"C, where were you the night of Monaka's murder?" I tap the recorder to let her know it's on.

"On top of my man. You?" She crosses her legs and bends over, allowing her breast to fall out of her loose-fitting robe.

That's it. This interview's over. Trying to get a straight answer out of her without backup's a waste of my time.

"Working," I say, collecting my items. "Call me when you feel like cooperating." I drop my card on the table and stand to leave.

"They'll never find out who really killed Monaka," she says to my back. "The main stage being closed down for her investigation's putting us all in a tight space. If this shit goes on for another week, I'm going to have to go back to dancing at the Palace permanently."

"We'll see about that," I say, struggling to get through the front door. She's locked every single bolt—is that to keep people out, or her victims in?

C gets up, opens her robe, and allows it to fall to the floor. "Don't you miss dancing for Drew?"

"Yes, I do." Our entire relationship started with a lap dance, but she doesn't need to know that.

C looks at her naked reflection in the wall of mirrors, and then back at me.

"I hear there's an opening down at the Spot. Want your old job back, Brandy?"

"I can't believe that even you could be so cruel, C," I say. "Let me out."

C blocks my escape, breathing hard into my ear. "Believe it. It's a bitch-eat-bitch world out here—literally."

C pins my back to the door in a full frontal. If she were Ian or Drew, I'd be completely turned on. But she's not, and this broad needs to get off of me.

"Back up, C." I try to push away from her, but it's no use. If she doesn't move, I'll have to hurt her to get out.

"You know you miss all of this," she says like a cat toying with its prey. "Want to jump on my pole?"

The last time some shit like this happened, I was young, stupid, and lit.

"Back the fuck up," I say again.

This time, she backs off. I straighten the crushed bag in my hand and smooth my dress down. Finally she opens the front door and I cross the threshold.

"You'd better watch yourself, C. I'm not the same trick you knew and hated."

"Oh . . . I think you are. You're just buried inside of that fat suit, but I'm sure we can find ways to work it off. I have a new daddy who'd love to meet your chubby ass, just like Big Jim." C lets out a disturbing laugh more akin to a roar, sending shivers down my spine.

I wonder if HoneyMama knows exactly how crazy this chick really is. I doubt it. If she did, I'm sure she would've fired her ass a long, long time ago.

Chapter 31

*I*T TOOK ME ALL NIGHT TO FALL ASLEEP AFTER VISITING C YESTERDAY. Her scent, and the smell of Ian in my sheets, had my mind twisted all night long. Drew added to the mix by calling me twice. I let them both go to voicemail. Like with C, our confrontation can't be avoided forever, but I'm not ready yet. First we need more answers for Monaka and Tiramisu. Everything else will have to wait.

I asked Pete to help me sift through the paper's archives this morning, our only real day off. I told him about my pointless interview with C, leaving out the raunchy details, and that's when Pete revealed he started seeing Tiramisu on a regular basis after his first visit to the Spot, much to my surprise. He strikes me as the golf club, yacht, and polo type of guy, not T's vibe at all, but stranger things have happened. Pete's as concerned with finding her attacker as I am.

"How's Tiramisu doing?" I ask, looking around the newsroom for Charlie, who's nowhere in sight, thank God.

He's been on me to dig up dirt on Mr. Graves, which doesn't exist. I can't wait to tell him how wrong he was to listen to Margeaux's neo ass.

"Still critical, but better," Pete says, forcing a slight smile. "Her parents took the kids, so they're good, too."

"I'm glad to hear that." I place my belongings on the table, ready to work. I need a distraction to make me forget about yesterday's visit with C.

"I found these pictures from a cold case in Riverdale, another slain stripper," he says, handing me the black-and-white photos of the familiar rooms.

It looks like the same house where C kept the girls that wanted to get away from the norm and allow a man—or woman—to have his or her way with them at will. If memory serves, nothing was off limits. Whips, chains, handcuffs, collars: the more tools for submission, the better.

"Do you have the article?"

"Right here, along with the reporter's notes," Pete says, handing me the slim file. "Margeaux was the assistant on this updated crime story, too."

"*Too?*" I say, sifting through the loose photos and papers. "She's not the assistant on my story."

"Put the claws away, Keke," Pete says. "Margeaux just wants to help. Don't you remember how eager you were when you first started?"

"Yeah, I was sent straight to death duty, not assigned to work on a major story."

"Speaking of which, how'd you move from being a stripper to a journalist?" Pete asks, propping himself up on the corner of the table, causing it to tilt to the left. "I know there's a good story there."

"Not really," I say, closely examining the article. "I always wanted to be a journalist; I became a journalist. End of story."

"Okay, but how did you end up at The Honey Spot, Keke McCoy? And make it poetic. I want to hear some Pulitzer shit," he says, deepening his voice and frown.

I laugh at my coworker's impression of our boss. The article that landed my then-coveted position at the *Metro Journal*'s located in the archives somewhere. I click the mouse and search the database.

"Here you go," I say, showing it to Pete. "Read your heart out."

"Nope, I want to hear it from you."

I print the article and pass it to him. "We've got work to do," I say, closing the file. "You can read it later, after we catch the killer."

"'An Epitaph for Jezebel,'" Pete says, reading the title. He folds the pages in half and places them in his satchel. "Kinda creepy you named your article 'An Epitaph' and now we're finding them at the scenes, huh."

"Yeah, creepy," I say. The irony hasn't escaped me, nor the fact that I'll have to mention this to Drew later—another uncomfortable topic to add to the list.

"Anything else stick out?" Pete asks, scanning the evidence box for clues.

"Not really." I carefully look through the musty box for anything that might shed some light on recent events.

"Check this out," Pete says, finding an envelope with a note tucked inside. "Looks like another epitaph."

"I knew it," I say, snatching it from his hands. "There's no such thing as a coincidence."

"Careful, Keke. We need to get it to the detectives as soon as possible," Pete says, just as excited as I am.

"Doubt there are any prints left, but there might be a handwriting match. I'll have them check the paper and ink as well," I say, carefully eyeing the aged note. "Our perp might be loyal to a particular brand." I can't wait to nail this bastard to the cross.

Pete removes the lens cap from the heavy camera hanging around his neck and takes several shots of the evidence.

"Wait a minute," I say, noticing another smaller box tucked in the same space against the wall, almost as if someone tried to hide it behind the first.

"Well, what do we have here?" Pete takes the dusty old box out and places it on the table next to the other.

"It's not even marked." I remove the top and eye the contents. "A picture of red stilettos. That's it?"

"Yeah, but they're very similar to Monaka's shoes, and Tiramisu's," Pete says, looking closer.

"We've got our work cut out for us if this is all that's left of

Mocha's investigation," I say, shaking the box, hoping to find something else hiding inside. "I'm telling you, C knows more about both of these murders, and T's attack, than she's letting on."

"Well, if she does, it'll come out during the interrogation. I heard the detectives say they were looking for a way to get a warrant for C's apartment and the Palace." Pete scans the files for more clues. "If you're right about C, then she's a dangerous woman."

"Even if I'm not, she's still dangerous," I say, shuddering at the memory of yesterday's encounter. "I'm glad to know that they're finally turning in the right direction."

I reach inside of my purse and take out my cell to call Drew. It goes straight to voicemail. "Drew, we found something very interesting while looking through the archives for clues regarding Mocha's murder. Meet me at the lab in an hour."

"I think you may be onto something here, Keke," Pete says, grabbing his satchel on our way out. "I'll be at the hospital, if you need me."

"Thanks for your help today," I say, following him to the elevators. "In the meantime, I'm going to see what else I can dig up. Hopefully, there's something that can link C to Monaka's last dance."

"I'm just glad it wasn't T's last dance."

"So am I."

"Where are you two lovebirds off to in such a rush?" Charlie asks, exiting the elevator with Margeaux in tow. He's not usually here on the weekends, unless there's a big story that requires all hands on deck.

"We're headed back to Indian Springs," Pete says, holding the door open for me.

"Why are you going?" Charlie asks Pete. "The gardener did it—case closed. All we need's more dirt, and that's Keke's job. Right, McCoy?"

"I need to get some more pics." Pete looks to me for backup. Usually, I'm against covering his ass, but given the circumstances, I'll make an exception.

"It would be easier if Pete could cover the photos, in light of the new lead and all," I say, letting Charlie draw his own conclusions." The sooner we get out of here, the better.

"Make 'em some good ones, and find some older ones, will you? Preferably of the gardener working before he got busted. One with the vic would be perfect."

"Charlie, did you know that there was another attack last night? What if Mr. Graves didn't do it?" I ask, looking dead at Margeaux. "We're persecuting an innocent man until he's proven guilty, which he won't be, because the actual murderer's still out there."

"Keke, the man's the prime suspect, plain and simple," he says, taking a sip of the sweet tea Margeaux's holding. "I want that story on my desk, come Monday morning, you hear? And don't forget to do a little exposé on the girls. This could be an ongoing story all the way through the trial, if we're lucky."

Margeaux's eyes light up at the prospect of having anything to do with my story. I'll be damned if this little heffa misuses The Honey Spot to launch her career.

"Charlie, the story's not about the girls. It's about justice for the victim." I repeatedly push the elevator's CLOSE DOOR button, but Charlie continues to hold the door open, damn the loud buzzing.

"Yeah, well, from your notes thus far, the victim sounds boring as shit. What about the violent love affair between her and that Mexican gal. Darcy, Danny . . ." Charlie snaps his fingers, like he's trying to remember.

"Dulce," I say, losing my patience. "And she's Puerto Rican."

"Yeah, that one. Let's use whatever you've got on her to fill in the fat."

"No," I say. "Dulce's not relevant to the murder investigation."

Margeaux and Pete both look like they want to shrink into the floor: they know Charlie's about to blow.

"Ms. McCoy, it'll do you some good to remember your place." Charlie's yellow teeth grind the worn toothpick as his bloodshot eyes home in on mine.

"I'm very well aware of who I am, and where I stand." I'm so tired of his chauvinistic shit, and today's not the day to fuck with me. If he wants a fight, I'm down.

"Ms. McCoy, I've been more than sympathetic of your nostalgia for your former identity, but I couldn't give a shit about your damned feelings," he says, pointing the gnarled, wet stick at me. "You'll take the stories I tell you to take, and you'll accept my edits. In case you haven't caught on yet, that's how it works around here. You write, I edit, and Mark publishes. That's the chain of command. Deal with it or leave."

Like I said, I've had it with this prick and his paper.

"Fine. I'm leaving, and I'm taking my story with me."

"If you leave, there is no story," Charlie says, stepping back inside the elevator, fully blocking the door. "Margeaux can take it off your hands, and Pete can help her. Can't you, Mr. Harper?"

Pete looks from Charlie to me with guilt all over his tanned face.

"What the hell, Pete?"

"Keke, it's your story. It's always been your story, no doubt about it. But it's my story, too," Pete says, stepping one foot into the hallway, while the other stays planted inside of the elevator.

Pete just played me like a fucking fiddle, and I almost fell for it, bonding over T and shit. He's the same little punk he always was.

"No, Pete. They're your pictures, but the story's mine. I'll be damned if either one of you take it from me."

"Keke, no one's trying to steal your story," Pete says, attempting to calm the situation. "Let's put this into perspective. We all want the story to print as soon as possible."

"But only one of us seems to want the truth," I say, angry enough to cuss everyone out.

"Truth's subjective, Keke," Pete says. He almost sounds sorry, but not as sorry as he'll be once I rip him a new one.

"Actually, the truth's what I say it is." Unapologetically, Charlie reaches for the few pages still in my hand and snatches them away, much like the paycheck I'm giving up if I leave on principle.

One of the first lessons I learned as a dancer's that principle don't pay the bills, but I can't let him do this to HoneyMama or anyone else at the Spot—not again.

"Not this time, Charlie," I say, reclaiming the crumpled pages from his plump pink hands. "Good luck getting the dancers to talk to this prick after they realize he lied to them, especially since your professionalism's been compromised, fucking one of them and all."

Pete's face turns from beet red to snow white as the truth settles in the air like microwaved fish. I wave the papers at him as he quickly realizes that the dagger he just planted in my back can twist both ways.

"What the hell is she talking about, Mr. Harper?"

"Oh, Mr. Harper failed to mention that he's been screwing one of the dancers on the paper's time?"

"Leave Tiramisu out of this, Keke," Pete says between clenched teeth. He must really be digging his first taste of chocolate honey to defend her at his job.

"Tiramisu?" Charlie repeats like he just tasted shit. "What the hell kind of a name is that? Boy, you're some piece of work. I need to talk to Mark about your conduct and what kind of liability you've just opened this paper up to."

Margeaux's silent, but I can tell she's taking mental notes. The woman misses nothing.

"Charlie, it's not like that," Pete says, suddenly nervous. I guess his daddy paying the bills isn't all it's cracked up to be. "My father doesn't need to know about this. Tiramisu won't say anything, I promise."

"I told him hiring family was a bad idea. You can't keep your dick in your pants for shit! And don't call her Tiramisu anymore," Charlie says, spitting on the floor as he steps out. "That's not a name, goddammit!"

I push the button for the lobby and wait for the ancient doors to close. Finally I can leave this hellhole and follow up on the few leads I have. My work here's done.

"Keke, remember what I said. Make sure your article gets to print by Monday morning." Charlie points at me like I didn't just quit. "We've got a suspect in custody that also happens to work at the strip club, and the dead chick's girlfriend's a hot piñata. It's a good story, follow?"

"I already said no," I say, tired of his sexist and racist bull. "Kiss my Black ass, Charlie. That goes for you, too, Pete. Good luck, Margeaux!" I wave through the closing doors.

The girl looks shocked, but she'd better toughen up if she plans on staying in this field. The weak always get plucked first.

"Keke, don't be so damned emotional," Charlie says, again blocking the elevator doors. "When people read the news, they look for sympathy, they look for recognition, and they look for people like them. These good Southern Christians ain't gonna sympathize with the murder of this whore, no matter how you spin it. They want the sensationalism, the blood, the sex, the violence—that's what wins awards," he says, echoing C. "And that's exactly what we've got in your exclusive—another accolade to add to your résumé."

"You just don't get it," I say, looking at the three of them.

"These opportunities don't come around often, McCoy," Charlie says, stepping back into the hallway with Pete next to him. "This is a career-defining moment, and you're blowing it. I'm disappointed in you, girl."

"I'm not your *girl*!" I yell. We can call each other girl out of endearment, but Charlie will never have that privilege. "I'm a grown-ass woman, so is Tiramisu, and so was Monaka. They deserve the dignity and respect of telling a credible story."

"Fine, you want my respect, you've got it. But the paper's done funding your hooker hoedown, pun intended," Charlie says, opening the newsroom door for Margeaux. "Get me the story by Monday morning, McCoy. After that, you're on to the next thing."

Finally the elevator door closes when a text comes through from Drew: **"Keke, come to the Spot. Walter's mother identified C."**

Charlie's right, these opportunities don't come around every day. And if anyone's going to use this one to define my career, it's going to be me.

Chapter 32

"GIVE IT UP, C," DREW SAYS, SCOOTING IN CLOSER TO C'S CHAIR. "I paid another visit to Walter's mama and showed her some pictures of the dancers from the Spot, including Monaka." He slides three pictures across the table to C, who barley looks at them. "Funny thing is that she only recognizes you, C. She said, and I quote, that 'your influence has been bad for my baby boy.' End quote."

C's been sitting in that kitchen chair for all of five minutes and has managed to tell at least ten different stories about her association with Walter.

"She said she kept Walter heavily involved in the church, but eventually gave up all hope that he'd ever be 'normal,' again thanks to you," John says, crossing his hairy forearms across his broad chest.

"What do you mean by that?" HoneyMama asks. She, Dulce, and I are serving as unofficial witnesses to the interrogation. "'Normal'?"

"He's a she," C says, smiling at John's disapproving expression. "And a damn good one, too. I told you a million times already, I know Walter from the dancehall scene. He's as good as any of us on a pole, Monaka included."

"You're such a *bruja*, you know that?" Dulce says from across the room.

"Eat me, Dulce," C says, opening her legs wide to reveal a fresh wax job. "Oh, wait, you'd enjoy that too much."

"Okay, you two," HoneyMama says, putting her hands up. "That's enough. This shit's serious, C. I'm done playing games with you."

"Young lady, it would be in your best interest to cooperate with this investigation," John says, attempting to reason with C. He's yet to realize just how far out of his league he is with her. "We can make you a deal, if you behave, that is."

"And if I don't?" C stands like she's going somewhere. "Y'all ain't got nothing on me."

"But I do," HoneyMama says from her stool at the kitchen counter. "I've got your financial books, I've got your client list, and I've got plenty of dancers on speed dial who hate you. Wanna test me?"

C looks around the room, and for the first time, it seems that the gravity of the situation hits her. "I didn't know he was going to hurt Monaka," C says, reclaiming her seat. "He's never gone off like that before. I honestly didn't think he was capable of that kinda shit; that's why I didn't tell y'all about the session before." She snorts. "Seriously didn't think the wanker had it in him. Can I go now?"

"No, young lady, I'm afraid not," John says, removing a pack of Marlboro Reds from his shirt pocket, packing them hard. "We're just getting started."

"Is that a confession?" Drew asks, turning up the tape recorder. I've also got mine on as backup. "Did you set Monaka up for a private dance with Walter Adams, Mayor Conrad Carter's son?"

"No," C says, taking a deep breath. "I set up a session between Monaka and Queenie, one of my best clients and protégés. Walter's her other side, and I don't really know that dude."

The silence in the room's deafening. What the hell's C talking about?

"If this is our guy, I want to take him down tonight," Drew says to his partner. "He's too dangerous to let go. We need an immediate warrant for Walter's arrest."

"But we don't have any solid evidence linking him to either *Monaka's* murder or *Tiramisu's* attack," John says, pronouncing each name as a slur rather than the affectionate monikers they were meant to be. "And we already have another suspect in custody. You know the chief won't sign off on this one without all the facts, especially not with the new suspect being the mayor's son."

"We've got the handwriting samples," Drew says, pointing at the envelope on the table in front of me. "And now that his alibi's fallen through, we've got Walter's schedule wide open on the night in question, a potential witness in the hospital, and we've got C's confession. She's about to be arrested."

"But C didn't do shit!" she says in her own defense. "What the fuck am I being arrested for? All I did was hook Monaka up with a side hustle. I didn't know Queenie would hurt Monaka, I swear."

"No?" Drew says, slamming down various photos of C in all sorts of precarious situations. "You've been under surveillance all week, C, friends included. Remember her, Keke?" Drew says, showing me one picture in particular.

"The woman with the scarf," I say, recalling the strange lady who brought flowers to Monaka's shrine. "Queenie's Walter?"

"I don't know. Is it, C?" Drew asks, holding the photo up to C's face. "Is this your protégé, or your pimp?"

C refuses to answer Drew.

"Answer the man's question." Done with the legalities, HoneyMama walks over to the china cabinet, reaches behind it, and pulls out a rifle—she keeps one in every room of the three-thousand-plus-square-foot house. "Or get to stepping."

C looks at HoneyMama, and then at the detectives, weighing her options.

"Ms. Thibodeaux, I don't think all that's necessary," John says, standing between HoneyMama and her target. "We're gonna take her down to the station and book her for obstruction of justice. Once we arrest Walter, we'll add on aiding and abetting."

"Like hell you will." HoneyMama points the gun at one of the several NO TRESPASSING signs posted near the entrances. "C, if you don't do as Drew asks, you're no longer my employee. And if you have no legal business here, then you're trespassing on my private property. Ain't that right, Detectives?"

No one comes to C's defense. C looks at HoneyMama, who hasn't budged an inch. She knows HoneyMama's a woman who rarely makes threats, and when she does, they're never empty.

"Fine," C concedes. "Walter's the one who actually runs shit. He has connections, high and low, all with money to burn. They like exotic liquor, cigars, and dancers. Monaka was one of the clients' favorites, and the 'she' side of him, Queenie, wanted to be just like her."

Satisfied with C's answer, HoneyMama replaces the weapon behind the cabinet, much to Dulce's disappointment.

"Let's get C down to the station, and issue an arrest warrant for Walter," Drew says, reaching for his handcuffs.

"Not so fast, Detective Drew," John says. "All we've got is circumstantial evidence, even with her confession. You know the sheriff'll have Walter out in an hour, and I guarantee he'll be in the wind after that. We need Walter's confession or a murder weapon with his DNA to make the charges stick—preferably both."

"Damn it," I say. "I would've never guessed that Queenie was Walter." I stare at the pictures, searching for similarities between the woman in the photos and the man I saw at the Adamses' house a few days ago.

"I can get the confession," HoneyMama says. "Give me five minutes alone with him, and I'll get him to talk."

"No, HoneyMama," Drew says protectively. "I don't want you going anywhere near that son of a bitch, you hear me? He's a complete psychopath and will stop at nothing to get what he wants."

"I'm not afraid of him, Drew. And furthermore, I need to protect my business and my dancers. This young man's not going to scare me off that easily," HoneyMama says, tossing the picture down on the table. "I don't care how many skirts he wears. He's like any other man and can be manipulated to our advantage, I guarantee it."

"We could use her to get the information we need if she can get close enough," John says, thinking aloud.

"You want to put a wiretap on HoneyMama? Have you completely lost your mind?" Drew asks, shocked that his partner would even suggest such a thing. "I'll be damned if we send her to meet that freak alone."

"I'll go with her," I offer.

This is just what I need to break this story wide open, especially after Pete's betrayal. If I do decide to leave the *Metro Journal,* I want to go out with a bang.

"Never," Drew says, like he's still my man. "It was one thing when you were working to get info out of the dancers. The suspect's a whole other beast, Keke."

"Why not?" John asks. "I think it's perfect. With the two of them all dolled up, like him, Walter won't feel threatened at all. In fact, he'll probably feel more powerful and slip up."

"How do we get in?" I ask, ignoring Drew's objection.

I still haven't told him everything about my past with C's side hustles, and won't until absolutely necessary.

"Couverture, of course," HoneyMama says, staring at C. "I knew you were a lot to handle, but I never thought I'd see the day that one of my dancers was responsible for the death of another," she says, looking forlornly around the homely kitchen." "You need to make this right, C—for your own soul."

"Why do you care about that heffa's soul?" Dulce says, standing. "I think you should make her wear the wire, stupid bitch. I hope you choke and die from your own spit."

Dulce charges toward C, but HoneyMama holds her back with her free arm.

"I still say no to the whole thing," Drew says solemnly.

"And your objection is duly noted, Elijah," HoneyMama says, letting go of Dulce to take Drew's hand. "But we're still going in."

"We can have C set up a private event with HoneyMama and her latest protégé, Brandy," Dulce says, setting the whole thing up. "Those rich white men will pay anything to see HoneyMama get down in private."

"Won't they suspect something's up when the owner and

patron of The Honey Spot, who never gives private dances, offers herself up on a platter?" Drew makes a valid point.

"Not really," John says. "Business hasn't been great since the murders. They'll just figure, like most dancers, she's in need of some extra cash. Am I right?"

Drew looks at us, realizing the plan's not so bad after all. "If we do this, it has to be by the book. Do you understand the danger you're putting yourselves in?"

"Drew, I know how to handle myself, in case you've forgotten," HoneyMama says, smiling at her overprotective former security guard. He still takes his job seriously.

"Not at all, HoneyMama. Not at all," Drew says.

There were many times HoneyMama had to pull a gun out on a fool or two, very similar to how she just did with C a moment ago.

"And what about you, Keke? How do you suppose getting past Walter, when you two have already met?"

"Leave that up to me, *papi*," Dulce says, placing her wide ass on my lap. "I used to help Monaka transform from a shy girl into a fierce geisha that all the men loved. I can whip this dime piece into a diva in no time."

"Then it's settled," HoneyMama says, clasping her hands to seal the deal. "C, you'll make the arrangements for tomorrow night. The rest of us will get ready."

"Fine," C says defiantly. "Long as y'all make sure to tell the district attorney that I fully cooperated. I will take you to the house, but you have to be in full disguise, attitude included. And you have to be willing to completely submit to the game. You remember how, don't you, Brandy?"

Drew, HoneyMama, and Dulce look from C to me. Thankfully, they leave the unanswered question to linger. I just hope this plan works, without us having to go too deep. The last time I was under lock and key with C, I almost didn't make it out, and only she knows why.

C's a bit too volatile to fully trust, but I don't have much of a choice if I want to get the full, true story, and catch a murderer before there's another victim.

"I still think that we all need to give this plan some more thought," Drew says, Mirandizing and handcuffing C, and not in the way she's used to.

"Maybe you do, but I don't," I say, ready to get back to my room and pass out. "I'm willing to do whatever it takes to get this asshole off the streets."

"Me too," HoneyMama, says. She puts her arms around me and Dulce, locking us in her embrace. "Thank you, girls, for coming together for Monaka, and for the Spot. Let's get this motherfucker."

Chapter 33

ONCE DREW AND JOHN HAULED C OFF FOR BOOKING, THE THREE of us took a well-needed break before the late-night, one-of-a-kind after-show. We've been working on my disguise all evening, and I think we've finally got it down. HoneyMama provided the outfit, but the hair, makeup, and fake eyes—furry lashes included—are all compliments of Dulce.

"Oh, my goodness, Keke. You look like a completely different person, eye color and all," HoneyMama says, checking out my violet contacts. They're no match for HoneyMama's natural brights, but they're just what I needed to make the disguise complete.

"Yes, you do," Drew says, walking in behind HoneyMama, with John beside him.

"Wow, Dulce," John says. Even he has to admire her skills. "You may have a career in the police department if you ever get tired of dancing."

"That'll never happen, but *gracias, papi.*" Dulce admires her work one more time before handing me over.

"I hardly recognize myself." The red corset with matching panty hose holds in all of my jiggle and creates a svelte, confident look, completed by a long, silky ponytail hanging down my spine to highlight the curve of my back.

"Ma'am, may I?" John says before hooking the tiny microphone into the lining of HoneyMama's corset bustier.

HoneyMama shifts her weight, causing John's hand to brush against her right breast. He blushes and she's satisfied, for the moment.

"We should do a quick run-through just to make sure everything's working properly," Drew says, placing a thick black duffel bag on the dining-room table. He looks at my red heels and smiles: the added shoe bait was his idea.

"Where's C?"

"At the precinct signing some paperwork," John says. "That woman's a tough nut to crack."

"No shit." Drew takes a headset out of his bag and passes it to John. "Even after she agreed, it still took us hours to convince her that cooperating with our plan was her only way out of being charged as an accomplice. The DA's finishing up the deal as we speak." Me and HoneyMama also had to sign waivers stating that we're acting on our own volition on behalf of the police.

"So she's getting off scot-free, just like that?" Dulce says, visibly upset.

"I wouldn't exactly say 'scot-free.' She'll be on probation for five years, and has to perform community service, only if this thing works. If not, the whole deal's off the table."

"Greetings, bitches," C says, startling us. "Miss me?"

"What I say?" Dulce says, walking out of the back door with a cigarette in hand. "Scot-fucking-free."

"Where's the gratitude?" C says as Dulce brushes past her and damn-near knocks her off her feet. "I'm possibly messing up very lucrative relationships so y'all can snag this punk, and I ain't no rat."

"You can't be serious, C." I'm ready to slap her, my damn self. "This is on your head almost as much as it's on Walter's."

"Monaka was so young," HoneyMama says. "You were supposed to protect her like a little sister, not treat her like old bait."

"No disrespect, HoneyMama. But Monaka wasn't no spring chicken. Atlanta breeds strippers from a very young age, and she was one of the best in the game because she knew how to play," C says, tightening her corset. "Everyone's either a pimp, a ho, or a hustler in this business. Niggas have them girls as young as eleven dancing at private parties, teaching them how it goes down."

"There won't be any girls there tonight, will there?" Undercover or not, I'll only go so far.

"You have to wait and see, Brandy," C says, pulling two metal locks out of her purse. "Come here and let me tie you up properly. I know you haven't forgotten how to bind yourself, but I want to make sure you get it right."

I was one of the submissive ones back in the day, and I'm not ashamed. Still, I don't want everyone to know about it, least of all Drew.

"Keke, you've done this before?" Drew asks, shocked. I can see him doing the math—it was at the end of our relationship, and we were both doing our own thing.

"Yes," I confess.

Drew looks truly hurt, but what can I say? All relationships have their games, and mine was making money while he was out fucking around.

"Well, I haven't done this before," HoneyMama says, also blindsided but less salty about it. "Can one of you explain how this all works?"

"All of the dancers start out in corsets," I say, admiring my instant hourglass figure. "Only very special girls receive locks and keys." I tug at the lock to make sure it's secure.

"The masters and mistresses take turns holding each other in bondage, always at the master's whim," C says, staring at my reflection in the window. "The hostess makes sure that everyone with a key gets to the right lock."

"Whoever has the key's in control." As I recall, being told what to do and how to do it has its advantages.

HoneyMama allows C to pull her corset even tighter before looping the satin strings through the lock and securing everything in place.

"Let's go," C says, clicking the padlock closed. "The men are

holding the keys tonight; they don't like it when we're late." She
opens the door and steps outside. HoneyMama follows.

"Be careful, ladies," Drew says, kissing HoneyMama on the
cheek. "And remember, we'll be right outside. Say the code
word when you feel threatened or just want to get out."

He looks at me hard, as if he's saying a thousand times "I'm
sorry," all at once. I accept his strong, warm embrace, also sorry
for my part in our demise. But all of that's over and we need to
focus on the present.

"See you on the other side," I say, the last one out the door
and into the crisp night air.

HoneyMama drives the five miles up the road, and thank
goodness for that. I've never grown accustomed to driving on
the dark, dirt roads out here. There are no city lights and barely
any streetlights, to speak of. She parks the SUV on the road side
of the front gate, just in case we need to make a fast escape. The
Carter estate's a little more than double the size of Honey-
Mama's property, with twice the buildings. There are eight former slave cabins behind the mansion, which takes up half the
land all on its own.

"HoneyMama, you go in first. Just do what you do every night
at the Spot, and everything will be okay," C says, leading us to
the back of the main house. "I sent Walter a text letting him
know we're here."

"Hell no," I say, already regretting working with C. She can't
be trusted. "We stay together. That's the deal."

"Brandy, this ain't amateur night," C says, pinching the back
of my arm hard, like my mom used to do when I was out of line.
"You know how this shit works. They call the shots, not us. If they
say it's a social night, then we all meet in the same room. If it's a
private night, matching locks and keys are alone in the same
room. And tonight's private, got it?"

HoneyMama runs her fingers over the hidden mic and taps it
twice to let Drew and John know we're here. "I'm a big girl,
Brandy," HoneyMama says, but I'm not reassured. "Remember,
the end game's to get a confession and evidence. We've got

this." HoneyMama enters the larger of the two adjoining cabins. The door locks behind her, leaving me and C outside to await further instructions.

"Where's your lock?" I ask, noticing her lack of accessories.

"I'm the hostess. I only entertain under special circumstances, just like HoneyMama," she says with more than a little venom behind her words.

"Hostess or not, you should have to serve, just like the rest of us," I say, remembering the house rules. She's no HoneyMama, no matter how hard she tries. What the fuck is she really up to? "If it comes down to it, you get in that room and do as you're told, just like the rest of us."

"That's where you're wrong. I don't have to do a damn thing to make a daddy come or a bitch jealous, including you, Brandy," C says, stealing my personal space, much like she did yesterday.

"Fuck you, C." I take a step back and nearly lose my footing in the five-inch heels. It's been a minute since I had to walk in these for longer than a few minutes and the sweat dripping down my forehead's not helping my balance.

"There she is! There's the Brandy I know and love," C says, grabbing my ass and forcing us closer. "Keke would never say no raw shit like that."

"More fresh meat," Walter says, opening the door to the adjacent cabin. He pauses for a moment to take in the sweltering heat. "Lovely choice, C. Just perfect."

"Brandy, meet Walter, our very generous and handsome benefactor for the evening," C says, introducing us.

Walter's dressed in a three-piece all-white suit similar to the two men seated inside. "May I?" he says, gesturing for me to turn around.

"My pleasure." I offer my back to him for inspection.

Walter tugs at my lock, at first. Once he's sure that it's secure, and that his key fits, he takes his time inspecting the antique piece. Then, using the lock as his compass, he turns me around so that we're face-to-face.

"Are you willing to submit to your master, Brandy?"

"My will belongs to you." I haven't said those words in over a decade.

"'Bout time y'all gals showed up," Mayor Carter says, biting the tip of his cigar. "Have some tequila, ladies." He pours two shot glasses full and directs us to take them to the head.

Here goes nothing.

"Think you can handle all that dark meat, Mayor," a potbellied, short man says. His diamond-encrusted pinky rings remind me of those worn by Jimmy at The Pimp Palace.

"Shit, Don," Mayor Carter says, taking out a fat wad of cash and tossing it onto the coffee table. "I know you ain't talking shit. The last party almost gave you a heart attack. Too bad that Oriental Negro's dead. Now, she knew how to entertain."

I look at Walter, who says nothing, but winces at the mention of Monaka. "What would you like to see first, gentlemen?" he asks, taking a seat in one of the oversized armchairs on either side of the couch and crossing his legs.

Now I can see a little bit of Queenie. How'd I miss it before?

"How about an icebreaker to set the mood," the mayor says, blowing smoke circles in the air.

"I want to see you two eat each other out on the pole," Don says, loosening his belt buckle.

"Our pleasure," C says, all too eager to oblige. C guides me to the pole in the center of the room. She takes a spin, expertly slowing her way back down the pole while popping her pussy in my face.

Oh, hell no. I didn't sign up for all of this.

"I thought we were being paid to dance and host, not fuck," I whisper, trying to remain calm.

"Ladies, house rules," Walter says, pointing at a sign hanging above the fireplace, similar to the one at the Spot, but sadistic. "You're not being paid to talk."

The men are not impressed as we wind our way around the pole. I don't know what to do, short of letting this bitch either go down on me, or saying the code word and blowing my cover.

If HoneyMama can keep her eyes on the prize, which I'm sure she is, then so can I.

"C, I thought you said she was trained?" Walter says, clearly irritated.

Don and the mayor look at me, their patience wearing thin.

"She is, Walter. You know how apprehensive virgins can be at first, but they always spread their legs in the end. Have another drink," C says, pouring a double shot. "It'll calm your nerves."

I down the drink and close my eyes, attempting to find my lost nerve. Silently Walter reaches for my lock and pulls my corset ribbon as tight as it'll go. After a moment, he releases his grasp and lets C take over.

"I don't feel so good." The room begins to spin, and I can't catch my breath.

"Just lay back and take it." C pushes me down and spreads my legs wide. "Trust me. You'll feel much better after it's all said and done."

Chapter 34

WHEN I COME TO, THE FIRST THING THAT I NOTICE IS HOW QUIET it is, wherever I am, with the exception of the clinking sound the handcuffs make against my lock.

"Brandy, you okay?" HoneyMama asks. Her voice is weak, but alert. I can feel that she's nearby, but can't see a thing in the dark space.

"I think so." My head's throbbing, and my entire body's sore. I try to move, but soon realize that I'm handcuffed to the same pole C and I were dancing on before, the memories resurfacing in vague bits and pieces.

"What happened?" HoneyMama sounds as lost as I feel.

"I don't really know," I say, only telling half the truth. "I lost time."

"That's because you were drugged," HoneyMama says. "We all were."

My eyes adjust to the darkness and allow me to make out the familiar figures. HoneyMama's on the other side of the pole with me, and C's slumped over the same chair Walter sat in earlier.

"C doesn't look too good," I say, looking around the small cabin for Walter's crazy ass. "Why haven't Drew or John come for us?"

"Walter disabled the mics somehow when the music started. He sent the detectives on a wild-goose chase across the lake, giv-ing him plenty of time to play with us and them."

Shit. How the hell are we going to get away from Walter, and, better yet, how will I get his confession?

"Is our sleeping beauty awake?" Walter enters the adjoining door between the two cabins. "You deserved a good nap, Brandy. You and C put on quite the show."

Instead of the Southern gentleman from a few hours ago, the odd female admirer from Monaka's shrine appears in his place. "Couverture, my beloved," she says, checking on her partner in crime. "What have you been up to, naughty girl?" She pulls C's weave back hard; her limp neck's no support for the heavy updo.

"What the hell are you going to do with all three of us, Walter?" I plead, scared for us all. There has to be a way out of this.

"He hasn't thought that far ahead, have you, Walter?" Honey-Mama says, her voice trembling, but still fierce.

"It's Queenie, you lying wench!" she screams into Honey-Mama's face. "You're just jealous because I can dance better than any of those fat bitches who work for you. Admit it."

Queenie mounts the pole and skillfully makes her way to the top. "Should've hired me when you had the chance." She bends her head back and kicks her legs parallel to the pole, executing a perfect inverted split.

"I'm beautiful, HoneyMama, aren't I?" Queenie winds back down the titanium rod. "Say it! I'm the most beautiful girl in the world."

"If beauty's synonymous with crazy, then yes. Yes, you are." I couldn't help myself. Besides, if I can distract him long enough, maybe HoneyMama can make a run for it.

"Crazy is as crazy does." Queenie dismounts, steps on Honey-Mama's right thigh with the tip of her gold-tipped stiletto heel, and then punches me in the face with a fistful of brass knuckles.

"Shit," I say under my breath. "Try that shit without the hand-cuffs and see how far you get." Blood trickles from my bottom lip and I can feel my right eye begin to swell. Queenie may look like a woman, but she definitely hits like a man.

"Brandy!" HoneyMama screams. "You won't get away with this, you fucking punk!"

"I tried everything! I wanted to prove myself by working at the clubs in the city, have you rescue me, like you did all of those unworthy whores!" Queenie shouts, clearly not afraid of being overheard this deep in the cut. Little does she know that somewhere this conversation's being recorded, if all went according to plan, that is. "But no one wants to see a flat-chested dancer, isn't that right, HoneyMama?"

"What the hell are you talking about, Walter?"

"Queenie!" she screams into HoneyMama's face. "My name's Queenie, you stupid cunt! Walter will be back later, just in time for the finale."

"Queenie, from the short story, A&P?" I say, reaching for the pen and notepad tucked inside the back of my corset. If I can keep her talking I can buy us some time. "That's one of my favorite characters."

"Mine too," Queenie says excitedly. She steps away from Honey-Mama and back over to sit with C's unconscious body. "She was so misunderstood, just like me. You see, most people don't know that I'm Mama's miracle baby," she says, twirling C's dark curls between her lavender stiletto-style fingernails, the same shade T said the suspect's toenails were painted. "Mama got pregnant in high school. Daddy, the devil that he is, wanted her to have an abortion, but there weren't any clinics in the area, and she didn't have a way out of town. Naturally, she attempted suicide, wrote a note and all. Very dramatic, but it didn't take." Queenie giggles, like it's a joke and not the villainous origin story that it is. "We survived. Mama went on to live a life devoted to the Lord, while Daddy went into politics, as you know. He married a wealthy socialite, had four daughters, all belles of the ball. Walter's the only son and the mayor spoils us rotten, as long as we don't call him Daddy in public, of course."

"No wonder you're such a twisted fuck," HoneyMama says, barely able to cough up a laugh due to the pain in her bloodied leg. "My daddy got around, too, but he loved and claimed all of his kids equally."

"Do you ever shut up?" Queenie picks up one of the leather whips hanging on the wall filled with rider's equipment and casts it across HoneyMama's upper body, face included.

"Ah!" HoneyMama cries out. "You'll pay for this."

"Already have," Queenie says, displaying both inner forearms covered with an array of scars.

Queenie releases the whip and focuses on me, coming closer to my side of the pole. "You look familiar to me, Brandy. Have we met before?"

"No, I don't think so." I keep my eyes low while working the pen and pad down my spine. We've got to find a way to get out of here and fast. This dude's about to completely snap.

"Of course, we have," Queenie says, forcing my head back by the jaw to look her in the eye. "You're that reporter from the city, aren't you, little girl?" She slaps me again, this time hard enough to make my left contact fly out of my eye and hit the floor. "Detectives and a reporter, C? You've been a very busy girl."

"Leave her alone," HoneyMama mutters.

At least he moves on from us, for the moment, and toward his accomplice. As far as I'm concerned, C deserves whatever's coming to her.

I manage to free the small wire-bound notebook and my favorite fountain pen, which I reclaimed on Ian's last visit. I pass the notebook to HoneyMama. Hopefully, she can use the wire to work her handcuffs loose.

"C," he says, slapping her awake. "I thought we had an understanding. I think you forgot that the one who holds the key is master of all."

"It was Monaka, not me. You know we're two of a kind, Queenie," C begs, her voice crackling with fear. "I've always had your back."

"Until now." Queenie steps behind C's chair and crouches low. "But a little birdie told me that you've been singing to the DA about our midnight marauding. Tsk, tsk, little nightingale."

"You're one twisted motherfucker, Walter, you know that?" C shouts, to no avail. The cabins are too far back into the woods for anyone on the main road to hear.

"And what shall I say about my dear, dear friend Couverture—as superior as the chocolate she's named for—when she's gone?" Queenie removes a dagger from her corset and licks the narrow blade, quite possibly the same weapon used to kill Monaka. "Should I say how I was truly inspired by her fierceness, or how her stature brought me to my knees every time she mounted that unholy stage?" Queenie crosses C's face with the sharp tip and forces her to kiss it.

I've never seen C look so terrified. I bet she didn't know her best client had this much crazy in him.

"You were supposed to strip HoneyMama's business to its core so we could take it over," Queenie says, letting it all out. "I was supposed to be the baddest bitch on the pole the South has ever seen, and your only job was to cripple the competition."

"Why not just start your own business and leave mine alone?" HoneyMama asks.

"Because you wouldn't rescue the likes of me, even though I was on the streets every night, working those back alleys just like the whores you have onstage every night," he says, turning to HoneyMama. "No, no, no. She wouldn't hire Queenie, the girl with the dick, no matter how fierce I was on- and offstage. But Monaka," she crackles, the natural deep voice betraying her. "That whore was turning tricks in between dances, and she still got saved. The fuck?"

"Because I could tell even back then that something was off about you, and I was right," HoneyMama says, risking another whipping.

"You're wrong, you know," I say, trying to hide the shaking in my voice. "It wasn't because you have a dick in your panties."

"What are you talking about, reporter?" Queenie says, stroking C's tearstained cheek with the blade. "You're telling me that HoneyMama hires men? Never!" She laughs.

"She hires women, even if they used to be men or still are, technically speaking," I say, still buying time. I hate betraying Dulce's trust, but desperate times call for desperate confessions. "Monaka was using the money she earned here to finish the process. She only had two more surgeries to go."

As Queenie allows the truth to sink in, HoneyMama and I work fiercely to unlock our hands.

"Lies!" Walter screams into the back of C's head, all traces of his feminine voice gone. "You're next, reporter, after I'm done with C."

"Queenie, please! You don't have to do this!" C struggles to free her hands and feet from the thick rope, but it's no use. She's too weak to fight in her condition.

"It's too late for me and you." Queenie's left hand moves swiftly from the right side of C's neck to the left, leaving a trail of red liquid in its path.

C stops struggling. Her corseted body falls completely limp into the plush leather chair.

"No!" HoneyMama shrieks, dropping the wire on the floor behind her before freeing herself.

Thick blood flows down the front of C's body, dripping onto her pink Swarovski crystal–laden bustier.

"Your turn, Brandy, Keke, or whatever you call yourself," Queenie says, moving in. "I'm going to make you watch me kill all of your girls, and then I'll finish you off," Queenie says to HoneyMama, who looks like she wants to pounce. "Monaka, Tiramisu, Couverture, Brandy. I'll save Praline and Dulce for the encore."

Good thing he doesn't know that Tiramisu's still alive. He probably would've tried to finish her off at the hospital if he did.

"You're a sick, twisted bastard," HoneyMama says, crying. "I hope you burn in hell."

"Me too, HoneyMama. Me too," Queenie says, crossing my face with the bloody knife, forehead to chin, cheek to cheek. "But until then, let's play."

With one final push, I manage to unlock my handcuffs with the fountain pen. Lucky for me, I've seen all the John Wick movies multiple times.

"What was that clicking sound?" Queenie says, nervously looking around the wretched scene. "What was that?"

"My lock, you sick fuck."

I remove my right hand from the handcuffs with the pen in tow and jab it into the side of her neck until the knife falls from her hand. Walter, Queenie, or whatever they ultimately wanted to be called, falls to the bottom of the pole, eyes wide open, just like Monaka.

EPILOGUE

*F*OR THE FIRST TIME, I BECAME A PART OF THE HEADLINE INSTEAD of the writer. It's been a week since I nearly killed Walter, but my constant headache's a reminder of just how close I came to being his next victim. C's still in a coma, and Tiramisu's finally out of the ICU. Drew and John have been overzealous about protecting HoneyMama, who left the hospital as soon as she was able to and is receiving private care at home, and making sure that Mr. Graves gets the justice he deserves for being wrongfully accused and incarcerated.

It's no surprise that Mayor Carter and Miss Adams have been radio-silent concerning their crazy-ass son. They haven't so much as sent a sympathy card to HoneyMama or any of his other victims, but no worries. They'll have plenty to answer for, once my article's printed and his trial begins. There won't be any- where to hide when I'm able to follow up on a few questions that are still lingering in the back of my mind: Did they know about Walter's alter ego, Queenie? And if so, for how long? Did they know he worked the streets in the city as a teenager? And how could they not know their only son was a homicidal maniac?

Pete walks into the hospital room and adds another vase filled with flowers to the cluttered hospital bureau. Charlie's sent them every day since I was admitted for a severe concussion and internal bleeding, and my mother's gardening club and Drew's department went overboard, too. Shelley's been by a couple of times, but one person's been MIA, as usual: Ian.

"How you feeling, Keke?"

"Like writing," I say, propping myself up in the sterile bed. I haven't forgotten about what a little shit Pete can be, and he's making up for it by being my butler until I'm back in the office.

"Here are the pictures and notes from the case, just like you asked," Pete says, handing me the thick file. "I also read your first article, and I was right. Pulitzer shit. You should check it out."

"Thanks, Pete, but I already know how it ends."

"Well, here's to new beginnings. Happy writing." Pete places the infamous article on top of the stack and leaves me alone with my work.

Guess it couldn't hurt to re-read my old words. Besides, even if it took a long, hard road to get here, the ending's much sweeter than I could have imagined, and justice was finally served for Monaka. Once I get out of here, and with Drew's help, I'm going to investigate Mocha's murder next, and then others like her that died under suspicious circumstances. Monaka's story is just one of many that needs to be told the right way.

An Epitaph for Jezebel

I DON'T KNOW WHAT IT IS ABOUT HOT WEATHER THAT MAKES PEOPLE SEEM-*ingly lose their minds—me included. My mother was convinced that Satan himself had got hold of her only child that fateful summer I turned sixteen. My entire world shifted and would never return to the normalcy I once knew. Outkast, Ludacris, and Trick Daddy dominated the airwaves, and I was caught up in the rapture of it all.*

My mother didn't allow the Devil's music—as she referred to anything other than gospel—in her house. Luckily, my neighbor's parents weren't as strict. When my mother wasn't home, I'd go over to Tony's house, and he'd play deejay for me in his garage while I escaped reality through dancing. Tony was the first guy who loved to watch me move, but far from the last.

While other sixteen-year-old girls were preparing for their cotillions and enjoying the freedom that summer brings most kids my age, I was forced to work at home. My mother didn't believe in fancy balls for young girls, saying that's what their future weddings were for. The truth is, we couldn't afford a coming-out dance, and she was just too proud to admit it. I couldn't care less about the unnecessary social gathering. All I wanted was to get out of Covington, Georgia, for once in my life. The city of Atlanta was only thirty-five miles away from our country town, but with no buses or MARTA trains linking us to it, Atlanta might as well have been New York City. And my mother was convinced that all cities were full of sin, which is why we rarely ventured across the county line.

My mom thinks I went astray, dancing for men and whatnot. If she only knew the power that lies in hussy hips—as she calls them—Daddy might've willingly stayed with her, and they could have lived happily ever after. In the end, I think my daddy simply gave up on having joy and settled for his mundane life as my mother's husband. My father left her twice. Both times, my mother knew he'd come back, and she never let him forget it. My mom blamed Daddy for everything she viewed as wrong in the world, including my love of food and our middle-class lifestyle. And I blamed her for making my daddy leave.

After the second time Daddy left, my mom and I had the nastiest fight ever. I didn't blame Daddy for leaving her—again—and said exactly that. As a result, my mother slapped me harder than she'd ever slapped me before, which was quite often due to my smart-ass mouth. Maybe that's why when pimps would smack me back in the day—or a couple of broads, for that matter—it didn't faze me like it did the other girls. Mostly, I'd just slap them back and keep it moving. But no matter how mad I got at my mom, I was never that crazy.

It was a fun summer, until my mom found out what I was up to when she wasn't home. Like her parents, my mother believed that idle hands were the Devil's workshop, and therefore she made sure that I was always busy. I had a constant checklist to be completed during those hot and lonely afternoons.

I had sex for the first time in her house, which was more than a sin: it was an abomination. I also had it in the garage, on the service porch, and next door at Tony's house. She never suspected that I was doing anything of the sort because my chores were always done by the time she returned from her socializing and other official church duties. What she didn't know was that I had help doing them, leaving me plenty of time to play. After all, the newspapers I loved to read stopped coming when Daddy left. What else was I supposed to do with all of my free time?

I was always very careful to clean myself and any other evidence well before the bewitching hour came. The only thing I overlooked were my ashy knees from the rug burn I endured during one of our afternoon escapades. My mother immediately noticed the indentations on both of my legs and demanded to know what happened. I didn't bother lying, because by then, I didn't care one way or the other.

My mother snapped and dragged me out of the house. With my thick ponytail in one hand, and a switch in the other, she beat me on the front porch for all to see—including Tony. The next day, she dropped me off at my great-aunt's house in East Point to stay for the remainder of the summer.

By the time my mom was ready to bring me back home, it was too late. Her strict rules and fake-ass ways were a thing of the past for me. At my great-aunt's house, I had a type of freedom I'd never known—the exact opposite of what my mom expected. During the day, I'd walk to the local library and read to my heart's content. My daddy found out what happened and would come visit every chance he got. My mother, on the other hand, never called once. I missed my parents, but I didn't miss living in Covington. East Point was a bus ride from Atlanta, and I fell in love with the city.

Once my aunt Esther fell asleep, my cousins and I would sneak out through a back window and stay out all night long, doing nothing and getting into everything. My older cousin, Doug, introduced me to his then-girlfriend, C, a dancer at The Pimp Palace—a strip club in downtown Atlanta famous for the ballers who frequented the joint, and the pretty girls who worked there. C made the life seem very appealing. I didn't know that was part of her job, and that Doug was also her pimp, but it didn't matter. I was stuck on the fairy tale, and they knew it.

It took three years for my daddy to go back home. He wanted me there with them, but by then, I was grown and happily out on my own. I graduated from Southeast Atlanta High School with honors, while dancing with C and Doug at night, and loved every minute of it. I went back home a few times while I lived with my great-aunt, who loved having another working body in her already-full household, but there was too much friction to stay.

My parents blamed each other for my newfound profession, which I never hid. They were already on the verge of killing each other before my dad left, but their anger hit an all-time high when I refused to come home. I don't know exactly where my dad was living before he moved back to Covington, but wherever it was took years off of his life. Perhaps that's why the last time that I saw him alive, he looked more like his father than mine.

My mother didn't shed a tear at my daddy's funeral, but I was a wreck. As a final tribute to my father, I wrote the longest obituary ever and submitted it to the Metro Journal, *his favorite paper. Even when money was tight, he maintained his subscription. Ironic, isn't it? That was my first published piece, and it is because of him that I now write this article for the very same paper. When my mother read my solemn words reminiscent of two lives passed—her husband's, and the daughter she once knew—she looked up from the page and asked me what she should write on my tombstone when I died, which she was convinced would happen sooner rather than later due to my scandalous ways. Should she write an epitaph for the smart, good daughter I once was, or one for the Jezebel that I'd become?*

That evening, I left her house in tears and didn't return until she sold it two years later. My mom demanded that I come and get my things, or she'd put them out on the curb with the rest of the trash. It wasn't until several years later, after I'd left the dance scene, that we reconnected, speaking every Saturday morning before her gardening club. I had finally become a respectable woman, in her eyes, with my Jezebel days, buried in the past, never to be mentioned again in her presence. If she only knew how strongly Jezebel still called my name.

Once I moved on from The Pimp Palace, I happily worked at The Honey Spot in Indian Springs, Georgia, while I attended college part-time. I needed more peace in my life after Daddy died and wanted to go back to school to honor his memory. Chris Rock can make fun of women who strip as a way of putting themselves through school all he wants, but it's no joke. I paid my college tuition from tips alone, with the rest of my salary going to books, gas, and other living expenses. As far as I was concerned, I had it made in the shade and was very happy living a life I'd never dreamed of—dancing at the most exclusive club in the South.

Even though The Honey Spot was not your typical strip club, it still was what it was. The game grew old and I was tired of playing it. More than that, I wanted to make my daddy proud of his little girl. I wasn't raised to be a Jezebel, nor did I want to be known as a stripper for the rest of my life.

When a newbie like me, Mocha, was murdered, all I could remember was how the media turned it into a salacious report that demonized the victim—my friend, coworker, and a good mother to her children. To the reporter who briefly summarized her death in a few lines at the back of the paper, Mocha was nothing more than a cheap whore who deserved the brutal fate she'd received. No one deserves to be left for dead in the bushes for dogs to find.

To this day, Mocha's killer has never been found, and the police never gave a damn enough to find out what really happened to my girl. This is why I initially wanted to become a journalist: to honor the stories of the untold, and that's just what I intend to do. When I finally do leave this world, my epitaph will read:

Keke McCoy:
Jezebel turned journalist for the unsung

HoneyMama's Sweet Potato Biscuits

2¼ cups all-purpose flour (extra ¼ cup sifted flour for sprinkling)
1 tablespoon baking powder
½ teaspoon salt
⅓ cup softened butter
1 cup mashed sweet potato (orange)
¼ cup milk or cream (more if needed)
1 tablespoon honey

Preheat oven to 425°.

Sift 2 cups flour into a large mixing bowl, and then sift again with the baking powder and salt.

Using a pastry cutter or a butter knife, cut butter into dry ingredients until mixture resembles cornmeal.

Mix in the mashed sweet potato and milk or cream.

Sprinkle about half the extra flour onto parchment paper or cutting board.

Turn dough onto the floured surface and (gently) knead several times. (If dough is sticky to the touch, sprinkle a small amount of remaining flour onto dough until it easily separates from surface.)

Using a floured cookie cutter (or drinking glass), cut dough into biscuit shapes.

Place on ungreased cookie sheet.

Bake 12 to 15 minutes or until biscuits are lightly browned and puffed.

Drizzle with honey and serve warm.